DEADLY SECRETS

What Reviewers Say About VK Powell's Work

Line of Duty

"Ms. Powell is an expert at writing police procedurals, and with this book, she also shows us just how talented she is at combining that with a lovely romance."—*Rainbow Reflections*

"I love a sexy butch cop, and Finley Masters was everything I needed. Not only was she damn hot, but she was a tormented soul, and that, my dear friends, just made her even sexier."—*Les Rêveur*

"I find myself wanting to reread the book, because the path each character takes is unique. The series of moments where their beliefs are tested and transformed are both big and small. I loved the pacing and I enjoyed that nothing ever felt like filler. ...I like to think of reading a story as entrusting yourself to the pilot of an airplane. You're in highly capable and talented hands here. I am already looking up other VK Powell books to buy."—*Lesbian Review*

Second in Command

"I love the family at the centre of the Fairview Station series, and their various careers in and around law enforcement and other public service professions. ...I greatly enjoyed the scenes involving the whole Carlyle family and was cheered to see various of the more peripheral members find their own place in the scheme of things."
—*The Good, the Bad and the Unread*

"I enjoyed the storyline and felt like the plot twisted more than once and made turning the page more exciting. The secondary characters in this book (and *Captain's Choice*) were excellent, and I thoroughly enjoyed every time the Carlyle family get around the dinner table."
—*Les Rêveur*

Incognito

"[F]ast paced, action packed and keeps you glued to the page."
—*Lesbian Reading Room*

"*Incognito* by V.K. Powell is the kind of intrigue/thriller novel that I enjoy. ...If you enjoy a good mystery with interesting characters and a bit of romance, then try this book."—*Rainbow Reflections*

"Well written main characters with plenty of chemistry. A good supporting cast as well that provide some good laughs and emotional feels. A fun read with enough action and romance to keep you interested."—Kat Adams, Bookseller (QBD Books, Australia)

"The strongest part of the book was the interplay between leads. ...Both women learned to keep people at arms' length, Frankie with her abilities to become almost anyone, and Evan with her almost obsessive need for rules and order. They clash, because Frankie's often mischievous behavior is so out of what Evan thinks she needs. But they are attracted to each other, and it does blow up their world view a bit."—Colleen Corgel, Librarian, Queens Borough Public Library

"If you're in the mood for a fast paced romantic intrigue novel with action, romance and humour, this might be one for you."
—*C-Spot Reviews*

"[T]his book is exciting and fast-paced and the chemistry between the two main characters is great."—*Jude in the Stars*

Take Your Time

"The last book in the Pine Cone Romance series was excellent, and I reckon VK Powell wrote the perfect book to round up the series. ...If these are the sex scenes VK Powell can write, then I have been missing out and I will definitely be checking out more because WOW! All in all... Fantastic! 5 stars"—*Les Rêveur*

Captain's Choice

"VK Powell is the mistress of police romances and this one is another classic 'will she won't she' story of lost loves reunited by chance. Well written, lots of great sex and excellent sexual tension, great character building and use of the setting, this was a thoroughly enjoyable read."—*Lesbian Reading Room*

Deception

"In *Deception* VK Powell takes some difficult social issues and portrays them with intelligence and empathy. …Well-written, enjoyable storyline, excellent use of location to add colour to the background, and extremely well drawn characters. VK Powell has created a great sense of life on the streets in an excellent crime/mystery with a turbulent but charming romance."—*Lesbian Reading Room*

Side Effects

"[A] touching contemporary tale of two wounded souls hoping to find lasting love and redemption together. …Powell ably plots a plausible and suspenseful story, leading readers to fall in love with the characters she's created."—*Publishers Weekly*

About Face

"Powell excels at depicting complex, emotionally vulnerable characters who connect in a believable fashion and enjoy some genuinely hot erotic moments."—*Publishers Weekly*

Exit Wounds

"Powell's prose is no-nonsense and all business. It gets in and gets the job done, a few well-placed phrases sparkling in your memory and some trenchant observations about life in general and a cop's life in particular sticking to your psyche long after they've gone. After five

books, Powell knows what her audience wants, and she delivers those goods with solid assurance. But be careful you don't get hooked. You only get six hits, then the supply's gone, and you'll be jonesin' for the next installment. It never pays to be at the mercy of a cop."
—*Out in Print*

"Fascinating and complicated characters materialize, morph, and sometimes disappear testing the passionate yet nascent love of the book's focal pair. I was so totally glued to and amazed by the intricate layers that continued to materialize like an active volcano… dangerous and deadly until the last mystery is revealed. This book goes into my super special category. Please don't miss it."—*Rainbow Book Reviews*

Justifiable Risk

"This story takes some unusual twists and at one point, I was convinced that I knew 'who did it' only to find out that I was wrong. VK Powell knows crime drama, she kept me guessing until the end, and I was not disappointed at the outcome. And that's not to slight VK Powell's knack for romance. …Readers who appreciate mysteries with a touch of drama and intense erotic moments will enjoy *Justifiable Risk*."
—*Queer Magazine*

"*Justifiable Risk* is an exciting, seat of your pants read. It also has some very hot sex scenes. Powell really shines, however, in showing the inner growth of Greer and Eva as they each deal with their personal issues. This is a very strong, multifaceted book.—*Just About Write*

Fever

"VK Powell has given her fans an exciting read. The plot of *Fever* is filled with twists, turns, and 'seat of your pants' danger. …*Fever* gives readers both great characters and erotic scenes along with insight into life in the African bush."—*Just About Write*

Suspect Passions

"From the first chapter of *Suspect Passions* Powell builds erotic scenes which sear the page. She definitely takes her readers for a walk on the wild side! Her characters, however, are also women we care about. They are bright, witty, and strong. The combination of great sex and great characters make *Suspect Passions* a must read." —*Just About Write*

To Protect and Serve

"If you like cop novels, or even television cop shows with women as full partners with male officers…this is the book for you. It's got drama, excitement, conflict, and even some fairly hot lesbian sex. The writer is a retired cop, so she really writes from a place of authenticity. As a result, you have a realistic quality to the writing that puts me in mind of early Joseph Wambaugh."—Teresa DeCrescenzo, *Lesbian News*

"*To Protect and Serve* drew me in from the very first page with characters that captivated in their complexity. Powell writes with authority using the lingo and capturing the thoughts of the law enforcers who make the ultimate sacrifice in the fight against crime. What's more impressive is the command this debut author has of portraying a full gamut of emotion, from angst to elation, through dialogue and narrative. The images are vivid, the action is believable, and the police procedurals are authentic. …VK Powell had me invested in the story of these women, heart, mind, body and soul. Along with danger and tension, Powell's well-developed erotic scenes sizzle and sate."—*Story Circle Book Reviews*

"*To Protect and Serve* drew me in from the very first page with characters that captivated in their complexity. Powell writes with authority using the lingo and capturing the thoughts of the law enforcers who make the ultimate sacrifice in the fight against crime."—*Just About Write*

Visit us at www.boldstrokesbooks.com

By the Author

To Protect and Serve

Suspect Passions

Fever

Justifiable Risk

Haunting Whispers

Exit Wounds

About Face

Side Effects

Deception

Lone Ranger

Take Your Time

Incognito

When in Doubt

Deadly Secrets

Fairview Station Series

Captain's Choice

Second in Command

Line of Duty

DEADLY SECRETS

by

VK Powell

2022

DEADLY SECRETS
© 2022 By VK Powell. All Rights Reserved.

ISBN 13: 978-1-63679-087-9

This Trade Paperback Original Is Published By
Bold Strokes Books, Inc.
P.O. Box 249
Valley Falls, NY 12185

First Edition: February 2022

Credits
Editor: Cindy Cresap
Production Design: Susan Ramundo
Cover Design By Jeanine Henning

Acknowledgments

It would be impossible to engage in the "business" of storytelling without the support, encouragement, and expertise of the outstanding staff at Bold Strokes Books. During these COVID-ridden times, thank you for finding new ways to keep your authors and our stories accessible and available to our readers. Words can never express my gratitude.

To my patient and entertaining editor, Cindy Cresap, you are the best! You make my screw-ups manageable. Thanks for everything.

Always, my heartfelt appreciation to sister author D. Jackson Leigh and friend Jenny Harmon for beta reading my work and making it so much better.

Thank you to every reader who has read my books, listened to them in audible form, tuned in to an online event, and kept in touch. You make writing books fun and more rewarding than I ever imagined.

CHAPTER ONE

The rappel master signaled, and Rafaella Silva dropped her deployment bag to the wooden dock jutting out into Badin Lake below. She pivoted 180 degrees on the skid of the stealth-modified Black Hawk helicopter, crouched in position, and looked back inside at her team. They'd belly-crawled through rainforest and desert, fought revolutionaries and terrorists, conducted recon, and executed medical evacuations and diplomatic extractions in locations worldwide. These men represented the closest thing she had to family but weren't. Odds favored them never being together again until one of them died.

"Team, present arms," the rappel master said.

The men snapped quick salutes, and Rafe reciprocated, her throat tight and eyes clouding with tears. "Thanks, guys."

"Ready, Major?"

She nodded, positioned her brake hand in the small of her back, and reached up to grab the rope over her head with her guide hand. Her pulse quickened anticipating the rush of adrenaline that encouraged and cautioned her about jumping out of a perfectly good helicopter. Nothing rivaled the rush of anxiety and excitement. Replacing the feeling would be one of her greatest challenges in retirement.

"Go."

Rafe flexed her knees and pushed away from the skid gear, allowing the rope to pass through her brake and guide hands. She descended at roughly eight feet per second and halfway to the ground began braking. Despite the double-layered leather rappeler's gloves, the friction from the rope warmed her palms. The heat usually keyed her to the impending fight, but this time it signaled the end of her combat days.

Glancing down at the dock that protruded from her small piece of property, she released tension on the rope and moved her brake hand out to a forty-five-degree angle to slow her descent. She landed solidly on the hardwood surface and cleared the rope through the rappel ring. The rappel master confirmed she was off the line, dropped it away from the helicopter, and she flashed another salute, a final farewell to the team.

Rafe planned her operational exits and reentries at night to avoid questions from nosey neighbors. She scanned the area and sniffed the air—remnants of burned wood from fireplaces and campfires and the rotten egg smell specific to the water of Badin Lake. She peeled off the layers of her sweaty uniform along with deposits of Middle East dirt that stung like microscopic nettles. Plunging into the cold lake water, she held her breath and dove deep until her lungs forced her up for air. The water refreshed but never dissolved the details of her final mission or all the ones before. But now service to her country was over.

Civilization awaited—sleeping on a mattress, not lumpy and hard from rocks, eating anything except MREs, drinking water without the chalky metallic aftertaste of a desert still, and living peacefully. Long ago, she sacrificed the hope of a normal life and love for a top-secret career with impossible missions and acts so clandestine she could never share them. She cringed at the danger she'd left behind and the empty unknown ahead.

When her skin pruned from the lake water, Rafe hoisted herself onto the dock, grabbed her bag and discarded uniform, and sauntered to the travel trailer she called home. The silver Airstream resembled a mushroom from the air and a misshapen loaf of bread up close, but she loved its compact features and simplicity. She connected the exterior power, water, and sewer hookups in the dark by touch. She unlocked the door, and the staleness of a long absence and burned toast welcomed her, so she opened the windows and while the night air cleared the mustiness, she went back outside. She hadn't walked naked and felt the air caress her skin for six months, and the urge to yowl like a feral animal and bay at the moon rippled through her.

She pulled the outside shower free and hosed herself down to dislodge the final grains of sand and to luxuriate in a shower with plenty of water and no one sneaking around to catch a glimpse. Before going back inside, Rafe tugged the cover off her black Kawasaki Ninja and checked it was still chained to the camper. She traced her hand along the sleek lines and knuckled the cushioned seat. After hibernation, she'd take it for a spin around the curvy lake roads, blow out the cobwebs, and celebrate her freedom.

Dawn painted the sky in pinks and oranges before Rafe stowed her gear and went back inside. Her personal cell phone rested on the countertop where she'd left it and flashed with unanswered calls and messages, but she ignored it and collapsed on the bed. Major Silva replayed the mission until the adrenaline waned, and Rafe's eyes flagged.

When she woke would she feel any different as a civilian than she had as a soldier? For twenty-five years, she lived with clear goals that defined every aspiration from choosing a meal to getting her next promotion. The blank space of her future outside the army gave her a floaty feeling, not totally unpleasant, but not easy either. The future disappeared in a second in war zones, but now she needed a mission, a purpose. She yawned. Tomorrow, she'd work on filling in the blanks.

Jana Elliott glanced at the blanket wadded up with her sofa pillows, magazines on the floor, cereal bowl on the counter, and closed her condo door. Tidying could wait. She reached for the lobby button on the elevator, but her cell rang. "Hello."

"Hi, boss, any chance you could pick me up this morning?"

Her assistant's usually chipper voice croaked with stress, and Jana immediately alerted. "Camille, is everything okay? Angie? The baby?"

"They're both fine, but Angie's car is in the shop and mine just died in the driveway. I hate to ask because I know you walk to work."

"I'll be there in five minutes." She hung up and pushed the *UG* button for the parking deck. A few minutes later, she unlocked the door of her Mercedes SUV for Camille in front of her Dunleath neighborhood home. The bubbly brunette filled so many roles Jana often wondered if the company paid her enough—scheduler, researcher, planner, mediator, secretary, caterer, deliverywoman, and always a friend. Today she looked tired and distracted. "Are you sure you're okay? Is it more than the car? You can tell me. Anything you need, just ask."

"I know." Camille squeezed Jana's hand and fastened her seat belt. "The baby kept us up all night again, but I wouldn't send her back for anything."

"That's good to know. She's a cutie. Do you need some time off? You *are* allowed maternity leave."

"Stop trying to take care of me. I'm good," Camille said. "Besides, Angie enjoys alone time with her for the moment. I take over after work and give her a break. If she gets overwhelmed, she'll have no problem yelling for help. Trust me." She gave Jana an up-and-down appraisal. "Two things. First, who are you wearing today? I don't recognize the designer."

They played this game most days, and Jana struggled to stump her astute assistant. "You don't know? Well, how about that."

Camille fingered the sleeve of Jana's jacket. "Wool or wool blend. Nice lines. Spill."

"It's an Elie Tahari. He's an Israeli designer, and this is my first of his. So far, so good. And the second thing?"

"Who were you out with last night?" Camille wiggled her eyebrows.

Jana honked at a slow driver in front of her and passed on the right. "Why does it suddenly feel like this five-minute drive is taking hours?"

"Because you're dodging my question. I know your fresh-fucked look and I'm trying to live vicariously through you. God knows when I'll get lucky again."

She really hoped no one else could read her so well. "Nobody you know."

"You didn't pick up a stranger in a bar?" When Jana didn't answer, Camille squealed. "You did!"

Jana stopped in front of the Alumicor building and waited for Camille to get out, but she didn't move. "Okay, I went out with some friends for dinner, then we hit the bar for a couple of hours. I met a single out-of-towner…"

"Perfect for you."

"You make me sound horrible. It was just a nice evening of mutually agreeable sex."

Camille grinned. "Like I said, perfect. It keeps things simple. You don't do commitment."

"That's not true." Camille's stare cut off further objection. "Maybe you're right." She was exactly right. Jana played her role as an extrovert well, and it was the perfect cover. She talked a good game, people thought she was approachable and felt like they knew her, but she never really let anyone close. Closeness opened the door to intimacy, and in her experience, intimacy led to eventual abandonment and pain. She wanted a real partner but wasn't sure she could be that trusting. "Are you getting out or am I paying you to sit in my car and grill me about my sex life?"

"If I have a choice—"

"Get out." She playfully shoved Camille. "I'll be back as soon as I park the car. And tell Sonya I'd like to review the Kitamura merger first thing."

Camille gave a mock salute and hurried to the front door of the polished granite high-rise.

As Alumicor's executive vice president and chief commercial officer, Jana handled all commercial strategies, global procurement, and business development. Her current project involved a merger with the Japanese company that could garner them both billions. Jana allowed her second, Sonya Duncan, to manage the details, but final approval rested with her and CEO William Fergus.

By the time she got to her office, Camille had herded Sonya and her assistant into the glass-enclosed conference room, procured an array of breakfast sandwiches and pastries from the downstairs restaurant, and had two large pots of coffee brewing. Jana dropped her carryall in her desk chair and joined them. "Where do we stand, Sonya?"

"Good to go, boss." The petite blonde sat up straighter. "Everything is ready for our attorney's final review. Dayle Hargrave will be here when her current trial wraps up."

Dayle—intelligent, single, strong butch—another mutually agreeable sex partner. Jana's earlier conversation with Camille prickled the back of her mind. Had her personal life become a series of convenient rendezvous with no serious attachments and no future?

Camille cleared her throat, and Jana rejoined the conversation. "The Kitamura attorneys have signed off already?"

"Yes, ma'am," Sonya said. "When will you present the paperwork to Fergus?"

"You can decide since you'll be making the presentation with Dayle."

"Me?" Sonya's face and neck flushed a deep shade of pink. "Why me?"

"Because you've done most of the legwork on this project and deserve an opportunity to be heard. You're my second right now, but one day, you'll sit in the big chair. Time to step up."

"Are you sure I'm ready?"

"I have absolute confidence in you, Sonya. It's time you did as well. Show him what you've got." She rolled her hand in the air. "But if it'll make you more comfortable, we can go through the proposal page by page to double-check."

"Yes, please," Sonya said.

Jana leaned back and listened, but her mind wandered to last night's companion and Dayle Hargrave's pending visit. Her body tingled at the prospect of seeing the company attorney again.

CHAPTER TWO

Heat warmed the side of Rafe's face, and she sniffed the air for camel dung, moisture, or decaying vegetation to get a sense of where she was. Iraq, Afghanistan, India, or the alligator-infested waters of the Bolivian wetlands? She tuned in to her body—soft bed, enclosed space, comfortable temperature—and opened her eyes. Pine trees and hardwood leaves swayed in a brisk breeze outside the window of the tiny nest she called home. She released a long breath and relaxed back onto the mattress.

The sun topped the trees to the east, so she guessed the time around 0900. A bronze maple leaf separated from a branch and fluttered to the ground as reality sunk in. She was no longer part of a whole either. Her life was totally her own again after twenty-five years. A free agent with no purpose or plan. Nobody needed her anymore or had a claim to her time, but that was a good thing, right? She stretched sideways to turn on the coffee pot on the counter. Baby steps. Caffeine first. Life plans later, much later.

Rafe fluffed the pillows behind her and settled back with her coffee, listening to the lake come alive. The whizzing sound of morning fishers casting lines in the still cove next to her dock. Boaters revving their motors as they sped along the main channel, and the occasional wave runner skimming and bouncing across the surface of the water. No bombs or weapon fire in the distance. Her little piece of heaven fit all her criteria—isolated and compact with lock-and-leave capability. What more could she need?

What she wanted—a woman she loved and a home—and could realistically have were entirely different, so she settled for what she needed. Her life was about duty, service, teamwork on the job, and solitude otherwise. Her career and relationships didn't mix because speaking about her missions was a criminal offense akin to espionage. How could she share her life when she couldn't even talk about most of it?

A child's yelp drew Rafe's attention to her neighbor's dock where the young boy, Teddy, and his mother, Brenda, stared down into the water. He pointed, crying for his mother standing nearby to "get it."

"It's gone, Teddy," Brenda said.

Rafe's mind flashed back to another child, breaking from a group of orphans and darting toward an open field in Afghanistan. Guilt and grief gripped her as it had that day, and she bolted from her bed.

"Noooo," Teddy cried louder, wiping tears from his eyes.

Rafe pulled on a pair of swimming trunks and a sports bra and walked to her dock. "What happened, Brenda?" she asked.

"He dropped his dad's watch in the lake. I told him a hundred times it's too big for him until he's older."

"Mom—ma." Teddy's voice quivered. "Please."

Rafe jumped in the water, swam over, and looked up at Teddy. "Do you know where you dropped it?" He pointed straight down, and Rafe nodded. She shucked off her dog tags and handed them to him. "These are the most precious things I own. Hold on to them for me. If I don't come back with your watch, you can keep them. Deal?"

Teddy nodded, closed his small hand around the dog tags, and clutched them to his chest as if they and her promise might also be lost.

Rafe floated and stared down through the murky water trying not to stir any more sediment from the bottom. When her eyes adjusted, she spotted the shiny band of the watch caught on a stump protruding from the ground. She dove and snagged the band in the crook of her index finger and kicked toward the surface. Teddy screamed when her hand holding the watch came into view.

"You did it."

He jumped up and down until Rafe pulled herself up beside him. "Want to trade?" She offered him the watch, opened her other hand, and he dropped the dog tags in her palm.

"Thank you."

"Yes, thank you so much," Brenda said. "How can I ever repay you? His father was killed in Afghanistan three years ago, and that watch means the world to him."

"No payment necessary, ma'am. I'm a veteran, so I understand." She slipped the chain back over her head and rubbed the dog tags between her fingers. She lived, breathed, and bled orders and operations, helping people, sometimes literally saving them, and maybe herself a little in the process. Being a hero was who she was. What now?

When she got back to the nest, her cell was chirping with a new message. Time to face the real world. She thumbed through her text messages deleting the spam. Voice mails were next, again, she deleted all but the final one.

"Rafe, it's Ben. Call me."

Bennett's voice caused a pleasurable swell in Rafe's chest. She'd spent the safest and most loving time of her adolescence with the Carlyle family. They provided her first real home, and she kept in touch with them as her schedule allowed, never wanting them to forget the pivotal part they played in her life.

She hit Bennett's number and smiled when she answered.

"Bennett Carlyle."

"What's happening, Chief."

Bennett chuckled. "Still a captain, as you know."

"I live in constant hope you'll run the place someday. What's up?" They were closer than Rafe and the other siblings by virtue of their ages, and neither wasted time with pleasantries.

"If memory serves, you're now a retired woman, so come for dinner tonight. Kerstin and I will ease you back into civilian life. I'll grill whatever Kerstin says."

Rafe poured another cup of coffee and settled at the small table overlooking the lake. "I don't know, Ben. I'm a little rough around the edges. Just got in last night."

"Come on. We'll make it an early evening. We've missed you."

The heartfelt words brought tears to her eyes, and she cleared her throat. "I'll…be there in a few hours." Rafe hung up and reconsidered her decision. She loved Bennett and Kerstin and wanted to see them, but they asked questions she couldn't answer, personally and professionally. "Too late now."

She spent the afternoon packing the military gear she wouldn't return into storage boxes and unpacking civilian clothes. The army took the decision of what to wear every day out of her hands, and she loved it. From the looks of her wardrobe, her new uniform would be jeans, cargo pants or shorts, button-down shirts, and T-shirts. Perfect. After a quick shower, she grabbed the outfit on top of the stack, pulled on her boots, and unchained her motorcycle. She cranked the first time, and Rafe relaxed into the lush seat as she hit the blacktop heading into Greensboro.

"It's so great to see you again." Kerstin lunged at Rafe the minute she opened the door and smothered her in a tight hug. "I've missed you. How are you?"

Bennett laughed. "She has to be able to breathe to answer, babe."

Kerstin stepped back and brushed blond curls from her face. "Sorry. You're *so* tanned."

"Desert life tends to do that," Rafe said and closed the door behind her. "Thanks for the invite." She pulled a bottle of Hangar 1 vodka from her jacket and gave it to Kerstin.

Bennett whistled. "You went all out, pal. That stuff isn't cheap."

"Neither is your wife." Rafe gave Kerstin a quick peck on the cheek before hugging Bennett. "You two look great. Married life still agrees with you." They looked at each other, and the answer was written on their faces. Was she capable of that kind of love or had her childhood and the military hardened her into a solitary being?

"Beer?" Bennett asked.

"Just one. I'm riding the bike."

Bennett reached into a cooler filled with ice behind the bar, pulled out two bottles, and passed one to Rafe. "Let's sit on the patio since it's nice. I'll cook after we catch up. Kerstin has everything else ready." Before Rafe settled in the old-style metal rocker, Bennett asked, "So, what are you thinking about doing as a retired woman?"

Rafe chuckled. Just like a Carlyle, goal driven and direct. "Did you miss the part about me just getting home last night? Can I have a whole day to think about it?"

"Best to strike while the iron is hot," Bennett said. "Your experience in counter-terrorism, hostage rescue, high-value target protection and extraction is bound to be good for something."

"Like what exactly? The military is a lot like law enforcement. It doesn't really prepare you for anything else, not even civilian life." Her comment sounded bitter, verging on angry, and she sipped her beer to think of something more positive. "Private security is the big thing for retirees right now, and it pays obscene money, but we'll see."

"We're hiring at the department," Bennett said.

"You're just proving my point, Ben. Besides, carrying a gun requires the same level of responsibility and accountability regardless of the employer. If I wanted that, I'd reenlist."

"Would you seriously consider another tour?"

"I'm not ruling anything out yet. It's early days, and I have no idea what the job market is like for someone like me. The military transition team offered suggestions and counseling, but I'm just not sure what I want at this point."

Kerstin rested a hand on Rafe's. "There's no rush. In the meantime, how about something more sociable like dating? I have several single friends who would be—"

"Kerst, you promised you wouldn't," Bennett said.

"And you promised you wouldn't grill her about work."

Rafe grinned at them. "You two are perfect together." She took another sip of beer. Could she even begin to explain to her best friends why she would probably never find a partner? "Sometimes I wonder if I joined the army because of how I was raised or if the army chose me for the same reason. Does that make sense? I went into a career that values teamwork but punishes individuality and pretty much guarantees to fuck you up and destroy any chance of a normal life. What does that say about me?"

This time when Kerstin touched her hand, she didn't let go until Rafe looked at her. "It says you were doing the best you could to make a life for yourself, and you have. What happens now is also your choice. No one else gets to tell you what to do or how to live. And yes, my friend, you will find someone who loves you just the way you are." She glanced at Bennett. "I mean, Ben did." They laughed together.

"Hey, what does that mean?" Bennett asked and then waved them off. "I'm going to put the salmon steaks on."

They shared a meal of grilled salmon, salad, and baked sweet potatoes on the patio and caught up on their lives as the evening cooled. "How's the rest of the family?" Rafe asked.

Bennett laughed. "G-ma is ornery as a caged cheetah since she and Ma turned the food truck business over to Stephanie. Jazz and Emory are remodeling their house and bring samples to every Sunday brunch. The dining table looks like a home improvement display until G-ma yells for the all clear."

"And that brother of yours and the twins?"

"Simon is the biggest kid in the family but still moving up in the fire department. Since Stephanie took on the food truck, he's around more for the kids, but Ryan and Riley are smart enough to be on their own, according to them."

"The Carlyles are nothing if not independent," Kerstin said.

"And your gorgeous baby sister, Dylan?" Rafe asked. "How's married life treating her?"

"She and Finley are great. They were clever enough to move out of Fisher Park, so they have more privacy than the rest of us. Who knew the baby girl was the smartest of the bunch?"

Rafe chuckled. "And you and Kerstin? What's happening on the baby front?"

Bennett glanced at Kerstin, and she answered. "We're still looking for the perfect donor, if such a thing exists. If we could just fuse our eggs, we'd have a perfect child."

"Wow. TMI. Just keep looking," Rafe said.

"Will do." Bennett pushed her plate away and yawned.

"Guess I better help with the cleanup and head back to Badin Lake." Rafe collected their plates and placed them in the dishwasher, and Bennett and Kerstin walked her to the front door.

"Promise you won't be a stranger, Rafe," Kerstin said and kissed her cheek.

Bennett clasped her shoulder. "Yeah, keep in touch. If not, I know where you live."

"Roger that, Chief, and thanks for tonight."

CHAPTER THREE

Jana read the obituary, dropped it on her desk, and stared out the window of her Alumicor high-rise office. Blue skies with bulbous white clouds belied the somber mood of the day. Old people with incurable diseases died, not vibrant men full of life and promise. A ridiculous assertion, but death made her twitchy and sweaty, funerals even more so. Now they invaded her workplace where she imagined herself safe and untouchable.

Travis Mills, company legend, started in the aluminum smelting pot room at the Badin Lake plant and worked his way up to management. They first met at an executive retreat before she moved to the Greensboro headquarters, and once here, they became friends as well as coworkers. Just a month ago, he'd stopped by her office, and they chatted briefly about old times. The announcement of his death haunted her, and she shivered.

Camille poked her head into the office and tapped her watch. "Are you ready, boss?"

Jana slung her oversized carryall over her shoulder and followed Camille to the elevator. "Can we walk? I need the fresh air."

"Sure."

Camille looked her up and down in a way that made Jana feel like the subordinate being scrutinized by the boss. "What?"

"Are you all right?"

"Yeah," Jana said. "Even though we didn't see each other every day, I'll miss Travis. He was one of the good guys."

"And death and funerals creep you out."

Camille knew too many things about her life—past, ex-lovers, her drink preference, even the foods she hated. Most of the time Jana loved and appreciated the familiarity until Camille brought up things she didn't want to face, like death. "Do you smell that? Luxe is grilling ribs. We should stop on our way back." She nodded toward the tiny restaurant as they passed.

"Sorry, shouldn't have mentioned death."

"No problem. I'm just starving is all." Food was the last thing on her mind.

"Anyway, I meant to tell you this morning, I love that suit. Alexander McQueen?"

"Do you sneak into my office and check labels when I'm in the toilet? I don't know anyone who's a bigger clothes horse than you."

Camille gave her the side eye. "Pot. Kettle. But you don't see me wearing two-thousand-dollar suits. Angie would kill me if I even looked at one too long, especially now with a tiny mouth to feed. She's convinced those fashion stores charge for window shopping."

"I'll ask next time." Camille could bring levity to any situation, another talent for which she should be handsomely compensated. And Camille was right, she wasn't good with death or funerals, and seeing Travis so recently made her wonder if there had been another reason for his visit. She'd sensed he wanted to say something else but couldn't draw him out.

"How many random people do you think will be at the funeral? Let's bet."

Jana arched an eyebrow. "Is that even a thing?"

"Totally. Folks go to show off new clothes, to do something different, or meet new people, and a big one is for the food. I've also heard scam artists weasel their way in to select their next bereaved target. That's pretty low."

"Please stop. I need to put on my game face." She nodded toward Hanes Lineberry Funeral Home and the cue forming in the parking lot. Before she and Camille reached the back of the line, one of the funeral home employees motioned her to the door.

"I'm Jonathan Lineberry. Are you Jana Elliott, executive vice president and chief commercial officer at Alumicor?"

Jana nodded. "And I'm sure Shelby insisted you address me just that way, didn't she?"

Lineberry smiled and waved her in. "You know your friend well. Mrs. Mills has requested you join her for a few minutes before the service."

Travis and Shelby were practical people but talking about business at the funeral seemed unlikely. Maybe she just needed to see a friendly face before the hordes descended. "Yes, of course." Jana glanced at Camille.

"Just you, I'm afraid."

Camille nodded. "I'll join the other folks from the office and save you a seat."

Jana's stomach roiled as they approached the funeral home entrance. Mr. Lineberry led her down a hallway reeking of embalming fluid and too many flowers, and she choked down the urge to wretch.

He opened a door and waited for her to enter. "Let me know when you're ready to begin, Mrs. Mills."

Jana gasped at the sight of Shelby Mills dwarfed in a cushioned chair in the center of the windowless room. Her skin was ashen, cheekbones jutted from beneath black-rimmed eyes, and her suit coat sagged at the shoulders.

"I know. I look like a scarecrow." She held out her hands to Jana and started to stand.

"Please, don't get up." Jana knelt and hugged her. "I'm so sorry, Shelby. Travis came to see me recently, and I had no idea he was ill. He looked tired, pale, and possibly worried about something, but I didn't ask if he was unwell."

"*Unwell?*" Shelby spat the word, and Jana recoiled. "Guess you could say that. Potroom asthma early on. Then PAH buildup over the years finished him off with kidney cancer. Yeah, he was *unwell.*"

Jana masked her surprise and withheld further questions about Travis's ailments and why he might've visited her. Shelby had enough to deal with. "I'm sorry, Shelby. I didn't know."

"How could anyone? Travis was the master of denial, hiding his problems and carrying on for the good of the company."

"He was a beacon for us all. And how are you holding up?"

"Don't worry about me. I'm just venting." She wrung her hands in her lap. "But I need you now. Can you help me? Will you?"

Jana pulled a side chair closer. The set of Shelby's jaw and the steeliness in her voice alerted Jana the request would not be a simple one. "Anything, but maybe you should talk to someone else about benefits or—"

"Not that." Shelby's eyes glistened with tears. "I don't care about benefits. Travis provided everything I'll ever need. This is more serious, and you may decide not to help once you've looked into the problem."

"The problem?" Jana's instincts tingled with something akin to fear. "Travis didn't mention a problem when he came by." She tried to get more out of him because he was sweaty and restless, but he promised to get back to her later.

"He never wanted to involve you, but now it's unavoidable." Shelby slid a shoebox held together with masking tape from under her chair and nudged it toward Jana with her foot. "I can't keep these secrets anymore."

Jana wasn't sure she wanted to touch the object at all, afraid of what its acceptance might mean. The whole conversation unsettled her. "What is it?"

"Marian sent this by messenger to Travis along with a note. It arrived the day after she died. She wanted him to handle the problem and not involve you. He said he never opened the box, and I certainly haven't. I suspect it contains whatever they found out about the company. He didn't talk about it much, but I knew it wasn't good."

"My mother?" She glanced at the box and felt sick when she recognized her mother's handwriting. "Why would you give this to me *now*?" Part of her wanted to rip the box open and search for answers about her mother's death. The other part feared what she'd find.

"After Marian died, he planned to confront Fergus about the situation but he got sicker."

"I don't understand, Shelby. What situation?" Jana breathed slowly to keep from hyperventilating.

"Maybe this will help." She pulled a folded sheet of paper from her suit pocket and handed it to her.

Jana unfolded the Alumicor letterhead with a list of names on the left and right sides of the page. One was titled *Denied for pre-existing conditions* and the other *Died before resolution.* At the bottom of the last column was the name Marian Elliott. Jana sucked in a sharp breath. "What is this about exactly?"

"I think that paper says it all."

"This is a list of names to which someone has assigned labels, Shelby. Am I supposed to assume some company wrongdoing? And what does it have to do with my mother? Why is she on this list? She committed suicide a year ago."

"Did she?"

"If you know something new about my mother's death, tell me." Jana's patience was reaching a breaking point.

Shelby jabbed at the paper. "Everyone on that list is either dead or dying, and I'm afraid Alumicor is covering up the reason while more people suffer. Your mother was not immune."

Jana dropped the paper, and it floated to the floor in an eerie slow-motion taunt. "*What?*" Maybe Shelby's grief demanded accountability for her fifty-five-year-old husband's early death. That had to be the reason for these random assumptions. Jana leaned forward and took her hand. "Today is a stressful day in what I'm sure has been a long line of the same recently. Why don't we talk after you've had time to grieve properly?"

Shelby glared at Jana, and her eyebrows knitted together. "Don't you dare patronize me, Jana Elliott. Do I strike you as an overreactive person or one who reaches conclusions without justification?" Jana shook her head, and Shelby continued. "I'm not a grief-stricken widow looking for a scapegoat. I'm an educated, intelligent woman searching for answers as to why my husband is dead and my friends are dropping like flies."

"Why specifically are they dying, in your opinion, Shelby?"

"Exposure to hazardous waste at Alumicor plants, unlined dump sites, and runoff into lakes and streams. And maybe that"—she stabbed her finger at the shoebox on the floor between them—"can help prove it. Your mother was an honest, principled woman, and if she uncovered evidence—"

"Wait." Perspiration dampened the collar of Jana's blouse, and she fanned herself with her hand. "I'm afraid you've caught me off guard. Alumicor addressed the hazardous waste issue years ago, or so they told me. Proof of remediation and appropriate compensation were conditions of my accepting this position. Shelby, I saw the original documents. They even smelled old and musty."

"They fed you a load of malarky."

"If what you're saying is true, I'm not the right person to look into this."

"You're an executive vice president of the company, and the only one I'd trust not to be corrupt or complicit," Shelby said.

"The benefits officer manages the administration of claims, settlements, and appeals. Even the reports from the insurance company to the CEO don't identify specific employees because of HIPAA restrictions. I don't have the authority to access that information or medical records." Jana wanted to run from the room and pretend this conversation never happened, but she couldn't. If what Shelby suspected was true—a company coverup—she wouldn't run, especially if her mother was involved or the CEO lied to her.

"Let me worry about those details," Shelby said. "Find out what the company knew, when they knew it, and what they've done about it since. You're the inside man. If you decide you can't or won't get involved, I'll understand. You've got a lot more to lose than I do. Travis was the most important thing in my life." Shelby wiped tears from her cheeks, pushed herself up, and hugged Jana. "I'm sorry to drop this on you, but I don't feel right holding onto it. Open the box when you're ready or don't. Maybe it will answer some of your questions. And if we're both lucky, maybe it's nothing, and we can get on with our lives."

"If the contents of this box are so valuable, why didn't my mother use it? Why didn't Travis use it after she was gone?"

Shelby raised her hands in the air. "Aren't you listening? After they made this new *discovery*, Marian submitted a lab request that took forever, and then she got sick. A couple months after she died, we found out Travis was ill as well. He just didn't have the strength to take on another fight. But mark my words, something is going on because William Fergus came to my house the day Travis died to *pay his respects*." She finger-quoted the air. "He'd never visited before, and he asked if Travis had any company files at home? Odd question out of the blue, don't you think?"

"And you believe he was after whatever is in that box?" Jana grappled to put everything Shelby was saying into a coherent picture, but her mind wouldn't grasp it.

Shelby shuffled toward the door. "Your guess is as good as mine, but I knew not to give Fergus anything. Once you've thought about this, we'll talk more, in person. Never on the phone, please. Travis and I have a great deal of respect for you, Jana. We have faith you'll do the right thing, as your mother tried to do." She patted Jana on the arm. "Guess I should get out there. Unfortunately, they won't start this sideshow without me."

Jana reached for the shoebox, withdrew, and finally picked it up before following Shelby into the auditorium. She found a seat with Camille and the other company folks, her conversation with Shelby still reeling through her mind. Was Alumicor knowingly covering up hazardous sites and disregarding EPA recommendations and sanctions resulting in more illness and death? Had her mother known about it and been a victim as well? Did this tattered box hold evidence against the company and/or information about her mother's death?

Jana was a loyal employee of what she believed was a reputable company. If Shelby was right and Alumicor was shady, what did that mean? What would a loyal employee do? Should she tell her bosses about the conversation with Shelby or investigate the claims herself first? She was so preoccupied by the box and Shelby's distress that the service was over before she fully engaged. The walk back to the office passed in a blur with Camille chattering beside her.

Jana was so disturbed by Shelby's accusations that she could think of little else. Still, she waited until everyone left the office for the day to do some research. Why was she being so clandestine? The answer displeased her. She *was* her job. It afforded her the safety and security she missed without her mother, the means to travel, wear nice clothes, drive expensive cars, seduce women across the globe, and live in a penthouse. But being a successful executive in a major corporation taught her not to rock the boat, to be a team player, and not question what other departments did. Stay in her lane. A lot was at stake. Too much. If she waded into this situation and caused trouble for the company, she could lose everything.

Shelby was grief-stricken, looking for someone to blame. Maybe in a few days she'd feel better and forget about her suspicions. But the shoebox with her mother's writing on the edge of Jana's desk taunted her. There was more than one way to approach any problem. First, she'd try to prove Shelby wrong.

A computer search for recent entries pertaining to hazardous chemicals, denied insurance claims, and/or lawsuits turned up nothing. She typed in the username and password to access the archives as a last resort. If she didn't find anything, she'd go home with a clear conscience.

The only entries she found pertained to the information she'd been told when she was promoted—abatement orders, remediation efforts, and four failed lawsuits from former employees—all documentation exonerating or reflecting favorably on the company. She copied the files she hadn't seen onto a flash drive and closed the system, wanting to take a closer look at home, just to be sure. She tucked the shoebox under her arm and exited the office. Halfway to the elevator, her phone rang. "Hello?"

"Jana, this is William Fergus."

Jana froze in front of the elevator, her finger poised to push the down button. The CEO of Alumicor, a man she'd spoken to seldom in her twenty-year career, didn't call to chat. "Yes, sir?"

"Are you still in the building?"

"Just leaving my office. How can I help?"

"Have you been in the archives tonight?" His voice sounded tight and gruff.

"Reviewing the remediation information pertaining to the old Badin Lake plant."

"I'd like to see you in my office at nine sharp tomorrow." He hung up before she could reply. That couldn't be good.

Chapter Four

The next morning, Jana unlocked her office door and froze. Her computer rested in the middle, not on the right side of her desk, and books had been rearranged on the shelves. Small flags from her mother's protest days were out of place. Subtle changes probably unnoticeable to the casual observer, but she was a stickler for details. She took a shaky breath and pulled on the desk drawers she'd locked the night before. They opened easily. After a quick search to determine if anything was missing, Jana headed to Fergus's office for the nine o'clock meeting.

William Fergus stood by the tall windows overlooking downtown when Jana entered. His lean frame and black mane gave him a menacing air, and when he leveled his dark gaze on her, she cringed.

"Good morning, sir." She positioned herself between Fergus's desk and the windows and clasped her hands behind her back so he couldn't see them trembling.

Fergus motioned for her to sit and started without preamble. "I didn't authorize any research into the archives."

"I didn't realize authorization was required, especially not for a vice president of the company," Jana said. "How did you know?"

"We upped our security since negotiations started with the Japanese. Every keystroke, document, expense, vehicle, phone, and flash drive is tracked, especially now."

"But everything I accessed was public information, and the same documents you gave me when I was promoted. What's the issue?"

Fergus looked at her like she should already know the answer. "The merger with Kitamura. But Sonya has handled the details, so maybe you're not quite up to speed." The jab was intentional. "This deal is worth billions, so we can't afford any negative publicity, present or past. You've always been a team player, Jana. Is there something I need to know?"

"No, sir."

"So why are you digging through the archives?"

She could just tell Fergus about Shelby's concerns, but what if they were true? Should she totally lie and keep digging? She settled for a compromise she could live with. "Seeing some of my mother's old coworkers at the funeral yesterday reminded me of the work she'd done on the remediation project. I was looking through her files, something to connect with her possibly. Nostalgia, I guess."

"Why did you make a copy? Why not just look at it here?"

"I didn't want to waste company time on something personal." Fergus's shoulders relaxed slightly. He'd be the first to agree that women were more prone to emotion than men.

"I can understand that, so just return the disk or whatever you downloaded the information to and that'll be the end of it," Fergus said.

If it was that simple, why had someone searched her office? She thought about asking the question, but if Fergus was playing dumb, maybe she should too, at least until she knew more. "It's at home. I haven't even looked it over yet."

"Even better. Bring it in first thing tomorrow, unopened, and do your reminiscing here, at least until this merger is finalized. Agreed?" Fergus waved her away. He didn't insist on a reply, and she didn't offer one.

The rest of the day was a blur with Camille doing most of the work and Jana allowing her paranoia to blossom. She checked under lamps and behind pictures for listening devices and taped a Post-it over her computer camera. By four o'clock, her suspicions had won. "I'm going home. If you need anything, call me." She left the building, glancing behind her at every intersection like a spy on a clandestine mission. The thought of being home alone creeped her out, so she texted her friend Bennett Carlyle to see if she and Kerstin were available for a drink.

K at architectural conference. At Fisher's Grill. Come by.

Bennett waved from the back of Fisher's neighborhood bar when Jana entered, and she made her way down the narrow space between the booths and bar toward her and another woman. "Thanks for the invitation." She offered her hand to the auburn-haired beauty with Bennett. "I'm Jana Elliott."

"Adena Weber, nice to meet you." She slid over and patted the bench.

"So, what's up?" Bennett asked. Ever the cop, straight to the point, but she could be forgiven for her bluntness because her concern was always well intended.

Jana studied the two women, and her professional instincts told her not to reveal company business to outsiders, but she'd never been spooked by something at work either.

What could she say? How much was too much? "You know, the usual corporate BS." She settled and waved for the bartender. Bennett had introduced herself and her wife, Kerstin, about five years ago at a charity event for the Police Officers' Association and they'd become friends. But other than hearing about Adena's reputation as a great attorney, Jana didn't know anything else. What she'd hoped to talk to Bennett about would have to wait.

"Adena and I are consoling each other on the absence of our spouses. Both our girls are out of town, so we took the rare opportunity to catch up," Bennett said. She clarified any potential for misunderstanding about having a drink with Adena, but Jana knew Kerstin had been her one and only love since high school.

"And Colby, my wife, is DEA, so she's gone quite a bit. We manage the downside of having successful wives, as they do." Adena raised her glass and they toasted. "Do you have a partner, Jana?"

"I haven't found a woman who won't let me push her away." Why had she blurted her truth so easily to a stranger? Maybe the day took a bigger emotional toll than she realized.

"She's out there. Trust me." Bennett studied Jana for several seconds. "You look a little stressed. Can we help?" Jana flicked her gaze to Adena, and Bennett caught it. "You can trust Adena with anything, but if you're worried…" The change from Jana's vodka martini rested on the tabletop, and Bennet slid it over to Adena. "There. Now you have attorney-client privilege."

Adena laughed. "I don't take it personally. Some people don't trust lawyers on principle. If you'd prefer, I can give you two some privacy."

Jana studied Adena a few seconds and gauged her own instincts. "That's not necessary. If Bennett trusts you, that's good enough for me." She looked around to make sure no one was eavesdropping and contemplated where to start. "I might've done something really stupid." She took a deep breath before launching into Travis's illness, Shelby's suspicions, her own efforts to research them, the fact she'd downloaded information from the archives and been caught, and the final piece—her office being ransacked.

"What did your boss say?" Bennett asked.

"He's concerned about a merger and doesn't want to risk any bad publicity, but I'm not convinced that's all."

"So, you're worried about your non-disclosure agreement? What you found? Or didn't find?" Adena asked.

"My NDA is pretty basic, so unless I release something that compromises the company's operations or divulges trade secrets, I'm fine."

"Are you worried Mrs. Mills could be right?" Bennett finished her drink and gestured for another round for the table.

"I'm mainly concerned about people being sick or dying, if what she says is true."

"The production of aluminum does have a history of releasing some pretty intimidating contaminants like toxic fluoride, cyanide, PCBs, and PAHs in spent potliner," Adena said.

"How do you know about potliner?" Jana asked.

"My office researched the process to represent a client a few years ago. Spent potliner is waste material from smelting, basically carbon and everything else not aluminum."

Bennett paid the bartender for their drinks and returned her attention to the conversation. "And what happened with the case?"

Adena studied her hands as if considering her answer and then met Jana's gaze. "The client died before the case came to court. Lung cancer."

"Jeez." Jana's stomach churned, and her drink rose in her throat. "I've never even told you and Kerstin this, Ben, but my mother, Marian, worked for Alumicor back when the hazardous waste issues first came to light. She documented the remediation efforts and coordinated with state authorities and the EPA to clear the contaminated sites. I have to know if Fergus hid anything from me, or my mother, about the company's culpability or the final resolution." She thought about the shoebox hidden in the back of her clothes closet and tensed at the prospect of opening it. The contents could put everything she valued in jeopardy and blow her world apart.

Adena nodded. "Because if he did—"

"Shelby Mills could be right. Alumicor may be aware of continued contamination that is affecting people around Badin Lake and could be covering it up," Bennett concluded.

"Exactly," Jana said.

"Could you ask your mother if she remembers anything?" Adena asked.

The familiar stab of pain mingled with anger flooded to the surface. "She's dead." Her blunt statement sounded harsh and unfeeling, but she couldn't delve into that emotional minefield right now.

"I'm so sorry," Adena said. "I didn't mean to bring up bad memories."

When Jana didn't respond, Bennett offered, "Is there anything we can do to help? Maybe you should let me hang on to the flash drive until you're sure of what you're dealing with."

"It's in a safe place for the time being. And I repeat, what's the problem? It's all out there in the public domain already. My source believes my mother and Travis found something incriminating… and what's in that shoebox could tie it all together…" Jana absently tugged on her necklace, unable to voice all the possible ramifications. "I can't think of anything I need at the moment, but I reserve the right to impose upon your good nature in the future."

"Anytime. You know that." Bennett squeezed her hand and gave her a smile. "Would you consider personal security, someone to watch your back until this blows over?"

"Definitely not," Jana said. "I don't feel threatened or unsafe." But she *had* scoured her office for listening devices and cameras and crept around like a fugitive all afternoon.

Bennett grinned. "You *have* seen *Erin Brockovich* and *The Pelican Brief*, right?"

"We're not talking about corporate espionage or government secrets here, Ben, so stop trying to frighten me."

"They searched your office, Jana. I'm not trying to scare you, just keep you safe. If anything happened to you, Kerstin would never forgive me."

"Thanks, but protection seems like an overreaction at this point. I might take you up on it if things escalate." She checked her watch. "I should get going. I'll keep you posted. And thanks for listening."

On the way home, Jana reviewed their conversation. Had she done the right thing involving others before gathering all the facts? She scanned up and down her street before keying the entry pad into her building. Nerves, just nerves.

Before she went to bed, she made a copy of the files on the flash drive and dropped the original into her briefcase to take back to the office. The information she'd taken was neither helpful nor harmful in proving Alumicor had knowledge of continued hazardous contamination around Badin Lake and contained absolutely nothing damaging to the merger. So why had Fergus increased security on the archives? Why was he so insistent she return the flash drive? And why was she so nervous about having it?

She disobeyed her boss and could possibly be fired. Her job was her identity and her security, but the potential consequences extended far beyond her. If there was a problem at Alumicor, people's lives and billions of dollars were at stake. Secrets that people worked desperately to conceal would be exposed. How far would they go to keep her quiet?

Bennett's question replayed in her mind. *"Would you consider personal security, someone to watch your back until this blows over?"* Maybe she'd been unwise to dismiss the idea so quickly.

CHAPTER FIVE

A loud bang woke Rafe from a fitful sleep, and she dove out of bed onto the floor of her camper. She shook the brain fog away, grabbed her gun from under the pillow, and knee-walked to the window. Peering through the string holes of the blinds, she pinpointed the source of the noise. Teddy wrestled another float from the boathouse next door, and the screen slammed shut behind him. Mystery solved, she fell back against the counter and reached up to turn on the coffee pot. Was her achievement of the day jumping to conclusions?

During deployment, she and her team filled off hours by working out with makeshift equipment, watching pirated movies, sending dumb videos home, and betting on everything. Not an efficient use of time, but anything to pass the days in Trashcanistan. Guys with families or significant others spent time on X-rated webchats, and those without retreated to Porta-Johns with porn magazines. She exercised, ran, and studied schematics of the area or upcoming operations. Now what? Her stomach responded with a growl.

Rafe pulled a loaf of bread and sandwich meat from the refrigerator and filled her coffee cup. Mustard. She reached back into the fridge and then snagged a butter knife from the cutlery drawer. She settled at the table and flattened half of a paper towel in front of her. Two slices of bread. She flipped the Dijon mustard upside down and dropped a full squeeze on each slice before smoothing it out with the knife. She counted twelve slices of super-thin honey-baked ham, uncurled them, and laid them alternately length- and width-wise on the bread. Cheese. Back to the fridge for pepper jack, a piece over the meat, one under. Add top bread slice, trim the crust, and voila, breakfast of champions. She glanced at her watch. Damn, only took five minutes.

She forced herself to eat slowly and enjoy her surroundings. Never sure of her next meal on deployment, she always wolfed down too much too quickly with an eye out for trouble, but now she had time to savor, to…to what? The guys talked about home projects, honey-do lists the wives saved for their return. Rafe scanned her tiny space. Even a deep clean inside took less than an hour. Outside projects maybe? She ate faster.

Rafe pulled on a pair of shredded jean shorts and a tank top and stepped outside. The morning air was crisp, invigorating. She stretched and took a deep breath—no gunpowder, latrines, or decaying corpses. She loved her home, and she'd trained the neighbors to respect her privacy unless she expressly invited them over. Today would probably not be one of those days because she needed to accomplish something. She tugged a water hose, soft-bristled brush, and car wash soap from a storage compartment and connected the hose to the outdoor spigot. With the hose coiled through her belt loops, she climbed on top of the camper, wet it down, and started cleaning.

After the camper scrubbing, she pressure-washed the small deck around the nest and the dock before daring to check her watch. Two hours, really? Who said boredom didn't kill? Her phone vibrated in her jeans pocket and then chirped like a sick bird. Thank God. "Yeah, Silva."

"You sounded friendlier when you were deployed," Bennett said.

"Very funny." Rafe dried her hands on her jeans and leaned against the side of the camper in a shady spot. "What's up?"

"I thought you might be bored by now. A friend of mine and Kerstin's has gotten herself into a bit of a jam and needs some close-quarters security. Interested?"

"Depends on who she is and the type of jam she's in. You know I'm not big on celebrity or high-profile execs. The further I stay from the limelight the better, especially until I put some distance between me and the army."

"I understand. She might've discovered some wrongdoing by her company and is considering exposing a coverup."

"A whistleblower. I don't know, Ben. Depending on the company and the nature of the coverup, things could get public quickly. Doesn't really sound like my thing."

"I know, but I'm hoping it'll be short-term and honestly, I haven't even..." Her voice trailed off as if she was about to reveal a deal-breaking detail.

"She doesn't want protection, does she?"

"Damn, you do know me. She might be a little reluctant, but she needs security, in my opinion. Her boss has already grilled her about copying public information, demanded its return, and searched her office. What do you think?"

Rafe didn't need to speculate. Seemingly innocent file transfers or duplications in the service often resulted in criminal and administrative charges against the perpetrators followed by swift court-martials. Bennett's friend had been warned. "I know you're worried for her, Ben, but I won't take on a protectee who doesn't want help. It makes matters worse and never ends well."

"But if I get her to agree, would you do it? For me?"

"That's a low blow."

"I know, but she and Kerstin are really close, and I make it a point to never disappoint my wife." Bennett cleared her throat, a tell that Rafe recognized as an attempt to cover emotion.

"No promises, but I'm willing to discuss the possibility, *if* she agrees."

"Fair enough. I'll get back to you. And thanks, pal."

Jana met the dawn with a cup of coffee, her laptop on the kitchen counter, and the flash drive clutched in her fist. She spent most of the night jumping at familiar sounds but imagining they weren't and visualizing the haunted look in Shelby's eyes. Was she just grasping for something to explain Travis's death? She understood Shelby's pain. She'd floundered since her mother's suicide last year, so it was difficult to dismiss Shelby's concerns without at least trying to find out if they had merit.

Groggy and anxious, Jana wrestled with the same questions plaguing her since yesterday. Should she look at the files or return them unopened as Fergus demanded? What could she possibly find that wasn't already public knowledge? That was the troubling part. Why was Fergus so adamant about her returning the drive unread? Loyalty battled curiosity.

"Screw this." She slid the flash drive into the USB port and clicked on the file. Folders labeled by year filled the screen, and inside each folder were that year's documents—news clippings, lawsuits, abatement orders, toxicological and geological reports—relating to hazardous materials from the smelting of aluminum oxide. She opened the first file in the earliest folder, the official notification of dangerous byproducts from the process, and skimmed the contents but found nothing new.

She scrolled to the end of the document and was about to close it when a notation at the bottom caught her eye. Initials. *MAE.* She gasped. Her mother's initials in her handwriting, followed by the letters *IM* and a series of numbers, all legible and not nearly as faded as the type print. The digits didn't look like a date. Maybe another location, but she hadn't seen any such filing system in the company in the past twenty years. She scanned all the documents in each folder and became more confused. If the numbers noted entry into a digital system or another registry, all the pages should have numbers, but they didn't.

Jana sighed and stretched the kinks out of her back from hunching over the computer. Would the old shoebox contain answers? She'd have to muster the courage to open it first. She glanced at the clock hoping for another cup of coffee before work. *Eight thirty?* Coffee would have to wait, along with her usual leisurely morning preparations. Shower, throw on whatever was recently dry-cleaned, and get her ass to work, pronto. Fergus would be expecting that flash drive first thing.

"Well, somebody was in a hurry this morning," Camille said when Jana walked into the office. "Late night…or early morning?" She straightened the collar of Jana's white shirt from underneath the lapel of her tailored suit jacket. "Burberry?"

Jana blushed. "Please, stop."

"I'm just living vicariously through your wardrobe."

"Like you do my sex life." Maybe Camille's next performance evaluation should include a hefty bonus plus a free session with Jana's personal shopper. Or maybe the money would be more appreciated in a college fund for baby Skylar. She was always searching for new ways to express her appreciation to the woman who made her life so much easier.

Camille followed Jana into her private office. "First things first." She placed a cup of coffee, the perfect shade of beige, on her desk. "Now the bad news. Fergus has called twice. I told him you were on with the widow Mills. That shut him up but won't hold much longer." When Jana gave her an "I can't believe you invoked the recently bereaved look," she shrugged.

"Guess I better get up there." She took a couple of quick sips of coffee and fumbled the flash drive from her briefcase onto the desk like it was radioactive. "You'd think this damn thing was made of gold."

"What *are* you talking about?"

Jana checked herself. She hadn't confided in Camille about Shelby's suspicions yesterday or the fuss over the flash drive. Her assistant had enough on her plate at home with a newborn and hormonal wife without Jana piling on at work. And if something illicit came of her actions, she didn't want Camille implicated. "Nothing. He's just in a mood." She hurried toward the elevator trying to decide what to say to Fergus and coming up blank.

Fergus's secretary waved her in, and Jana waited in front of his desk while he finished a call. When he hung up, he held out his hand without comment, and she placed the flash drive in his palm. She had so many questions, especially after finding the strange notations her mother had written on the bottom of some of the pages, but something kept her from asking even one.

"I trust you haven't opened this."

"I haven't, sir." But she *had* opened and closely scrutinized the copy she'd made. Splitting hairs or lying by omission, Jana didn't see the harm in what she'd done. Fergus picked up some papers on his desk, signaling an end to the meeting, and Jana started to leave but changed her mind. She hadn't become a vice president of the company by avoiding the difficult questions.

"Sir, may I ask again why you're so concerned about archived material that's been in the public domain for years?"

Fergus lowered the papers in a slow, deliberate motion. "We've been over this, Jana. The merger."

"Surely, they already know about our history." Fergus straightened in his chair and his eyes narrowed. She'd gone too far.

"Maybe and maybe not. If they're too preoccupied or inept to conduct due diligence, I'm certainly not going to draw them a map. I can't risk anything surfacing that might harm the image of the company and interfere with this transaction. If you have a problem with that…"

The threat hung in the air between them. Toe the line or else. "I certainly had no intention of sharing the information with anyone. My interest was entirely personal, as I said yesterday." Her curiosity had broadened overnight and blossomed in the last few minutes, but she kept her tone congenial and waded in. "But something else has come to my attention."

"What something else?" Fergus gave her a hard stare, his lips tight.

"My mother left a shoebox and—"

"Congratulations," Fergus practically growled. "What's wrong, not designer?"

"I'm not sure what's in the box yet, but I've been told it could contain information about the company, unflattering information."

Fergus rounded the desk and came within inches of Jana's face. "If so, it's company property, and I expect you to hand it over for proper assessment by our legal team."

The hairs on Jana's neck rose. "Of course, sir, as soon as I remove any personal items."

"So, we understand each other?"

"I believe we do, sir. Thank you for your time." She understood that William Fergus was afraid of something. Whether or not it was connected to Shelby's suspicions, Jana had no idea, but she was certainly going to find out. And snooping when a high-powered man warned her off might call for backup. After the night she'd had, a little peace of mind would be welcome.

When she passed Camille's desk on the way back into her office, she said, "Hold my calls, please." She closed the door and dialed Bennett's cell. "Ben, you got a minute?"

"Sure, what's up."

"Do you have someone in mind for this personal security detail you mentioned?" She heard a door close on Bennett's end, and when she spoke again, her voice was tight with concern.

"Are you okay? Has something else happened?"

"I'm fine. Don't worry. I've decided to explore things further, and based on everything that's happened, I'm willing to entertain the idea of protection. I'm not committing at this point, just looking into the possibility."

"I understand. Let me set up a meeting with my candidate. Are you free for a drink this evening at our place around six? I would say dinner, but we have theater tickets at eight."

"See you then. And thank you, Ben."

CHAPTER SIX

Jana showed up at Bennett and Kerstin's thirty minutes early and swooned when Bennett opened the door wearing black tuxedo pants and a medium blue shirt. "You look…hot. Can I say that to a married woman? Would Kerstin be upset? Sorry I'm so early. I can come back later. Guess I'm more anxious than I thought."

"And rambling just a tad? Thanks. Yes. Kerstin would agree. No problem, and come in."

"Thank you, Ben."

Bennett hugged her and motioned her into the spacious great room. "You'll have to put up with me for a few minutes. Kerstin is… well, she's a gorgeous woman who likes to take her time dressing, especially when we're going out." She looked toward the stairs. "It's one of the many things I love about her."

Would a woman ever look at her with the love and adoration Bennett showed for Kerstin? Probably not since she spent her time bed-hopping instead of looking for a real partner. "And normally you'd be up there with her, enjoying the show, wouldn't you?"

A slight blush colored Bennett's cheeks as she moved toward a wet bar tucked in the corner. "Would you like a drink?"

"Vodka with anything would be great." She leaned across the counter to watch Bennett mix a generous pour of Tito's with cranberry juice, ice, and a lime garnish. "I'm sorry to bother you with this, especially tonight."

"Hey, we're friends. Any time is a good time." Bennett handed her the drink and clicked her beer bottle against the glass. Her smile left no doubt of her sincerity.

"I really hope you have something for me behind that bar," Kerstin said as she came down the stairs. "Besides your handsome self."

Bennett turned toward her wife. "Wow. You look *amazing*. That dress is—"

"Totally original," Jana said. The sapphire fabric contained golden threads running from the mid-calf hem and converging at the waist highlighting Kerstin's shapely figure and accenting her blue eyes. "Is that a Debbie Wingham? Sorry, I play this game of name the designer with Camille at work."

Kerstin blushed, splashing her cheeks and exposed décolletage with color. She flipped her blond hair off her shoulders and hurried to give Bennett a kiss. "Glad you like it, darling." Then she hugged Jana. "It's great to see you again. I've missed you. And yes, it's an early Wingham before she started using priceless jewels in her designs."

"The jewel is inside this one," Bennett said and handed Kerstin a martini. "Let's sit." Bennett waited until Kerstin and Jana were seated, and then joined Kerstin on the loveseat.

Now that the time had come to broach the subject, Jana felt like an overreactive, paranoid woman dodging shadows that didn't exist. She took a deep breath. If anyone could set her straight, it was Bennett and Kerstin. "I suddenly feel foolish for even considering the idea of personal protection."

Kerstin squeezed Jana's hand and gave her an encouraging smile. "Why don't you tell us what's happened since you last spoke with Ben and Adena?"

"Do you mind if we wait for the other guest, so I don't waste your time repeating everything? In the meantime, tell me something about this bodyguard."

Kerstin and Bennett exchanged a curious look before Bennett said, "A recently retired army major, seriously overqualified for this type of work, quiet, and one of the most efficient and responsible people I've ever met. You two will be a good match. I mean, Rafe is perfect for this assignment."

"Wow, that's quite a recommendation from Bennett Carlyle, but I'm not sure I can handle some testosterone overloaded man in my personal space." Bennett and Kerstin exchanged that look again, and Jana asked, "What am I missing?"

"You didn't tell her?" Kerstin asked.

Bennett grinned and the dimples beside her mouth grew deeper. "I didn't see the point until she made a decision."

"If you're trying to make me feel better, your bedside manner needs serious work. I can't be shadowed by the Incredible Hulk at work or in my personal life. He needs at least a modicum of tact, social skills, a non-judgmental attitude, and the ability to string words together in a coherent sentence. Tell me what's up." Jana had to stay in her own home, be free to come and go as she pleased, see her friends, and get laid occasionally.

"Rafe is very differ—" The doorbell interrupted her, and Bennett headed toward the door. "I'll let you judge for yourself."

Kerstin smiled, and her eyes sparked with playfulness and a hint of uncertainty. She'd had the same look when they'd crashed Bennett's bachelor party. Jana took a gulp of her drink and steeled herself to meet the man Bennett thought would be perfect to protect her.

"This is Rafaella Silva," Bennett said. "Rafe."

Jana turned to greet the new arrival, gasped, and sucked part of her drink down her windpipe. She coughed and pulled for air, feeling her face burn with the heat of embarrassment, surprise, and something she hadn't felt in too long, attraction.

Before she could catch her breath, Rafe knelt beside her and patted her on the back. "Can you talk?"

Jana stared at the woman's tanned skin and umber eyes and tried to think of something intelligent to say. What came out was, "You're hired."

Rafe backed away from the woman whose energy tugged at her like the blast wind from an explosion threatening to suck her into its orbit. The woman—blond, expensive clothes, and eyes a peculiar shade of blue—examined her with equal intensity.

"Rafe, this is Jana Elliott," Bennett said. "The friend I told you about."

Jana composed herself and offered her hand, but Rafe simply nodded and said, "Ma'am." Nothing rattled Rafaella Silva, not even the fear and urgency of battle, but something about Jana Elliott disturbed her. "Do you have any Gatorade, Ben?"

"Does a cat have climbing gear? I knew you were coming, so I stocked up." Bennett led the way to the wet bar, pulled Rafe's favorite from the fridge, and handed it over.

She drank and visually clocked everything except Jana Elliott. Bennett and Kerstin had completely renovated the old house and restored its Craftsman features—open floorplan, exposed beams, stained glass, and stone fireplace. The warm interior colors and comfortable furnishings made it feel homey, like the Carlyle family place. Would she one day have a real home, and if so, would it be filled with the love she felt here?

Rafe took another long gulp. The room had quieted, and everybody stared at her. She wiped her mouth with the back of her hand, avoided Jana's gaze, and addressed Bennett. "So, why am I here?" She hoped Jana changed her mind because Rafe *wondered* about her, in a personal way, and personal feelings had no place in her line of work.

"Jana thinks she—"

"Ben, I can speak for myself, thank you." Jana moved to the sofa opposite Bennett and Kerstin and motioned for Rafe to join her.

"I prefer to stand. If you'd tell me, please, what makes you think you need protection?"

"I'm an executive vice president of Alumicor, an aluminum production company. A friend suspects our company is covering up hazardous waste contamination from our plants which has and is causing illnesses and deaths. I downloaded some archived files, the boss demanded I return them, unopened, and doesn't want me to look into the matter further."

"Her office was searched too," Kerstin added.

"And I suggested other unfavorable information might exist. I don't know if it does, yet, but I've been told. And my boss asked about a box containing old files when he visited the home of a recently deceased employee." Jana sipped her drink and stared at the floor.

"You didn't mention that before, Jana." Bennett stood and moved closer to Rafe.

"Why would you warn him that you may have potentially harmful documentation?" Rafe tried to imagine any situation in which crucial information should be shared with a potential adversary.

"I wanted to see his reaction, and it was telling. I'm convinced he's hiding something."

"And now he knows you have something he wants," Kerstin said. "Oh, honey."

Rafe tried to decipher the bits of information. Either Jana was overreacting, or her boss really did have a problem. "Did he explain his request for locking down the archives?"

Jana raked her fingers through her wavy blond hair and sighed. "An upcoming merger. I don't buy it. The info I accessed has been in the public domain for years. The other company would be practically negligent not to research our history."

"Any threats?" Rafe asked. "Are you being surveilled?"

"Nothing overt, and I'm not sure about surveillance. I'm starting to feel a little paranoid, so everything seems suspect, but nothing probably is, really."

Rafe conducted a more thorough assessment as Jana spoke. Intelligent, well-spoken, and physically fit. A confident woman with a moneyed corporate career, enjoying the benefits of privilege, secure and proud of her ability to face adversity and handle problems. A woman of substance, but she was unaware of the shadowy underbelly of politics and business or the dark operators keeping those institutions and men in power. "Have your phones been traced or cloned?"

Jana's face paled. "How would I know?"

"Sorry. I'm not trying to scare you. Maybe you should tell me what you expect from me."

Jana wrung her hands for a few seconds before making eye contact with Rafe. "I want to feel safe again. If you could just watch my back, until I find out what's really going on, that would be great. And depending on what I find, I'll decide about going public, confronting the CEO, or leaving it alone entirely. I'm not afraid of being a tipster. The North Carolina False Claims Act protects whistleblowers from retaliation by their employers for filing a claim or assisting the state with a claim."

As Jana spoke, her eyes teared, and her lower lip trembled. Nothing tugged at Rafe's heart like someone who was afraid and needed help.

"And I'd want to stay in my place, be free to come and go, see friends, and occasionally entertain. Privately, if you get my drift."

"Have sex," Rafe said without hesitation or judgment.

Bennett stifled a laugh, and Kerstin elbowed her.

"Yes, have sex…with women, if that makes a difference to the threat level or whatever you call it." Jana maintained eye contact with Rafe.

"Everything you've said makes a difference to the threat level," Rafe said. "And for the record, women can be as deadly as men. What you're asking is impossible. Protection comes at a price, not just financial, but to your personal comfort and daily routines. Ask the president. Concessions have to be made because you're at risk from the very things you consider familiar and safe." Jana's eyes sparked. Rafe hit a nerve.

"So, you'd have me bound in bubble wrap and locked in a closet?"

"Not exactly," Rafe said. "It's entirely your call if and how you'd like to proceed. You haven't been injured or even overtly threatened yet. Maybe hold off on security because it could draw more attention than ignoring the situation at this point." Rafe placed her empty Gatorade bottle in the trash and headed for the door. "Good evening, Ms. Elliott, and good luck." She nodded to Bennett and Kerstin. "Hope to see you again soon."

Jana rose from the sofa and followed Rafe. "That's it?"

"I'm not trying to sell you anything. If you need me, Ben has my number."

"Stop." Bennett's captain voice halted Rafe in the doorway. "You both want the same thing really."

Rafe stared at Bennett like she'd lost her mind.

"Jana needs to find out if her company is knowingly hurting people, and you've fought the good fight all your life. You want to help people." Bennett pointed to each of them and added, "And you both like necklaces."

"Very funny, Ben." Rafe glanced at Jana's medical alert necklace and wondered why she wore it. None of her business. She reached for the doorknob, but Bennett didn't give up.

"Why don't you talk a bit more before making a final decision? Kerstin and I have to go, but Jana could take you to her place and let you see if what she's asking is totally out of the question. And you could give her some idea of what to expect. How does that sound?"

Jana regarded Bennett and Rafe for a few seconds, chewed her bottom lip as if considering her options, and said, "I could do that, if you have time."

Rafe nodded though her gut warned her to distance from Jana Elliott. In the field, she'd be double-checking her weapons, scanning the horizon for bogies, and preparing to fight, but these dangers were subtle, appealing, and too close. "Where's your car?"

"I walked from downtown. You?"

Rafe pointed to her Ninja motorcycle parked beside Bennett's SUV.

"Pretty. I love the lime-green tubes, but I bet you didn't buy it for beauty, did you?"

"Speed."

"Is it a two-seater?" Jana asked, stroking the sleek curve of the gas tank.

Rafe nodded. "For a single rider, the seat supports your hips at speed. And the *tubes* are actually part of the frame." She rolled her bike out of sight behind the trash bins in the driveway, grabbed her backpack, and motioned for Jana to lead the way. She shot a scowl toward Bennett and Kerstin in the doorway. She'd talk with Bennett about this setup later.

She and Jana cut through Fisher Park to Elm Street, and Rafe guided her close to the buildings and took a position on the street side. Caution flowed with the blood in her veins from years of precision training and live operations, and she constantly scanned for danger.

"You don't talk much."

Jana's heels clopped on the sidewalk, and Rafe cringed as the announcement of their position echoed off the buildings. "Sorry, I'm just not much for small talk."

Jana cocked her head and studied Rafe before speaking again. "Indulge me. I'm guessing you're a serious introvert, few close friends, live a hermit's life somewhere in the woods, and don't really like people."

"Nailed it." Jana had no idea how close she'd come to the truth of Rafe. She wanted to like people but didn't usually encounter the good ones in her line of work. Jana Elliott might be an exception, but Rafe couldn't allow herself to find out, especially if Jana employed her.

Jana pointed to a huge tan and beige block building with expansive windows and a scrolling marquee. "Our new Steven Tanger Center for the Performing Arts. The outside is too blasé for my taste, but when it opens, we'll see if the inside lives up to the hype. Do you go to concerts, plays, or shows?"

"Not really. Don't like crowds."

"How about open-air events?"

"Again, crowds, so no." Jana waved to a park across the street, and Rafe noticed the snug fit of her suit and the curve of her waist and hips. Jana was almost as tall as Rafe but fuller in the right places while still firm. She shouldn't be noticing any of that.

"Okay, nice talk," Jana said jokingly as she swiped a fob in front of the door lock on a high-rise building. Rafe held the door for her, and Jana said, "Home sweet home." She waved to the concierge. "Good evening, Jay. She's with me. No car."

Rafe scanned the entry cameras, other exits, and the monitoring equipment behind the concierge's desk. When the elevator arrived, Jana again swiped her fob and pushed the button to the tenth floor. The doors closed, and Rafe's skin prickled with conflicting sensations. Confined space. Limited egress. Jana's subtle lavender perfume wafted into every crevice like the pervasive sand of the Arabian desert. She backed into the corner, but it didn't help.

"You can only get to your own floor unless you're accompanied by a resident, granted access by the concierge, or buzzed up with our Air-Phone system that has visual ID and entry code capability. Secure enough for you, Silva?"

Rafe forced her attention away from Jana's distractions and back to the task at hand. "How many general staff have pass keys to the entire building? How many executives? How many employees of the offices downstairs?" Jana's confident expression turned to doubt.

"I'm not sure."

"How many people live on your floor? What are their names? Do they ever leave the stairwell door propped open for other guests in the building to visit?"

The space between Jana's eyes wrinkled into double lines. "Uh, I don't know." When they reached her door, Jana raised her key to the lock.

"Wait. Always check if the door is locked before you try the key."

Jana's hand shook as she reached for and tested the handle. Locked. She turned the key and preceded Rafe inside, holding the door open for her.

Rafe held her breath. Was she ready for this? She second-guessed herself around Jana in neutral spaces like Bennett's home, on the street, and in an elevator. Could she focus in the place infused with her essence? And *why* was Jana a problem? Maybe because Rafe had been around men most of her life and didn't know how to act in the presence of a refined woman. She hadn't dated anyone in years, so Jana's femininity and confidence were especially appealing. Rafe blocked the unproductive thoughts and concentrated on the one thing that always kept her focused. The job.

CHAPTER SEVEN

J ana held her condo door open and studied Rafe in the moonlight filtering through the floor-to-ceiling windows. Intimidating came to mind—hair the color of wet coal that absorbed the light and a body honed like a weapon. Jana shivered from the dangerous image and a hint of something else. What would it feel like to run her fingers along the shaved sides of Rafe's hair and tug on the unruly curls that fell across her forehead? She shook away the image and reached for the light switch.

"Wait," Rafe whispered. "Leave them off and stay here while I do a sweep." She closed the door, ducked into the kitchen for a few seconds, and then disappeared down the hallway to the bedrooms. In a few minutes, she returned. "All clear. You can turn the lights on now."

Jana flipped the switch and groaned. She'd walked out of her fuzzy bedroom slippers and discarded them near the front door. Her cereal bowl and open computer from this morning littered the kitchen island. Her favorite Sherpa blanket and lacy bra mocked her from the sofa where she'd abandoned them last night.

"Sorry for the mess. I wasn't expecting company." She kicked the shoes under the entry bench and hurried to retrieve the bra, her face and neck flushing with heat.

"Mind if I look around?"

"I thought you just did that." She tucked the bra inside her suit jacket and shuffled awkwardly like she was the visitor.

"That was just a security check. Now, I need to do a proper assessment to see if the place is defensible…in the event you decide to hire me…if that's okay with you."

"Sure, but can I change clothes first? I'd love to get into something more comfortable." Goddess, that sounded like a come-on.

Rafe shrugged. "It's your place. I'll work in here first."

"If you want something to drink, I have sodas in the fridge, alcohol over the fridge, and glasses to the right of the sink. Help yourself. Sorry, no Gatorade." Without waiting for a reply, she escaped to her bedroom and closed the door.

What did *I'll work in here first* mean? The living, dining room, and kitchen were open with a floor-to-ceiling sliding door the only exit. Rafe could stand in one spot and *assess* all she wanted. Jana's stomach knotted at a stranger rummaging through her condo—the place she loved and felt safe—and grading its deficits. She stripped off her work clothes and collapsed across the bed. Her skin was clammy, and her senses muddled. Too much had happened in such a short time and none of it made sense.

Rafe Silva rattled her nerves and made her pulse race. She was the type of woman Jana could be interested in…if. If Jana didn't hire her. If Rafe wasn't such a regimented ex-military specimen. If she ever talked about herself. If she was even vaguely interested. A question she hadn't considered in years rushed to the surface. Would Rafe be interested in her? What kind of woman would appeal to her after an army career eating, sleeping, working, and fighting with mostly men? "One who drinks beer, burps, and farts aloud and tells sex jokes?" *So* not me. Stereotype much? She chuckled and pulled on a pair of American Airlines first-class pajamas and went back to the living area.

Rafe sat rigid in the straight-backed chair at the corner window scribbling in a small notepad. Her position allowed a view of the entire living space and the front door. She looked up when Jana returned. "May I check the bedrooms now?"

"All yours." She squelched a flutter of unease by pouring herself a glass of wine as Rafe headed toward her bedroom. What would she think of the queen-sized bed cluttered with pillows, her colorful flip-and-pour paintings, and the work clothes piled on top of the old school desk ready for the cleaners? What would her choice of furniture, artwork, and accessories tell Rafe about Jana's priorities and how she lived? What did it matter? She settled on the sofa and sipped her wine. Rafe would be in her life briefly, if at all after tonight.

When Rafe returned to the living area, she again took the chair by the window and flipped through her notepad. "Would you mind telling me why you like this place?"

Jana started to fire off a defensive answer, but the tight line of Rafe's mouth and her narrowed eyes indicated she was still in evaluation mode. "If I can cook while we talk. I'm starving. Are you hungry?"

"I can always eat."

"Is an omelet okay? It's easy, filling, and total protein and veggies." She moved to the kitchen and scrounged the ingredients from the refrigerator. When she turned around, Rafe was sitting at the island watching her.

"I'm not picky. I've survived on MREs most of my life."

Jana chopped red and yellow peppers and onions and sautéed them in butter. "MREs?" She asked to mask the growling of her stomach.

"Meals ready to eat. Pre-packaged food like chili with beans, shredded beef in barbecue sauce, or chicken, egg noodles, and vegetables in mystery sauce. The list goes on. Filling but not tasty and predominately carbs for energy. Can I help with anything? I absolutely can't cook, but I'm good at breaking things. Eggs maybe?"

"Thanks, but I've got this." Jana cracked and whipped the eggs, poured them over the mixture, and sprinkled pepper jack cheese on top. "That's the most you've said since we met. You have a very confident and soothing voice." The truth was Rafe's voice reminded Jana of sex by candlelight, sultry, inviting, and just raspy enough to cause goose bumps.

"Thanks, I think." Rafe cleared her throat.

Had a simple compliment flustered Rafe? "If you want coffee, turn on the pot. The timing should be perfect. And grab a couple of plates and cups from the cabinet to the left of the sink." She liked that Rafe offered to help and took direction without question. Maybe all that regimented training had its benefits. Rafe set the plates on the island but then just stared at Jana's assortment of coffee cups. "Something wrong?"

"Do you have anything more…substantial? Reference my earlier comment about breaking things. These look fragile."

"Sorry, soldier, no metal cups or plates here." Jana chuckled. "Just pick one and do your worst. None of them are priceless heirlooms."

Rafe filled two cups with coffee and resettled at the island. "Back to the question."

"And just when I was starting to enjoy your company." Jana plated the food, slid one across to Rafe, and ate standing up. "Yes, why I like it here. I always wanted to live in a vibrant downtown with entertainment venues, restaurants, and people. Living in the middle of nowhere would drive me insane. I get the morning light and practically never lower the shades, even in the bedroom. Who can spy on me ten floors up? I also appreciate the lock-and-leave capability because I love to travel. The building is relatively secure, and there's only one door into my condo. The staff is friendly, helpful, and keeps the place immaculate. I have choices during downtown events—avoid them entirely by staying inside, enjoy them from my balconies, or immerse myself in the action on the street. What's not to love about my condo? Wait, I bet you're about to tell me."

Rafe referenced the notes she'd placed beside her plate. "The building entry isn't awful, as long as no one follows you in or hitches with another tenant to your floor. The staff would have to be vetted and all entry fobs accounted for. I'd want a list of the residents on your floor so I could check them out." She raised her eyebrows as if asking permission to continue.

"Go ahead."

"I would prefer the shades be down at all times, and I'd need to post myself in this room with eyes on the entry and hallway to your room. I'm not sure how you envision this arrangement working during the day since you suspect your boss isn't being entirely honest."

Jana dropped her fork and it clattered on her empty plate before falling to the floor. "I'd forgotten about that." How would she explain the handsome soldier to anyone in the office, but especially her intuitive assistant, Camille? Rafe's demeanor, her posture, even the way she spoke telegraphed intrigue, intensity, military. It would take years of reintegration before Jana could sell Rafe as a civilian. "Can't you just stake out the building? We're talking about a multinational corporation, not the mafia."

"They're called *body*guards for a reason." Rafe finished her omelet and collected the empty plates. "I'll clean up."

"Not a chance. Sit. Think about how to sell someone like you"— she waved her hand up and down in front of Rafe—"to a group of touchy-feely types in my office. I'll just pop these in the dishwasher."

"You like to take care of people, don't you?"

The observation caught her off guard. She hadn't expected any degree of personal evaluation from Rafe, but she was pleasantly surprised. "It's what I do, just like you do…whatever you do. Rescue, I'm guessing. I'm all about the human relations aspect of things." She hadn't thought herself so transparent, but Rafe drilled to the heart of who she was—a caregiver. Rafe Silva was more complex and interesting than Jana first imagined.

Maybe she was simply intrigued by Rafe's mystique. When you know nothing about a person, anything seems possible. She knew little about Rafe, while she knew too much about her—her job, where she lived, how messy she could be, that she could cook, liked taking care of people, slept with women, and possibly her bra size—everything except the type of woman she preferred, and she might've intuited that as well.

Jana busied herself with the cleanup. What was she thinking? This could never work, personally or professionally. Fergus would suspect a stranger in the company of being a spy for the merger, or worse, for the opposition. Her social life would become unrecognizable, and her friends would likely abandon her. She finished tidying and returned to the sofa. "This probably isn't a very good idea. A bodyguard will signal the CEO that I'm going against his wishes and fear retaliation."

"Why don't you sleep on it? Weigh the pros and cons, and if you still want to employ me, think about how I might blend in at your office. You know your company. In the meantime, I'll get out of your way."

"We haven't discussed your fee."

"That's another thing that might be prohibitive. I'm very expensive. Being a bodyguard means no off time, unless you want to hire a relief person, and requires total commitment to the protectee. That kind of obligation isn't cheap."

Jana liked the sound of *total commitment to the protectee* and for a second imagined the things she might possibly command her bodyguard to do. "Does that mean you'd have to do whatever I told you?"

The corners of Rafe's mouth rose, but she checked herself and brushed at the curls that fell across her forehead. "*You'd* have to obey *me*. Can you handle that?"

Jana's breath stuck in her throat at the thought of obeying the sexy Rafe Silva in another succession of arousing possibilities. "Might be an interesting test."

"Think about it. Women in powerful positions don't always adjust well to taking orders." Rafe rose and put her coffee cup in the dishwasher. "Thank you for dinner. It was an unexpected but much appreciated bonus. I'll leave my number on the pad by the entry."

Rafe headed toward the door, and with each step, Jana's pulse quickened. She'd provoked Fergus today with information she didn't have. Not her brightest move. And the talk about security, vetting staff, and ways to violate what she considered her sanctuary unnerved her. "I don't suppose you'd stay?"

Rafe turned back, her forehead furrowed. "Have I frightened you?"

"Maybe just gave me a reality check." Did she suddenly feel unsafe in her own home? Had Rafe's observations scared her, or was she seeing life through a different lens and realizing another possibility? "But I haven't hired you, have I? And you didn't bring any clothes, did you? Or your *tools*? Where would you sleep? Am I creating a problem?"

Rafe stared at Jana from her position by the door as if searching for something specific. She cocked her head to the right, appraising with those dark eyes that made Jana feel exposed and yet strangely calm.

She tried to blank her expression, but Rafe's gaze was too intense. An inspection that close deserved less space so Jana walked toward Rafe. For the first time, Jana noticed the fullness of her lips, the flecks of gold in her brown eyes, and a jagged scar near her hairline partially covered by errant curls. She cleared her throat. "Wh—what?"

"I asked if you always jabber like an automatic weapon when you're nervous?"

All Jana could do was nod. How could a single look make her feel simultaneously vulnerable and safe?

"No, you haven't hired me, yet. I did bring clothes." She hefted the backpack over her shoulder. "Necessary tools included. The recliner is fine if you'd allow me to turn it toward the door. I don't sleep much anyway. And you haven't begun to create problems yet, Ms. Elliott. Would you like me to stay?"

Jana prided herself on handling problems and taking care of people, not the other way around, but something about Rafe Silva said maybe just this once she could be the receiver. She released a deep breath. "Yes, please."

"Done."

"Thank you. I'll get a blanket and pillow. The guest bathroom is all yours." Jana's pulse returned to normal. When had she become so afraid? She was usually so capable and self-assured. Yesterday, she wouldn't have invited a stranger to spend the night with her, and today, it felt right. Was Fergus's secret worth the disruption to her life, her peace of mind, and safety? If people were at risk, it was worth whatever she had to do to expose the truth.

CHAPTER EIGHT

Rafe stirred from a catnap before the sun topped the horizon and assessed her surroundings out of habit. She listened before opening her eyes, inhaled the air and tasted it on her tongue, and then visually scanned for threats. High-rise condo. Two possible points of attack. Secure and currently danger free. She imagined relaxing in the unfamiliar environment, enjoying the sky and clouds, no grass or water at her disposal, and growing tolerant of the sounds of traffic and people below on the street, but the only thing that felt right about this place was the woman who occupied it.

G-ma Carlyle always said a person's home was a museum to their life, holding memories and revealing their nature. If that was true, Jana's expensive taste ended with her wardrobe. The furnishings were contemporary but felt warm, well-used, and welcoming. Actual photos, not an electronic gadget that flipped images, and hardback books populated the bookshelves. Rafe studied each picture—an older version of Jana at a rally of some sort, college friends at graduation, more recent updates of the same group, and two attractive women with a baby—people who mattered to Jana. If her clothes said extravagant and aloof, her home screamed function and hospitality. Which of Jana's contradictions was the truth of her, Rafe had yet to discover.

The lingering scents of Jana's flowery perfume and last night's omelet and coffee still filled the unit. Their evening felt like a date, or at least what she remembered of dates, until she saw the fear in Jana's eyes. Why was she so blunt in her assessment? Jana wasn't a soldier who needed hard facts or a government representative who'd spin whatever she told them to their own advantage. She was a woman who discovered her world was not exactly as it seemed…and feared it. But Rafe couldn't afford to sugarcoat the truth or indulge her latent emotions now. Jana needed, and deserved, her to be on top of her game.

She slid out of the recliner, returned it to its original position, and reached for her backpack, diverting to the kitchen to turn on the coffee pot before hitting the bathroom. The shower spray pounded her stiff shoulders with the pressure lacking in the nest. She'd missed this most on her missions, often going for days without enough water for minimal cleaning, much less the luxury of a shower. It never seemed to bother the rest of the team.

Were the guys on another assignment? Had they filled her position already? Maybe they could get together for a beer. A chill in the water temperature brought her back to the reality of her situation. Retired. Her quasi-family was gone, and she needed a new purpose. What had her service experience prepared her for in the civilian world? Being a bodyguard? Most corporations didn't require her specific skill set.

She turned off the shower, dried, and wiped down the tile with her microfiber towel, and then cleaned the drain and put everything back exactly as she'd found it. Force of habit. Leave no trace. A few minutes later, she was dressed and sitting at the kitchen island drinking coffee. The sound of the master bathroom shower preceded Jana's cushioned footsteps in the hall.

"Good morning. Thought I smelled coffee. Thanks. I've never tried sleeping in the recliner. How was it?" She paused. "Sorry, I'm jabbering, as you put it. Not used to anyone being here in the morning. Wait, that sounded weird." She filled her coffee cup but kept her back to Rafe. "I have guests, of course, but they don't often stay…I mean they're—"

"Stop." Rafe considered letting Jana ramble, because she was adorable when she was a bit edgy. At least Rafe wasn't the only one with a case of nerves. "You don't have to explain your life to me. Sleep well?"

Jana stretched and her silky robe gapped open revealing lacy underwear, her lean torso, and long, shapely legs. "The best sleep I've had in three days for sure. I can't thank you enough for staying. Did you sleep?"

Rafe shook her head.

"I imagine in your line of work sleep is a luxury you can't often afford."

Rafe nodded and took another sip of coffee. "Sleep is like a mini death, and it brings memories of too many others."

Jana stared as if grappling for a response to the morbid observation but decided against it. "Okay, then, how about I make breakfast?"

Rafe raised her cup. "I'm not much of a morning food person, just keep this coming and I'm fine." Jana took the stool beside Rafe at the island, and she got a whiff of her delicate perfume and freshly showered skin—a blend of flowers, fresh air, and rain—three of her favorite things. She turned sideways and breathed deeply to refocus before facing Jana again.

"I've been thinking about how we can get you into Alumicor," Jana said.

"Let's hear it."

"Last week we had a walk-in, what our security folks called a breach, but was actually a homeless man looking for food. He wasn't threatening or anything, just needed help. The boss wasn't happy with the company because we're card-access only, and they're supposed to man the front entrance at all times. I could pass you off as a security expert. It's what you do, right?"

"Not exactly but go on."

"I could say I've asked you to conduct an independent review of the incident to determine what happened and give us and the security company recommendations. It wouldn't be a lie to say some of our personnel were shaken by the incident. What do you think?" She took a sip of coffee and licked her lips, and again, Rafe looked away.

"It has potential, but wouldn't that require me to actually assess the building instead of watching over you?"

"Hmmm. I see what you mean. Somebody would need to show you around the place, and that could easily be me. And once you've conducted your evaluation, you can camp out in my office or adjoining conference room with your laptop to finish the report. I assume you do have a laptop?"

Rafe nodded. "Sounds like a plan. I can sell being a threat assessment professional."

"I'll call Camille and have her organize an access card. You can have your picture taken when we arrive." She studied Rafe for a few seconds, a look that made her skin heat and thoughts wander, before adding, "But we'll have to do something about your outfit."

Rafe looked down at the black heavy-duty cargo pants, T-shirt, and boots she'd worn as her unofficial uniform for years. "What's wrong with my clothes?"

Jana stuck her tongue between her lips and bit down to keep from laughing, but her blue eyes sparkled. "Can you say terrifying? You look like SEAL Team Six. Very attractive but still."

"Shut up." Rafe slapped her hand over her heart. "How dare you compare a member of Delta Force to those SEAL Team guys."

"Sorry? But my point is, people in corporate America like to feel comfortable, not intimidated by Commando Barbie. And you have to meet Fergus before our plan can work."

Rafe mentally inventoried her small stack of clothes in the nest and shrugged. "I don't have any business attire. I was a soldier and when I wasn't in uniform, I wore this."

"What did you wear on dates?"

Jana's cheeks turned a delicious shade of pink, and Rafe smothered a laugh with another sip of coffee. "I haven't dated in years."

"*Years*? You're kidding, right? But you've been out, hooked up, had some kind of…interaction…with whomever?" Jana's tone made it sound like she'd committed a crime.

"I couldn't exactly join dating sites in my line of work, and the places I was deployed didn't lend themselves to bars, alcohol, or cruising for lesbian company." She shied from Jana's stare and noted the ache in her chest. The service devoured her like a jealous lover and never cared about clothes, how she looked, or if her personal needs were met. Why did it matter now? Feelings were not part of her job. "Back to my wardrobe?"

"Sorry. I didn't mean to pry. I think I have something that will work."

"I've seen what you wear, and trust me, I'm not a designer suit woman."

"You don't have to be. Will you just trust me?" Jana rose from the island and motioned for Rafe to follow.

"I'll just go shopping on the way to your office."

"Where?" Jana asked. "Army-Navy surplus? None of the actual clothing stores open until ten, and we have to be at work no later than nine, though I'm usually in by eight."

She followed Jana down the hall, each step more uncertain than the last. Was she really doing this? Going into Jana's bedroom with the queen-sized bed? The most intimate room in her home, where she'd probably had sex with more women than Rafe even knew. *Stop. Focus.*

Jana pointed to a chair in the corner. "Sit while I work my magic." She kept talking as she stepped into the walk-in closet. "We're close to the same height, and similar size, just distributed differently."

Similar but so very different. Rafe couldn't resist the pull to look at Jana, and when she did, the closet light shown through the sheer fabric of Jana's nightgown and outlined the ways their bodies contrasted. "Damn." Rafe moaned and stiffened with an urge so unfamiliar it felt like something foreign awakening inside her.

"What?" Jana stuck her head out of the closet. "What did you say?"

"Not—nothing. This is just crazy."

Jana emerged with her arms full of options. "I think you'll like these." She smiled, and her eyes grew wide. "It's like a treasure hunt in there." She dropped the pile on the bed and tweezed out a pair of black jeans, a white button-down shirt, and a black and gray tweed jacket with leather-patched elbows.

"O—kay."

"Okay yes or okay no?" Jana asked.

"Actually, not bad." She'd found probably the only things in her exorbitant wardrobe that Rafe *would* wear.

Jana grinned. "You assess things your way, and I assess them mine. These are from my tomboy phase, before personal shoppers. Try them on."

Rafe grabbed the outfit and started toward the door.

"Where are you going?"

"The bathroom to change."

"Try them on here, so I can see how they fit and what needs to be changed."

Rafe shook her head. She did that a lot around Jana, unsure what to say or how to say it. "Not happening. I'll be back."

"What's the matter, don't trust me?" When Rafe didn't answer, Jana motioned to the other door in her suite. "Well, at least use my bathroom. We're running out of time."

Rafe could've sworn Jana laughed as she closed the bathroom door and stripped. She pulled on the jeans first, followed by the shirt. She'd try the jacket after Jana approved the rest.

When she stepped back into the bedroom, Jana froze holding a red T-shirt in front of her. "Oh. Wow. Those look way better on you than they ever did on me." She dropped the T-shirt and reached toward Rafe. "May I?"

"I guess." Rafe's body burned like flash paper when Jana lifted the shirt and tucked two fingers in the waistband of the jeans to check the fit. She puffed slow breaths to control her pulse. When was the last time she'd been touched other than in combat training or an actual fight? And she'd never felt skin as soft and tender as Jana's.

"They're perfect in the waist, maybe a little tight through the thighs but not at all unattractive." Jana ran her hand down the front of Rafe's leg and pulled at the fabric.

"Please." She sounded tense and needy. "Stop."

Jana stepped back. "Sorry. I guess you don't like to be touched."

The problem was, Rafe liked Jana's touch too much, but went with the offered out.

Jana put her hands on her hips and studied the shirt. "I think that's definitely too loose. Try this. I'll even give you privacy." She tossed the red T-shirt to Rafe and turned her back.

Rafe shucked the blouse off and pulled the T-shirt over her head. "Yeah, now you're talking. Great."

Jana turned. "Yes, it certainly is. It compliments that tanned complexion of yours and doesn't look like someone stole half of your breasts. Now, the jacket." Rafe's face heated, and Jana said, "You really should learn to take a compliment."

"Not my thing." She slid her arms into the jacket sleeves and tugged it together in the front. "A little snug in the arms but I can deal."

"Perfect. You look business casual, which suits someone in your line of work. Too dressed and you look soft. Too sloppy and you're unreliable. Now, go caffeinate while I get dressed."

Rafe took a couple of steps and stopped. "Thank you. You realize we might be doing this for nothing. You haven't even decided if you want to hire me yet."

"And I won't know until we pull off this scam. Think positively. And you're welcome. And thank you for staying last night. And—"

"Stop rambling and dress, Ms. Elliott."

Jana saluted. "Aye, aye, ma'am."

Rafe scooped up her discarded clothes from the bathroom and folded them neatly into her backpack in the living area. She poured another cup of coffee and tried not to think about wearing Jana's clothes. The guys called this the cheater's way into a woman's pants. She'd definitely been around men too long. Part of her prayed this job opportunity fell through, but the other part really wanted it to work. If it didn't, she'd have no excuse to see Jana again...and maybe that was best. No two people could be more different.

CHAPTER NINE

Jana waved to the concierge on the way out of the building with Rafe close behind. She was tempted to grab Rafe's hand so the women in the lobby would stop ogling her, but Rafe would probably freak.

"I need to pick up my bike from Ben's place," Rafe said as they walked.

"You won't need it. We're here."

Rafe gawked at the granite high-rise. "Easy commute. What is it, half a block?"

"Not even. I actually counted the steps once door to door, walking and running."

Rafe cocked her head to the side, sending curls dancing across her forehead.

"Slow day." Jana motioned toward the elevator. "We're on the ninth floor." Rafe tensed beside her as they squeezed into the packed space. "Relax. It's a quick ride if we go straight through." Rafe craned her neck to look at the floor indicator where every stop was illuminated. Jana shrugged. "Sorry. Are you ready for this?" She hoped to distract Rafe and take her own mind off explaining her companion to Camille.

"I will be once we're on site."

With each departure from the elevator, Rafe breathed more easily and seemed to fill the vacated space. She rolled her shoulders and flexed her neck right and left as if preparing for battle. "Remember, you'll be dealing with civilians, so—"

"No kicking ass and taking names?"

Rafe shot her a full smile, and Jana almost swooned. She'd never met a woman so confident, attractive, and vexingly unaware of her appeal. "Exactly. And please be extra careful with my assistant, Camille. She's very perceptive. If anyone smells a rat, it'll be her." The elevator pinged on their floor, and Jana said under her breath, "Here we go."

Camille was waiting with the ID printer in her hand. "I'm read—" Her gaze shifted from Jana to Rafe without a second glance at Jana's Armani suit much less a comment. "Wow. I mean. Uh…*you're* the—"

"Threat assessment expert," Jana said. "Close your mouth, Camille. This is Rafaella Silva of Silva Security Solutions. Do you have her ID?"

"Just need a photo." She pointed to the blank wall beside the elevator. "If you'd stand over there, Rafaella."

"Just Rafe."

Camille faced Jana and mouthed, *Oh, my God,* and gave her a thumbs up. She snapped Rafe's picture, and a few seconds later, the printer spat out the laminated ID. She attached a clip and took her time hooking it to the lapel of Rafe's jacket. "There you go, Rafe, your all-access, go anywhere anytime pass to everything Alumicor."

"Thank you, Camille. It's a pleasure to meet you. Ms. Elliott speaks highly of you."

Camille actually blushed, something Jana had never seen before. "Yes, thank you, Camille. Have you checked with Fergus?"

Camille didn't take her eyes off Rafe. "Yes, he can see you now. Both of you."

If she didn't get Rafe away from Camille, she might forget she was a married woman with a new baby. "Good." She inclined her head toward the private elevator at the end of the hall. "This way, Rafe."

As they walked, Rafe said, "Camille seems very nice."

"The best. She and her wife just had a baby girl." Why she'd offered Camille's personal status wasn't clear. Maybe to red flag any interest Rafe might have in her assistant, or maybe she'd been the tiniest bit jealous of the easy way Camille fawned over Rafe. Why couldn't she express her interest as freely? She certainly did with her usual liaisons, straightforward wham-bam-thank-you-ma'am sex.

She stopped in front of Fergus's door and circled back to the thought of family. "Do you have relatives here?"

"No," Rafe said in a tone so flat and sad that Jana hesitated to clarify.

"Not here?"

"No family. Period." Rafe nodded to the closed door. "Shall we?"

"Sure you're ready?"

Rafe nodded. "Don't worry, Jana. I've got you."

Jana's pulse trebled as she knocked on the door, and Fergus bellowed for them to enter.

"Good morning, sir. This is Rafaella Silva of Silva Security Solutions. Rafe, this is William Fergus, CEO of Alumicor. I've asked Rafe to investigate last week's security breach and make recommendations for improvement. Some of the staff were upset by the incident." Rafe and Fergus shook hands and sized each other up like fighters circling in the ring, and Rafe didn't flinch from his dark-eyed appraisal.

"Sir," Rafe said.

"Have a seat and tell me about yourself and your company." Fergus motioned to the leather chairs in front of his desk. "I couldn't find you on the internet."

"I recently retired from the military and started the company. It's strictly a word of mouth and referral operation at this stage. I plan to be selective with my clientele."

"Smart." Fergus turned to Jana. "And how did you hear about Ms. Silva?"

"Captain Bennett Carlyle of the Greensboro Police Department is a friend. I mentioned the incident of last week, and she referred me to Rafe."

Fergus nodded. "The Carlyles are good people. I knew her father and grandfather, both excellent cops. What branch of the service, Ms. Silva?"

"Army."

"I was army as well. Any special unit?"

"Combat Application Group," Rafe said.

Jana enjoyed the mini interrogation that afforded her a glimpse into Rafe's background.

"You were Delta Force?" Fergus nodded and leaned back in his chair. "That's a tier one anti-terrorist unit."

"As a soldier yourself, you know I can't comment on that."

"Well, you obviously know your stuff. The *security* company we're using apparently has no concept of what the word means. We're in merger negotiations, so I look forward to your rapid assessment." Fergus stood and shook Rafe's hand again, neither of which he ever did with Jana. "Welcome aboard. If you do a good job, I'll refer some of my top-tier clients to get your business started."

Jana clenched her teeth at Fergus's condescending tone. As if Rafe would need any of his cronies to establish herself, but Rafe's expression didn't change.

"Thank you, sir, I'd appreciate that."

As they neared the door, Fergus added, "Oh yeah, good initiative, Jana. By the way, did you bring the item we discussed yesterday?"

"The box?" Fergus nodded, and Jana continued. "No sir. I haven't had a chance to look inside it yet with this security breech and finalizing the Kitamura paperwork. But I'll get it to you as soon as possible."

She hurried Rafe out the door before Fergus could respond and then diverted into the restroom. She checked they were alone, locked the door, and leaned against the cool tiled wall. "I need a second to process. You may be used to this clandestine business, but I'm not."

"I thought it went well," Rafe said, her voice cool and confident.

"It went like clockwork, until he asked about the box. You totally own him."

"I researched him while you were sleeping this morning. Once I found out he'd been in the army, it was easy."

"Why?"

"People who've served share a bond. I knew if his first impression was good, we'd be fine. Army strong. Hooah!"

Without thinking, Jana grabbed Rafe in a bear hug. "You are totally awesome. Thank you." Her body caught up with her impulsiveness and warmed against Rafe. She felt good—strong, dependable, sexy as hell, and more than a little tense. Rafe was holding her breath. "I'm sorry." She backed away. "I'm just so relieved."

"Shall we get started?" Rafe exited the restroom without waiting for an answer.

Camille perched on the side of her desk when they entered her complex. "Jana, I was thinking maybe I could show Rafe around while you catch up on phone messages."

"That won't be necessary. I've got plenty of time." When Rafe turned to survey the complex, she waved her finger back and forth at Camille in a no-no motion. "We'll start in my office. Would you please bring us coffee? My usual and one black." She caught her mistake immediately, and Camille did as well.

"Will do, boss." She winked and sashayed toward the break room.

"She'll have questions," Rafe said from so close that Jana jumped.

"I told you she's sharp. Knowing how you like your coffee when we supposedly just met will be interesting to explain."

"Tell her the truth. She knows the employees, and I'll need her for access to your calendar and such without bothering you every time."

Jana settled on the sofa overlooking the eastern skyline and motioned for Rafe to join her. "That sounds perfectly reasonable unless you know Camille. She's very protective, which I love about her, but she's not trained or discerning in threat assessment like you. She'd insist on vetting and body searching everyone who wants to see me."

"Would that be a problem?" Rafe followed the question with an evil grin that nearly took Jana's breath. "The glass surrounding your office makes visual surveillance easy, but the problem will be audio coverage and walk-ins. I assume you have employees drop by with and without appointments."

Jana nodded.

"With access to your calendar, I can check the scheduled ones but not the others." Rafe swept the hair away from her forehead, and Jana caught another glimpse of the untanned scar near her hairline. "Any suggestions of how I might handle them without inside help?"

"Huh?" Jana was busy trying to find a way to ask about the injury. "Oh. Well, like I said before, I don't think anything is going to happen at work. Who sends a hitman into an office full of witnesses?" The thought sent a shiver up her spine, but she smiled to cover her discomfort.

"You'd be surprised. Could you set me up in there and allow audible access to your meetings?" Rafe pointed to the adjacent conference room with clear line of sight into Jana's office. "I'll sign an NDA if you prefer, though my contract will cover anything I see and hear during the course of my employment...assuming you employ me."

"After that performance with Fergus, of course I'm employing you. And yes, I'm fine with that arrangement."

Rafe studied her for a few seconds before asking, "Are you sure you don't want to wait and see if anything else happens before jumping into a protection detail? It's been several days since your office was searched and nothing since."

"Except Fergus's attempts to get his hands on that shoebox. Peace of mind is worth whatever it takes. So stop trying to talk yourself out of a job." Was protection necessary, or did she just want to keep Rafe close until she figured her out? Without thinking, she blurted. "How did you get that scar on your forehead?" The lines around Rafe's mouth tightened, and her hand automatically went to the injury. "Sorry. I obviously have no filter around you."

"Knife fight."

"Yeah, right." Jana almost laughed, but Rafe's expression didn't change. "Really?" When Rafe nodded, Jana plowed forward. "Have you killed people?" She wanted to know and didn't.

Rafe's mood turned as black as her hair, and she crossed to the window. "The army was my life for twenty-five years. I served in almost every war-torn country on the globe. What do you think?" Jana started to answer, but Rafe held up her hand. "It's not something I'm proud of. It took part of my soul. But when I joined, I wasn't even aware I had a soul, much less anything to offer the army. Honestly, I think I wanted to die, and going to war was the quickest way to accomplish that."

Jana stared at Rafe's back, unable to believe how candid she was about her past and how much her admission affected Jana. She wanted to reassure Rafe and encourage her to say more but didn't speak for fear of breaking their intimate bubble.

"But life is a jealous mistress that holds on to you. If you're lucky, she gives you hope. If not, she rips you apart bit by bit and feeds you to the dark side, which is what happened to me." Rafe turned to face her. "And on that uplifting note, that's all I can say about my former career." She glanced toward Camille's desk. "Maybe your assistant should show me around."

"I'm sorry I upset you." She watched helplessly as Rafe walked toward the door. "I don't have any appointments this morning, so I'll be here returning calls."

"Consider telling Camille the truth or at least afford me the opportunity to feel her out about it," Rafe said.

Jana cringed at the feeling out part but nodded. "I trust your instincts."

"Let's hope you're as agreeable with everything I say going forward."

Jana wrinkled her nose. "Not likely."

When Jana turned Rafe over to Camille and excused herself to make phone calls, she felt restless, no longer comfortable in her hallowed space. She delved into Rafe's past, got shut down, and distanced a potential ally. She needed a friendly voice, not one that constantly told her how terrible things could get.

Kerstin answered on the first ring, and Jana's voice caught in her throat. "Kerst—"

"Oh, honey, are you all right? What happened? Do you need me to come over? I can drop everything and be there in five minutes."

Jana fought back tears. It was so Kerstin to key in on her feelings with a single word. "No, I'm okay, but thanks for the offer. I'm at work."

"Well, you sound like you're about to cry. Tell me. Is it Rafe? I noticed her bike has been in our driveway all night. Did the two of you—"

"Nope. Nooooo."

"Sorry. Not the priority. So, what's got you so upset?"

When was the last time someone asked that question and actually wanted to know the answer? She bit her lip to keep from crying as the feelings of the past few days caught up with her. "I'm…I'm not sure. One minute I think I'm imagining any threat at all, and the next, I'm certain I'm being followed. And Rafe doesn't help. She's all about worst-case scenarios." She pulled a long breath and started again. "Does she *ever* talk about anything but problems, plans, and outcomes?" Kerstin's hearty laugh caught Jana off guard. "What?"

"You're talking about a retired army major. A member of Delta Force, the most elite group in the army. Most of what she's done throughout her career is classified. It's hard to share a life of experiences you're forbidden to discuss. I get the impression from Ben that the army has been Rafe's entire existence, and she retired less than a week ago. Maybe she doesn't know how to be any other way in the world."

"That's painfully obvious. I'd hoped to feel safer while I figured out what's going on at the company, but so far, she's made me even more paranoid and confused. You know me, I like to talk, get to know a person, but it's either our strategy or silence."

"I'm sorry, Jana. She's really pretty awesome when she's not working, but when she is, she's one hundred percent focused."

"I do believe nothing will get past her. Guess I just needed to hear a friendly voice and vent. Thanks for listening."

"Anytime, my friend. Maybe we can all have dinner and help her open up a little."

"Okay, but I'm not *interested* in her, just trying to communicate."

Kerstin stifled a chuckle. "Sure, I mean who'd be interested in a tall, olive-skinned woman with killer good looks and a body to die for? Really, Jana, have you checked your standards lately?"

"Stop it. I have to get back to work. At least you made me smile. Love you."

"Love you more."

Jana hung up and imagined a date with Rafe—gorgeous eye candy but no conversation. What would she be like as a fling? She shook the idea from her mind and refocused on work, but the office she'd fashioned into her personal comfort zone seemed unwelcoming. Someone had violated her space, searched her things. Were they still watching or listening? She disliked being alone here now and wanted the security of Rafe's presence. Were her fears getting the best of her, did Rafe really make a difference, or did Jana just like having her around, conversation or no?

Chapter Ten

I'd like to start on the ground floor where the breach occurred," Rafe said as she held the elevator open for Camille. "How long have you worked here?"

"Ten years, all of them as Jana's assistant, and I couldn't imagine working for anyone else. She's the most thoughtful, accommodating person I've ever known. Angie and I love her so much we asked her to be godmother to our daughter, Skylar."

When they exited the elevator, Rafe listened while surveying the entrances and exits of the building including maintenance and delivery points. "She seems like a decent boss."

"Decent?" Camille stopped and placed her hand on Rafe's arm. "Jana is the best. Totally awesome, always taking care of everybody. And that's why I need to know what's going on. We usually share everything, and I do mean *everything* from work to dating details… but not clothes." She flicked the sleeve of Rafe's jacket. "She doesn't share her wardrobe with *anyone.*" She didn't wait for Rafe to reply. "The past few days, she's been jumpy as a neurotic cat and avoiding eye contact. And then you come along all hot and gorgeous, but she's not looking at you like a date. You're something else. I don't want to ask her outright because I'm afraid it will upset her more."

Rafe studied the drawn expression on Camille's face and the sheen of tears in her eyes and pulled her into the stairwell. "Okay. I'm going to level with you, but you have to swear you won't share what I'm about to tell you with anyone."

"I swear, not even Angie."

"Jana received some threats and asked me to look into it. Before you ask, we don't know who or why yet. Since you're closest to Jana, you can be my first line of defense. Keep your eyes open for suspicious mail, phone calls, or visitors. Will that be a problem?"

"I open the mail and screen her calls anyway. Walk-ins are harder to manage."

"But you know almost everybody in the company who would want access to her, right?"

Camille nodded, and Rafe continued. "If someone you don't recognize shows up, stall, forward their details to me in the conference room, and I'll do a quick background check while they wait. One of the most important things is for you to act normal. Don't panic, treat people different, or let on anything has changed. If you can do that, I think we'll make a good team."

They arrived back on the top floor after checking each exit door to assure it was secure and alarmed. Camille stopped beside her, breathing heavily from the climb. "Thank you…for telling me. I'll… do whatever you need…to keep…her safe."

"Is there anything you can tell me about Jana's personal life that might help me do the same? People she sees on a regular basis. Places she frequents. Stuff like that."

Camille hesitated. "Well, she…I'm not sure I should answer that."

"She's already warned me that she enjoys her friends and wants to feel free to have women over for…to—"

"Yeah. She has a healthy appetite but not a strict diet, if you get my drift."

"She likes variety." The words tasted bitter, and Rafe wasn't sure why. What difference did it make how many women Jana dated?

"Definitely," Camille agreed.

Before they reached Jana's office, Rafe stopped. She didn't want to see Jana after verifying such an intimate detail of her life. It bothered her but strictly from a security perspective. "Tell Jana I'll be back at four thirty and not to leave without me. I have to pick up some things." Camille started to walk away, but Rafe caught her arm. "And remember, act normal. I'll inform her that I've briefed you."

On the short walk back to Bennett's to retrieve her bike, Rafe texted Jana that she'd told Camille about the threats, nothing about the flash drive or her suspicions about the company. A sound strategy dictated that the person closest to the target be in on the plan if possible.

Next, she called Kerstin and asked for recommendations of a reasonable place to buy business clothes. Since her employment was now official, she needed to look the part. Typical Kerstin, she offered to handle everything. After relaying her measurements and payment information, Rafe got the address and promised to collect her purchases when they were ready. Perfect. Knowing the right people solved most problems.

Rafe skirted through downtown traffic on her bike and edged into the flow when she hit the interstate. She hadn't breathed easily since meeting Jana Elliott, too busy focusing on her safety and ignoring the attraction. She desperately needed to decompress aka test her limits. She shifted gears, gunned the throttle, and maneuvered in and out of vehicles like stationary obstacles. The acceleration forced her hips back into the supporting pads like the welcoming thighs of a lover. She revved faster, certain no vehicle could catch her, not even the enhanced highway patrol cars that frequented the interstate.

In less than thirty minutes, she pulled onto the lot where her Airstream rested. With a few taps on her watch, Rafe disabled the security system and walked her bike in before resetting the alarm. No matter the mission, the outcome, or the next one looming, she always loved returning to the nest. She shucked off the unfamiliar clothes before setting a timer for fifteen minutes. A short rest and she'd be right again. She collapsed across the bed, all the tension and hypervigilance draining away. She'd survived on short naps while sitting, standing, or leaning on deployment, so her bed was like sleeping on a cloud. When the watch vibrated against her wrist, she woke refreshed, but her thoughts turned again to Jana. Damn it.

Rafe dressed in her own clothes, packed her go-bag, and headed back to the city. As always, en route to the assignment, she wondered if she was ready? Did she have all the intelligence on the job? Was she aware of the possible hazards? Had she planned enough? This time, she also questioned if she could succeed without the support of her team. She'd failed to protect an innocent once, and that time had almost killed her. An equally important question, could she focus on the task without being distracted by the woman?

During her career, she'd concluded that fate was cruel, now she understood it also had a sense of humor. Why else put Jana Elliott in her path, a woman she couldn't possibly ignore but had to for the sake of the mission? Jana's curious mind and nurturing nature threatened to pry Rafe open. And Jana's selflessness compelled her to risk her life for the sake of others. Why this woman? Why now? She scaled the stairs two at a time searching for answers she'd never find.

When Rafe burst through the stairwell door at Jana's office, Camille rushed toward her. "She's gone. I told her what you said, but—"

"But your boss doesn't like being told what to do. Is she alone?"

"Yes, but she's meeting someone at the Marriott Downtown Bistro 40 for drinks. Dayle Hargrave, one of our corporate attorneys, is in town overnight and they usually...you know. Here." Camille handed her a fob to Jana's building and a key to the condo. "She said to make yourself comfortable and not worry, because she'll be home before pumpkin hour."

"I see."

Camille pressed her lips together in a tight line. "I tried to reason with her. She said it was still daylight, she was only walking two blocks, and Dayle was a strong butch who could protect her if she needed help. I'm sorry, Rafe. I feel like I failed the first day of a new job."

"It's not your fault." Rafe squeezed her shoulder. "I'll see you tomorrow." She hurried to the condo, stowed her things, and made a few necessary preparations before walking to the Marriott. Jana Elliott didn't understand who she'd hired. When Rafe made a commitment, she took it seriously, even if her protectee didn't.

She entered the old firehouse section of the hotel that now served as a modern bar and located Jana and her companion in a back booth. They sat on the same side facing away from the entrance, so Rafe entered without being seen. She snagged a stool at the end of the bar, out of eyesight of the couple and away from the crowd. She felt like a stalker, but it was her job to keep Jana safe, despite herself.

Jana started to remove her suit jacket, and Dayle helped her out of it with the practiced moves of a player. Probably only the first item she'd help Jana out of tonight. "Not your concern," Rafe muttered, noting an uncomfortable twinge in her chest.

Dayle rose and hung the jacket on the end of their booth, and Rafe sized her up. Tall, probably a swimmer or gymnast judging by her broad shoulders and slender waist and hips. Dark hair, longer than Rafe's, but straighter. Androgynous. Jana Elliott had a type, and Rafe wasn't sure if she liked or disliked the fact that she fit the criteria. Didn't matter because that ship was never going to sail.

Dayle slid her arm around Jana's shoulder and whispered in her ear, and Jana blushed and tugged at the collar of her blouse. Rafe's stomach roiled. She was just hungry because she'd passed on breakfast, worked through lunch, and forgotten about dinner while on her bike. Maybe she'd have time for a sandwich before the lovebirds headed upstairs.

She scrutinized the couple again. Could she be as smooth as Dayle, helping Jana out of her jacket? After all she'd seen and done in her career, could she find the sweet or teasing words to bring a blush to Jana's cheeks? And why, after only a few days of retirement, was she interested in the first woman she'd come in contact with…and a client? Maybe because she *was* the first. Rafe would get over it. She had to.

"Let's take this party to my room," Dayle said a bit too loudly as she reached for Jana's jacket.

Rafe squeezed the corner of the bar with both hands. Did Dayle need to announce to the entire bar that she was taking Jana to bed? That was no way to treat a woman of Jana's caliber, but maybe she liked the rough around the edges type. Again, not her concern. She strained to hear Jana's response over the din of other patrons.

"We haven't eaten, and I'm starving."

"Trust me, gorgeous, I won't let you pass out. We'll order room service." Dayle looped her arm around Jana's waist and guided her out of the bar.

Rafe couldn't follow without being seen. She motioned for the bartender. "Could I get an Angus burger with cheese and a ginger ale to go. I'll eat in my room."

A few minutes later, she had her food and was on the way to the front desk. "I'm sorry, ma'am, but I've lost my room card. Dayle Hargrave." The key would give her the room number, and if something happened, immediate access.

"Of course, Ms. Hargrave." The lady programmed another card and passed it across the counter. "Have a nice evening."

Probably not going to happen. Camping outside a hotel room door while her protectee had sex wasn't her idea of a good evening, but she refused to examine why it bothered her so much. She'd done that and worse in her career, but this time it felt different. Personal.

CHAPTER ELEVEN

Why did the short walk to the hotel room for a tryst feel different from any other? Jana wanted to have sex with Dayle. They understood each other, and neither spoke of exclusivity or forever. More importantly, she'd been anxious and tense the past few days and needed to really relax.

Guilt crept in for leaving Camille to face Rafe and ditching her protector without an explanation, but she was perfectly safe with Dayle. And Rafe was her bodyguard, not her chaperone or lover. Jana had been up-front about her needs in the beginning, but she was paying Rafe an exorbitant fee for protection and should get her money's worth. Enough about Rafe.

Dayle opened her hotel room door and waved Jana in. "You okay, babe? You seem distracted."

Jana paused in the doorway and glanced at Dayle. She'd proved a good sounding board in the past, but could she risk being completely honest about her fears? "I've been thinking about my mother recently. She left me a box of stuff and I'm anxious about opening it."

Dayle tossed Jana's coat across a chair. "Why? What do you think is in it?".

"Maybe an explanation about why she killed herself."

"That might be hard to process. Didn't she work for the company at one time?"

Jana nodded.

"Could it have anything to do with that?"

Jana's chest tightened. Did Dayle know about Shelby's suspicions and Jana's disagreement with the boss? Fergus said he wanted their attorney to vet whatever company papers were in the box, if in fact there were any. She'd been totally bluffing to get a reaction from him. Was that why Dayle suddenly appeared for a meeting and layover? And was this liaison an attempt to find out what Jana really knew? Now she was just being paranoid. Dayle had been scheduled weeks ago specifically to review the Kitamura contract. "Not likely. She often stuffed old pictures and keepsakes in shoeboxes. That's exactly what I expect to find. I'm just nervous because her loss is still so fresh."

"I understand."

Jana ran her hands across Dayle's chest. Still, it wouldn't hurt to ask the question. "Why are you in town today? I thought you were in a trial."

"Kitamura. I was, but one of the other attorneys did the closing for me." Dayle encircled Jana's waist and pulled them closer. "Is that what you want to talk about?"

Despite her reservations, Jana's body responded to their closeness. "Definitely not."

"Good. What kind of mood are you in? What's your pleasure?" She kissed the side of Jana's neck, nibbled her earlobe, and then moved in for a deeper kiss.

An image of Rafe flashed through Jana's mind, and she sucked in a surprised breath but changed it to a moan she hoped sounded like passion. "I'm in the mood for less talk and more action." Jana pushed Dayle away and stretched out across the bed. "You know what I like. Do it."

"Yes, ma'am." Dayle loosened her belt and dropped it to the floor before unzipping her jeans and pulling them open just enough to reveal skin underneath.

"I love commando. So…" Jana paused. Why did she like knowing a woman was sans underwear? Accessibility? The constant teasing of flesh against fabric? "So easy."

Dayle laughed. "And I'm nothing if not easy?"

"Shush."

Dayle tugged her shirttail from her jeans and unbuttoned each fastener, easing the shirt off her shoulders to reveal firm, unconfined breasts.

Jana's center ached. "Lose the shirt and touch your breasts." She loved admiring a woman's nude body—the similarities and subtle differences, shades of skin, muscle versus softness, hair color, and their varied reactions to arousal and desire. And if she was honest, she delighted in controlling the strong, androgynous women who found her irresistible.

"Like this?" Dayle teased her nipples between her thumbs and forefingers, and Jana felt the sensation as if she'd been touched.

"Harder," Jana urged her. "Tug and twist. Show me how it feels." Dayle did as instructed, her face a mixture of pain and pleasure, and Jana pressed her thighs together to stay the surge of arousal. "That's it." She rocked against the seam of her trousers and almost came after a couple of thrusts. "Good."

More intrusive images. Rafe opening her shirt, touching her breasts, writhing in sexual agony, a hungry look in her eyes, and begging Jana to let her come. Would Rafe submit to Jana's wishes as freely as Dayle did? Her desire spiraled. "Lower your jeans and touch yourself. Just once."

Dayle dropped her jeans to her knees, ran her hand up to her crotch, and stroked slowly. "Jana, can I—"

"Once." Jana's voice was thick with the urgency of her need. "Are you wet?"

"God, yes," Dayle replied, her knees visibly trembling. "I could get off with just one more stroke. Please?"

"Get naked and come here."

Dayle was beside her before Jana finished the command. "Thank God. I was about to die." She reached for the zipper of Jana's trousers, but she stopped her.

"I want to ride your thigh like this while you come in my hand." Jana turned her palm up and wiggled her fingers for Dayle to follow her orders. When Dayle settled on top of her, Jana curved her fingers inside and felt Dayle close around them. "Don't come until I tell you."

"*Jana!*"

"Not yet." Jana barked as her sex tightened and she worked Dayle's clit faster. She closed her eyes and imagined Rafaella Silva on top of her—mouth open, breath erratic, and her olive complexion flushed with desire. The tremors caught her off guard and before she could speak, the orgasm ripped through her. "Oh, God." She left Dayle hanging. "No—now." She managed to eke out between spasms. "*Yes.*"

Dayle came on demand while clinging to Jana's shoulders. "*Jesus, Jana.*" She eventually went slack and rolled over, pulling for breath. "How do you get me so hot without even touching me? It's always so fast."

Jana didn't answer, still surprised and embarrassed by Rafe's uninvited appearance. Did she think about Rafe that way or had it simply been too long between dates? She settled on the latter and started to get up.

"Give me a few minutes and we can go again," Dayle said.

"Love to, but I can't. Maybe we'll have more time when you're here next."

Dayle propped up on her elbow. "So, that's it for me?"

Jana tucked her blouse and shrugged into her jacket. "Are you complaining, Hargrave?"

"Oh, no, ma'am, just wishing for more as always." She waved as Jana headed toward the door. "See you soon?"

Jana opened the door without answering and stopped short. Rafe sat propped in a chair against the wall opposite Dayle's door, a food wrapper and empty ginger ale bottle beside her on the floor. She wore her usual black outfit and a brown bomber jacket. The ensemble, finished off with black jump boots, made her look roguish but sexy as hell.

Without looking at her, Rafe rose and followed her to the elevator. "Done so soon? Hargrave got no stamina?"

Jana's mouth dried. "I...shut up." Damn it, Rafe heard them having sex. Was that a hint of jealousy in her voice or just mockery? "What are you doing here?" Rafe was too close after what Jana had thought during sex, so she moved to the opposite side of the elevator.

"You hired me for protection."

"And you thought I needed protection from…" She jerked her head toward Dayle's room.

Rafe didn't respond or speak at all as they walked the two blocks from the hotel back to the condo. She'd grown even more sullen and noncommunicative, and Jana hadn't imagined that possible. When she closed and locked the door, Jana said, "I apologize for ducking out."

"You did warn me, but if you really want my help, we need to talk about some things."

"Have you been watching me all evening?" How much had Rafe seen? Jana already knew what she'd heard and blushed at the memory.

Rafe nodded.

"I'm not sure if I'm impressed, annoyed, or terrified. How did you know where to find me?" Before Rafe could answer, Jana said, "Camille."

"Told you she'd be helpful."

"I'm going to change clothes, then you can throw your rule book at me." While showering the traces of Dayle from her skin, Jana attempted to rid her mind of the graphic fantasy of Rafe naked on top of her, but the shower spray only aroused her again. She patted herself dry and jerked on a pair of sweats before rejoining Rafe in the living area. "Would you like a drink or something to eat?"

"No, thanks."

Jana poured herself a glass of water and settled on the sofa opposite Rafe with a long sigh. "Okay, let's hear it."

Rafe dropped her leather jacket at her feet beside her chair, stretched her legs in front of her, and crossed her ankles. "Both our lives will be easier if you keep me informed. Enough said about that."

Jana nodded. The less said about her excursion, the better.

"I'm going to give you worst-case scenarios, but you need the facts. While you were out this evening, I attached a rappelling line to your bedroom balcony in case of emergency and—"

"A *what*? You mean like we'd go over the side? From ten stories up?" Jana glared, and her insides coiled in knots.

"Exactly, but don't worry. I've rappelled hundreds of times. You'd be totally safe."

"No way. We have a perfectly good stairwell for emergencies. I wouldn't even know how to hold the rope." Jana swallowed, but fear tightened her throat and she coughed instead.

"You don't need to. You'd be in a harness in front of me. I'd maneuver the ropes and get us safely to the ground."

"Absolutely *not*. How many times do I have to say no to this absurd idea?" Jana rose and paced in front of the windows. "Normal people don't jump off ten-story balconies." Her shoulders stiffened into ribbons of pain.

Rafe leaned forward and looked up at Jana. "This is new and frightening for you, but like I said, it's worst-case scenario. Hopefully, we could use the stairwell, but if someone comes in and we can't get out, I'd prefer not to kill them."

"*What?* No. No killing under any circumstances."

"Okay, so we need an alternate plan. I'll try everything in my power to keep us from going over the balcony, but if we have to, we will. And if we get separated, I want you to run to the northeast corner of LeBauer Park and wait for me. If the maintenance enclosure is unlocked, hide in there. If not, duck behind the brick wall beside it with vegetation in front. Stay hidden until I come for you. Okay?"

"Northeast corner?"

Rafe pointed behind her, and Jana made eye contact with her for the first time tonight. She felt an unexpected surge of confidence and safety like a protective shield. How could Rafe expose her to the potential of something so terrifying and then make her feel it was perfectly normal? Because it probably was to her. "Okay, I guess."

"Good. Now the other thing. Pack a bag with clothes and anything else you can't live without, enough to last a couple of weeks. Try to remember we might be rappelling, so pack only what you feel comfortable carrying."

Jana gave Rafe her most skeptical glare. "Seriously? Now you're really asking for the impossible. I love my clothes."

"I'm aware, but if we have to abandon your condo, you probably won't be going back to work immediately, so a couple of business outfits and the rest casual will be fine. And don't forget your coat."

"If we have to abandon my condo? Where the hell would we go?" This whole scenario went from bad to worse. She hadn't considered any of this when she agreed to protection, hadn't imagined anything would really happen. She just wanted to feel safe again in her home and workplace. "Maybe we're getting ahead of ourselves?" At least she hoped so. "Like you said, nothing has happened in several days, so maybe I'm seriously overreacting. And after this evening...maybe it's gotten a bit ridiculous. That can't have been comfortable for you, because it certainly wasn't for me when I saw you in the hallway."

"My feelings have nothing to do with the job, but if you've decided you don't want my services, just say the word and I'll go."

Damn, Rafe was frustrating. Would it kill her to admit a feeling, any feeling? Jana's emotions flooded her in waves. Was it the thought of Rafe leaving? Her own fear and suspicions? She did a quick self-check. No, that wasn't it. She'd *wanted* Rafe to care that she was having sex with another woman. When had that happened? She dismissed the notion and reconnected with the conversation. "I don't want you to leave until I know what's going on."

"Okay. We need to be prepared. Pack tonight and leave your bag by the balcony door." Rafe sat back in her chair. "That's about it for now."

"Thank the goddess," Jana said. Rafe stared out the windows, her gaze searching and her shoulders tense. "You're different tonight. Is it because of my vanishing act earlier? Or Dayle?" Why did she keep bringing up Dayle? Was that the reason Rafe was so distant? Was Jana hoping for something that wasn't there?

"I'm working."

"Okay, then." She started toward the bedroom, but Rafe cleared her throat. "Yes?"

"One more thing. You really need to find out what's in that shoe box, so we'll know if you were bluffing or if Fergus really has something to worry about."

"I can't deal with that tonight. Soon." The anxiety of the day, alleviated by sexual release, finally caught up to Jana and she yawned. "I'll leave you to it. I have to pack. You know where the blankets are. Good night." Rafe didn't answer, and Jana wasn't in the mood to coax her. She wouldn't consider getting involved with a woman who couldn't talk about her feelings—not that Rafe was offering—but she might entertain the idea of sleeping with her, especially if they were quarantined somewhere together. Like the last woman on earth type thing.

She grabbed her coat from the hall closet, packed some clothes in a designer bag, scrounged the old shoebox from the back of the closet, and placed everything by the door. She climbed into bed in her sweats and prayed for a swift and dreamless sleep without thoughts of Rafe. Just before she dozed off, a sharp, beeping sound ripped through the condo three times, and a disembodied voice bellowed.

"This is not a test. Fire has been detected. Please evacuate the building immediately using the emergency stairs. Do not use the elevators."

Rafe knocked on her bedroom door. "Get your stuff, Jana. We might not be back."

She grabbed her bag, shoebox, and laptop on the way out, and followed Rafe to the stairwell. "What, no rappelling?" A mass of knotted nerves, she followed Rafe down the stairs, a sheep to slaughter.

Outside, Rafe guided her away from the other residents and fire equipment to an empty spot in the parking lot. "Probably a false alarm. I'm sure it'll be fine."

"In the nine years I've lived here, we've had only one alarm that wasn't a test, and the unit next to mine was actually on fire. So, excuse me if I'm a little skeptical of your platitudes." She sounded harsh, but the thought of not returning to her place stripped her nerves raw. "I'm sorry, Rafe."

"No problem. You're scared." She pointed toward the building. "And you're also right. The firefighters are actively working the scene, so there is a fire."

"Of course, I'm afraid, but that doesn't excuse bad manners." Fear hadn't been part of her life until recently. She'd always assumed she was secure in her insulated bubble. Across the parking lot, firefighters hosed water into a small storage room at the back of the building, and her stomach churned. The cold wind carved through her clothing and peeled away her final layer of safety. "I've lost control of my life." She swayed sideways and reached for Rafe.

"Come here. You're freezing." Rafe propped her foot against the side of a retaining wall and pulled Jana into the warmth of her leather jacket like it was something she'd done a thousand times.

"Forgot my coat. Can't imagine why."

Rafe's body warmed Jana, and she started to feel normal again though she hated feeling needy. When the concierge gave the all-clear to return to the building, Rafe insisted they wait until most of the residents had gone back in before returning to the condo, and Jana didn't argue. She'd never felt this comfortable and right in a woman's arms.

When they made it back to the condo, Rafe said, "I'll do a quick sweep. Wait here."

Jana didn't reply but followed closely on Rafe's heels.

"Or not," Rafe mumbled.

Jana flipped on the lights and gasped. "What the hell?"

CHAPTER TWELVE

Sofa cushions dotted the hardwood floor like random stepping-stones, chairs rested upside down on the carpet. Drawers and cabinets gaped open, their contents littering the countertops and floor. Rafe spun, turned off the lights, pulled Jana inside and against the closed door. "*Wait here.*"

She tugged the Walther from her ankle holster and crept forward. "If anyone is here, come out now. I'm armed." Nothing. Ambient light from the windows created shadows in every corner. She crept so her boots made no sound and opened doors in a crouch to reduce her target size. Whoever had been here was gone. She holstered her weapon, turned on the lights, and went to Jana.

"Damn you, Rafe Silva." Jana flailed and kicked. "Being left... alone...wasn't comforting." She clutched the necklace at her throat and pulled for breath. "Why?"

She braced and let Jana vent. Rafe likened it to soldiers who exercised, drank, fought, or fucked to decompress following a raid or firefight. After a few seconds, Jana stepped back and stared at Rafe as if seeing her for the first time. She trembled, her cheeks flushed, and the pulse at her neck pounded.

"Sorry. I'm not usually violent. I have no idea what came over me."

"At least you're not a wimp, and that makes my job easier. The adrenaline from your fight-or-flight response made you lash out. Perfectly normal."

"Not for me." Jana blew out a long breath and wobbled sideways.

"I'm here." Rafe scooped Jana up and carried her to the sofa.

"What are you doing? I'm perfectly capable of walking. I'm not an invalid."

"And you're not accustomed to accepting help." She placed Jana on the sofa and fluffed a pillow behind her. "I'll get you something to drink." When she handed Jana the water, her hand shook, so Rafe settled beside her and held the glass while she sipped. She'd never been the nurturing type, but something about Jana called to instincts long buried or nonexistent. She relaxed against the pillows, and Rafe asked, "Better?"

"You went through that?"

"Everyone did after missions. Your body gets used to the constant highs and lows after a while, but they never stop."

"I can't imagine. It was like being on cocaine, not that I've actually used it, but I was so wired and felt like I could move a building." She took in the chaos. "Now, I've got to put everything back together."

"Take a few minutes before you stand up."

"Why would anyone do this?"

As much as Rafe liked being close to Jana, she moved to a chair nearby so she could think about the situation instead of how scared and vulnerable Jana looked and how much she wanted to take care of her. "I'm not sure. You said you returned the flash drive to Fergus, right?"

Jana nodded but didn't look at her.

"Jana?"

"I returned the original after making a copy, but IT has beefed up security for the merger, so Fergus probably knows. If this is his doing, he's definitely hiding a problem with the company. And I can't let that stand, Rafe."

Jana was fearless, and Rafe admired her for confronting an international company with endless funds, but she had no idea what she was getting into. "Would you check and see if the copy you made is still here?"

"It is."

"How do you know?"

Jana shucked the medical alert necklace over her head and tugged. The caduceus came apart in two pieces, one clearly a USB drive. "I keep it with me."

Brave and smart. What's not to like about Jana Elliott? "Have you examined the data again?"

"In case you haven't noticed, things have been a bit hectic recently." She put the necklace back on. "Do you think they'll return?"

"I'm guessing the fire was intentionally set as a distraction. If so, this was a brazen attack with people around." Anger and protectiveness raged inside her, but Jana needed to know what she was up against. "I think it's safe to say you need protection, and yes, I believe he'll return since he didn't find what he was looking for. Next time, he'll come for you."

Jana's eyes widened, and her bottom lip trembled. "Well, don't sugarcoat it, Silva."

"You deserve the truth."

Jana glanced around her ransacked condo, and her gaze settled on the shoebox she'd dropped on the floor when they entered. "And that confirms I need to look in that box sooner rather than later. It might provide answers...or not. But first, I have to straighten this place up."

Rafe stood and shook her head. "Why don't you try to get some sleep? I'll deal with the big stuff, and you can tidy up tomorrow. I'll be here, so you're safe. Have your go-bag and car keys handy and leave the balcony door ajar in case we have to jump."

"I'm not sure how much more excitement I can take." Jana placed a hand over her heart. "If you're sure, I won't argue." When Rafe nodded, Jana picked up her bag, shoebox, and laptop and slogged toward her bedroom but turned back. "Thank you. I don't think I fully appreciated what you're doing for me until tonight. I'll try to be a better client."

The quiver in Jana's voice broke Rafe's heart. The people she'd rescued in the service were already traumatized, desperate, and willing to do anything for relief. But Rafe witnessed the slow, insidious invasion of Jana's life by doubt, suspicion, and finally outright attack and wondered which was worse. Her job now was to see it went no further.

Jana retreated to her bedroom, and Rafe grabbed her keys and hurried downstairs to collect camera footage from the concierge. When she returned, she righted the furniture, collected her go-bag, and camped outside Jana's bedroom door. Strategy dictated that forewarned was forearmed, but an opponent might also assume his adversary wouldn't expect a second attack so soon or in the same place. Rafe didn't make assumptions, especially when Jana's life hung in the balance.

When Jana's light went out, Rafe eased the door open. Their exit needed to be quick and quiet. An intruder would try to sneak in and get as close as possible to his target instead of rushing in, giving Rafe more time to get them over the balcony.

She settled against the wall and texted Bennett. They'd both always slept lightly and gone back to sleep easily, a trait that served them well in their careers.

Intruder at J's condo tonight. Might need help later today. Good for now.

A reply came quickly. *Whatever you need.*

After a couple of hours, Rafe relaxed, and her eyelids drooped. Maybe she'd been wrong. Then she heard the soft click of the door handle and a subtle change in air pressure as the door opened. She rolled into Jana's room and locked the door behind her. She placed her hand over Jana's mouth, relieved to see she'd worn sweats to bed. "Put this on." She handed her the belt with carabiners attached and rushed to the balcony. "Grab your bag and come to me."

Jana followed her instructions without question, her eyes large, and her movements jerky but efficient. Rafe harnessed herself in position on the opposite side of the balcony and dropped down to give Jana room to come over.

"I'm not...sure I can...do this, Rafe." She pointed down and glared at the harness and belt crisscrossing Rafe's body.

"You can." Rafe clicked carabiners to the ones on Jana's belt. "Just put your legs over and hug me. I won't let you fall." She opened her arms, waiting and mentally calculating how long before the intruder burst through the locked bedroom door and charged them. If he was armed, they'd be easy targets dangling from a rope. "Please, Jana. Hurry."

Jana pulled her coat tighter, grabbed her bag and the shoebox, and climbed over the railing into Rafe's arms. "If you drop me, I won't be happy."

"Cross your arms over your chest, close your eyes, and hang on. We're going down fast."

Jana started to say something else, but Rafe released the line and in seconds, they were on the ground. She unclipped the ropes, left them, and urged Jana forward. "Run to your car. Stay close to the building. I'm right behind you." Rafe looked up. The intruder, illuminated by streetlights from below, was male, white, mid-thirties, dressed all in black. He peered over the balcony and scanned the ground below, but they darted around the corner in time to avoid being spotted.

Jana stumbled in her house slippers like a newborn calf on spindly legs. Rafe steadied her as they approached the car. "Keys." Jana tossed them to her, and Rafe clicked the doors open. A few seconds later, they zigzagged from street to street heading north.

"Where are we going?"

Rafe constantly checked for a tail and eventually parallel parked in a space in the Fisher Park neighborhood between two other cars. "Here, for now. Recline your seat and relax for a few minutes. I don't think he got a look at the car, but if he did, we're better off trying to blend in than making a run for it on deserted streets this time of night."

She scanned the area for movement before glancing at Jana. Her face was pale, and her eyes were wide with shock or horror. "You okay?" Jana nodded, laughed, and kept laughing. Definitely shock.

When she finally stopped and caught her breath, she said, "No, I'm obviously not okay. Look at me. My clothes are inside out. My hair is a nest of tangles. And I just went off a balcony ten floors up. Nothing about this is okay."

Rafe reached toward Jana but stopped, raised her eyebrows to ask permission to touch her, and waited until Jana nodded. She slowly cupped Jana's hands. They felt cool and clammy, and she pulled them inside her jacket for warmth. She wanted to nestle Jana against her chest and warm her as well, but this wasn't the time. "But you did great. I've rappelled with soldiers more rattled than you."

Jana studied her as if deciding if she was just blowing smoke. "If you're trying to make me feel better, Silva, it's working. What now?"

"It's almost daylight, so we need to decide on our next move."

Jana withdrew her hands and gestured back toward her condo. "After what happened tonight, I'm looking in that damn box before I do anything else. Shelby thinks it might be valuable, and it's time to find out. This can't be about a few archived papers."

"Sounds like a starting point. Where would you like to do this?"

"Ben and Kerstin's? Do you think they'll be up this early?"

"I'm sure of it. I've already texted Ben this morning." Rafe shot a text to Bennett, checked the street again, and started the car.

"How the hell did this guy get in the building in the middle of the night, to my floor, and into my condo? Somebody is going to pay for this."

"Somebody already has," Rafe said. "It's too easy to bribe minimum-wage employees when you have unlimited funds. I'm betting there will be no helpful camera footage either. After he didn't find what he wanted during the fire evacuation, he probably came in through a service entrance, covered his face, and was keyed directly to your floor."

"Then I want to know who helped him."

"And what good will it do to fire some peon?" Rafe asked. "Will it get us any closer to the person who hired him or the real reason you're doing this?"

Jana glared at her. "You're a frustratingly rational and controlled woman. Can't I just rant for a while without being taken so literally?"

"Just keeping it real," Rafe said as they pulled into Bennett's driveway.

Bennett and Kerstin met them at the door, Ben in flannel bottoms and a T-shirt, and Kerstin in a pair of Super Woman pajamas. Kerstin ran to Jana. "Are you all right?"

"I rappelled off the balcony," Jana said and grabbed Kerstin in a hug.

CHAPTER THIRTEEN

Kerstin guided Jana into the den warmed by a large stone fireplace. They settled on a sofa, and she hugged Kerstin closer. "I'm sorry to show up so early."

"Don't be silly. We're here for you. Would you like some coffee? A drink?"

She barely heard Kerstin's questions but nodded anyway. Her mind reeled with the thoughts and images of things she'd just done but never imagined possible. She shivered from raw nerves. "I *rappelled*." She looked around for Rafe. "Didn't I? Or doesn't it count if I'm cowering in your arms? It happened so fast. Yesterday was totally surreal. I took Rafe to work, wearing *my* clothes, and Fergus hired her on the spot as a security analyst. Camille was smitten. I met Dayle for a drink and…never mind about that."

Bennett offered Rafe a cup of coffee and raised an eyebrow.

"Don't ask," Rafe said.

"When we got back to my place, Rafe and me, not Dayle, the fire alarm went off. We waited in the parking lot half the night until the fire trucks cleared. Somebody trashed my condo while we were outside. Can you believe it?" Jana accepted a small glass of amber liquid from Kerstin and knocked it back. She sputtered and coughed. "What was that?"

"Brandy. It'll calm your nerves," Kerstin said, rubbing circles on her back.

Jana looked at Rafe standing with Bennett by the kitchen island and asked, "Rambling?"

"It's fine. You've been through a lot."

Jana handed the glass back to Kerstin. "Again. Then someone broke into my condo, and Rafe took me over the balcony. And you know the rest." She drank the second glass of brandy just as quickly and blew out a long breath. "What the hell has happened to my life? I can't even have sex without someone lurking outside my door." Damn it, she hadn't meant to bring that up again, but her diarrhea of the mouth worsened when she was nervous and drinking.

"What?" Kerstin lowered her voice. "You obviously left out some details."

Bennett and Rafe hunched over the island looking at something on a laptop with their backs to them. Jana pulled Kerstin closer. "Dayle and I hooked up earlier. Rafe was outside the hotel room door when I left. Just sitting there. I felt so…I don't know. Cheap? Embarrassed? And I'm not sure why."

"What did Rafe say?"

"She asked if I was finished so soon because Dayle lacked stamina." Kerstin laughed, and Jana shushed her. "Maddening. Totally maddening."

"So, what's happening now?"

Jana pointed to the frayed shoebox next to the sofa. "I'm opening this Pandora's box."

She reached for the lid, but Kerstin stopped her. "Are you prepared for what's inside? What if it's to do with your mother's death? Have you thought about how that could affect you? And what if it's bad for the company?" Rafe and Bennett turned and waited for her reply, but Kerstin continued. "What are you prepared to do?"

Jana tapped her nails against the brandy glass. "I'm not in this to punish anyone. I want to uncover the truth about Alumicor and expose it publicly if they won't accept responsibility. More importantly, I want to know how the company figures into my mother's death. If she died for what's in that box, I have to see it through."

"And if it comes to public exposure, what about your job?" Bennett asked.

"Whistleblowers are protected by law, but I'll worry about that when the time comes. After this, I might not want to work for Alumicor anyway."

Kerstin placed her hand over Jana's. "We'll give you some privacy."

Jana glanced at Rafe. "Would you stay with me?"

"Of course." Rafe closed the laptop and moved beside Jana on the sofa.

"Let us know if we can help," Kerstin said and kissed Jana's cheek before following Bennett upstairs.

Jana's palms were sweaty when she picked up the box and rested it on her lap.

"Finally, the mysterious box," Rafe said. "I wondered but didn't want to pry."

"My mother left this with Travis Mills last year." She wiped her clammy hand across the lid, and a mixture of hope and dread made her stomach lurch. The contents of this box could answer some painful personal questions, vindicate or condemn Alumicor, or simply be a waste of time on all counts.

"Any idea what's in it?" Rafe asked.

Jana shook her head. "I didn't even know it existed until Shelby Mills gave it to me at her husband's funeral. I've been a little preoccupied since then, and if I'm honest, when I think about opening it, I feel an overwhelming sense of dread. I'm terrified of what I might find."

"One thing you are not is afraid, Jana Elliott." Rafe smiled. "Let's find out what your mother left you together."

Jana swallowed a sob. "The...important thing is...she *left* me."

When Rafe spoke, her voice was soft, almost apologetic. "Maybe I'm missing something or can't interpret nuance, but I don't understand what you're saying, Jana."

"My mother went to the Outer Banks on a freezing day in December, stripped off her clothes, walked into the ocean, and was never seen again. For a year, I foolishly believed she'd show up one day and have a perfectly credible story for where she'd been." She looked at Rafe and saw her own agony reflected in her eyes. "My mother killed herself. She left me after I'd grown to love and depend on her." Rafe reached for her, and Jana couldn't prevent the tears any longer.

"I'm so sorry, Jana." Rafe rocked her in her arms. "Let it out."

Jana purged the grief she'd thought long gone. When she sniffled, Rafe handed her a tissue, and she kept crying. "When the person I loved most vanished, everything else in my life seemed fragile and uncertain. Work became my safety net." She looked at Rafe, and her eyes were full of concern and helplessness. "I'm sorry to dump this on you."

"I just wish I could help."

"You are. Listening helps more than you know." Jana wiped her eyes. "After my mother died, I never felt truly safe with anyone, so I distanced from people because the risk of getting close was too painful."

"So, your bevy of beauties is a ruse?" Rafe asked and winked.

Jana almost laughed. "You're not the first to suggest that. Being an extrovert is my camouflage. If you're approachable, people feel comfortable. You're better at this than you think, Silva. You picked up on my defense mechanism *and* distracted me quite nicely."

Rafe mimicked tipping a hat. "Glad to be of service, ma'am."

Jana dried her eyes again. "Enough. Time for action."

"Are you sure you want to do this right now?"

"There you go with that nurturing gene. Careful or I'll think you like me."

She retrieved the box Rafe had placed on the coffee table, pulled a deep breath, and lifted the lid. On top lay the last picture of her and her mother together. They printed it as a Christmas card for friends and family, before she walked into the cold water of the Atlantic. Underneath the photo were tattered brown pictures of distant relatives. Miscellaneous items littered the bottom of the box—a lock of her baby hair, teeth she'd lost as a child, school pictures, and a locket she gave her mother on her last Mother's Day. A rolled manila envelope tied with a ribbon was the last item in the corner of the box. Jana lifted it out and handed it to Rafe. "Would you open that while I look through this stuff one more time?"

Rafe loosened the ribbon and unrolled the envelope. "You might want to do this."

Across the front of the envelope was written in her mother's hand, *Baby pictures*. "I'm not in the mood for more photos of myself. Go ahead."

Rafe opened the folder and pulled out a stack of typed pages with handwritten notes attached. "Definitely not baby pictures and totally meant for you."

Jana looked at the first note. Her mother's handwriting and the date—the day before she died. Her vision blurred again. She stared at the opening line and read aloud. "*My dearest daughter Jana.*" She wanted to scream, but her chest tightened. "I feel like ripping the damn note into a million pieces without reading it." She shoved the paper back at Rafe. "Will you?"

❖

Rafe eased the faded stationary pages from Jana's fingers and smoothed them out in her lap. "Are you sure you want *me* to read this?"

When Jana nodded, she began. "*My dearest daughter Jana. First, please believe you are and always have been my world. The day I gave birth to you was the best day of my life. Sharing our adventures was more than I ever imagined, and I'm sorry to leave you alone. I hope you will be able to forgive me someday.*"

Jana choked back a sob, and Rafe cupped her hand. "Let me know if I need to stop. We can do this slowly or in segments if it'll help."

"Let's just get through it."

Rafe squeezed her hand and continued. "*You'll want to know why. For years, I worked for a company I believed was reputable, honest, and caring. They are not.*"

"Damn you, Fergus." Jana clutched Rafe's hand tighter. "Go on."

"*Alumicor has known for decades that the spent potliner from aluminum smelting contains toxic fluoride, cyanide, PCBs, and PAHs. They gave lip service and feigned attempts to correct the issue, and when it became too expensive, covered up the problem entirely.*"

"Sounds like Shelby Mills was right."

"Hold on." Rafe raised the note in her hand. "There's more. *I provided information behind the scenes to state and local authorities to identify the workers and residents affected by these hazardous chemicals, including myself. Alumicor investigators discovered my involvement, and Fergus threatened to ruin me and have you taken away. You were just a child. I couldn't bear it."*

"My mother was sick too. What a disgusting man." Jana wrung her hands. "I want to—"

"I know," Rafe said, "and we'll have time for that later." The tight lines around Jana's mouth telegraphed her anguish more clearly than any words, and Rafe would've given anything not to put her through this torment.

"Keep reading. I'll try not to interrupt again."

"My darling, this has not been a short or easy road, as the enclosed pages will attest. Maybe by the time you find this, the laws and sensibilities of society will be such that something can be done. Too many friends, coworkers, and neighbors have suffered and died from Alumicor's illegal and unethical operation, and my own inability to help is devastating.

"You may think I'm a coward, but I can no longer fight a conglomerate with no conscience. My physical and mental health won't sustain me as the effects of exposure take their toll. Use these documents as you see fit or destroy them for the sake of your own sanity. Whatever you decide, I trust your judgment and again ask for your forgiveness. All my love, Mom."

"I can't believe this," Jana said. "And sadly, I can. It all makes sense now. My mother's final months were not happy ones. She'd been ill and tormented, but I never knew how badly or why. So, Alumicor was indirectly responsible for my mother's death."

"Why do you think she put the letter to you with this company stuff and left it with Travis?"

Jana shook her head. "Maybe she wanted to give me time to grieve? Maybe she thought Travis would handle everything before I found out. Or maybe she simply wasn't thinking straight. Near the end, she wasn't herself. I just wish she'd told me about all this. I could've helped…done something."

"She was probably trying to protect you. Isn't that what mothers are supposed to do?" Rafe flipped the note over. "There's a postscript. *Travis and I suspect the Badin Lake drinking water supply is contaminated from plant runoff. We've submitted a sample for analysis."*

Jana stared at Rafe, and her mouth moved wordlessly.

"I know what you're thinking," Rafe said. "They're still hurting people."

"If the water samples support Travis's and Mom's suspicions." Jana shuffled through the other notes. "Travis must've written these because they're dated after Mom's death. Here's a report from the Charlotte Water Environmental Lab Services, but it's a year old."

"What does it say?" Rafe leaned closer to read over her shoulder.

"Dangerous levels of cyanide, fluoride, lead, and cadmium, some of the same chemicals from the aluminum smelting process. This is much worse than I thought. I can't believe I've worked for this company so long...and had no idea. Have I been blind?"

"You just trusted a deceitful man. We've all been there." Jana's pain was too raw, too cruel, and Rafe hugged her, unable to stay away. "I'm here. Whatever you need."

"Just hold me?" She rested her head on Rafe's shoulder. "I'll never forgive Fergus."

"Was he CEO during your mother's employment?"

Jana nodded.

"We'll get through this. One step at a time, Jana. First, we examine these other documents for ammunition. Then, we plan our attack." She held Jana until she indicated she was ready to continue. "We'll start with the earliest information on top and work our way to the bottom. Do you want to read or take notes?"

"I'm a visual person, so I'll read, if you'll organize the information into some kind of coherent timeline." Jana cleared the coffee table of everything but the pages from the envelope.

Rafe grabbed a pen and notepad from the side table and leaned back. "Ready when you are." Jana was fragile from the new information about her mother's illness, her attempts to do the right thing, and confirmation that Alumicor continued to knowingly injure people, but still determination burned in her eyes. She'd persevere because they were on a mission to find the truth and ultimately vindicate her mother.

"This is a newspaper article," Jana shook a paper in her hand, "that says former employees witnessed discard piles burning for days and were instructed to dump smelting waste into unlined pits on plant property. And this is a memorandum to Fergus about that article and what was done to downplay the impact to the company." Jana dropped the pages in her lap.

"What? What?" Rafe asked.

"The letters *IM* on the bottom of some of the documents I downloaded. I think they mean internal memos, these memos. For each complaint from an employee or a concern from the public, Alumicor officials sent private internal memos to management about the issue and what could be done within the company's fiscal limits. Can you believe they're more concerned about saving money than lives?"

"Yeah," Rafe said. "Unfortunately, I do believe it. Money drives too many things in the world."

"But, Rafe, they had forty dump sites around the area, none with liners. Hazardous materials directly contaminated the soil and leeched into the ground and nearby streams and waterways. Some of the sites were eventually fenced and soil, straw, or clay applied on top, but those were only temporary fixes."

"From what I know about hazardous materials," Rafe said, "they have to be excavated from the soil and taken away completely. And they can cause all kinds of cancers from blood to brain and lung."

Jana sighed. "My mother kept copies of these internal memos and arranged them by date with the corresponding issue and company response. No wonder Fergus threatened to ruin her and didn't want me digging into the past."

"And what better place to hide evidence than in plain sight in the archives? No one could ever prove intentional company wrongdoing without your mother's notes. They tie everything together. And now we have a more recent violation." Sensing Jana's growing anxiety, Rafe slid closer. "Are you all right? Should we take a break?"

"Not until I know everything." She pulled another page from the stack. "Look at this. Alumicor received numerous extensions on abatement orders and is still using zombie permits for water discharge pipes under the facility that continue to pollute the waterways."

"Zombie permits?" Rafe asked.

"Expired but somehow extended by the state. Unbelievable."

"Doesn't the Department of Environmental Quality investigate and enforce issues like these?" Rafe asked.

"They're supposed to. Someone was well compensated to look the other way, or Alumicor has done an excellent job of covering it up. Either way, it's wrong."

"Trust me," Rafe said. "They won't get away with hurting people when we're on the case." She nudged Jana's shoulder.

Jana picked up the last legal document. "The cyanide levels in Badin Lake still exceed North Carolina water quality standards. The county posted advisories against eating fish caught in the lake."

"Our next move is comparing these memos with the documents you downloaded from the archives and show a correlation between them," Rafe said.

"I agree." Jana reached into the box. "The only thing left is a newspaper clipping from Mississippi where Alumicor had another plant until a few years ago. According to this, they had fifty-one environmental violations and paid penalties of over three hundred forty-four million dollars and almost nine million in settlements. The penalties in North Carolina are minimal by comparison, and no one has even come close to that level of compensation."

"They probably died before their cases were adjudicated," Rafe said.

CHAPTER FOURTEEN

Jana clenched her fists beside her on the sofa. Rafe's last statement sparked an anger she never knew she possessed. "*We need a plan*," she said through clenched teeth.

Rafe rose without a word and went to the bottom of the stairs. "Ben, Kerstin, can you come down here?"

Footsteps sounded on the second floor and in seconds, Bennett and Kerstin joined them in the den. "What's up?" Bennett asked.

"Alumicor is so bent they're practically a circle," Jana said. "We need to put our heads together and come up with some options for next moves."

"Maybe you should…" Rafe pressed her lips together.

"Say whatever is on your mind. We're brainstorming at this point." Rafe's usually dark brown eyes were tea-colored, and Jana gazed into them as if searching for leaves at the bottom to read her future. Instead, she saw only golden flecks sparkling in the dawning light like a treasure she would never uncover. "Go ahead."

"Maybe you should fill them in first."

Jana nodded and briefed Kerstin and Bennett on what they'd found in the shoebox. When she paused, Bennett rubbed her chin. "Spit it out, Ben."

"The threat is real, not just suspicion anymore. I've been in touch with a fire department source this morning. The fire at your building was intentionally set in the trash room on the ground floor, and the suspect posed as a fireman. He ditched the turnout gear in the dumpster on his way out. The gear and poor camera angles prevented facial identification."

"Is there any good news?" Jana asked.

Bennett shook her head. "I'd recommend you take a couple of weeks off."

"Or quit," Rafe added.

The suggestion might've made Jana angry yesterday. Her company was corrupt, and they were causing injuries and deaths. And her career and life as she knew them would soon be over. "You're probably right."

"My folks have a place at Badin Lake you can use," Bennett said, "but don't drink the water." She tried for a laugh, but it fell flat. "It's small, on the lake, and easily defensible."

"Defensible? You make it sound like I need to move into Fort Knox. You expect me to leave my job, friends, basically my life, and disappear?"

Before Bennett could respond, Rafe said, "Yes."

Jana pushed up from the sofa. Rafe started toward her, but Jana placed her hand on her chest to stop her. "You're not intimidating me, Silva."

"That's the last thing I want to do. In case you've forgotten, you were running for your life a few hours ago. That guy wants the thumb drive and will hurt you to get it. And now we know why Fergus wants the contents of the shoebox, which makes the situation worse."

"What we don't know is how far back all this goes. We need to compare the archived documents, my mother's notes, and Shelby's list. Together it should provide a timeline. That's our proof." Jana tried to breathe normally as she registered the heat of Rafe's chest against her palm, the steady beat of her heart, and the gravity of her words. Did nothing upset this woman? "There you go sugarcoating things again."

"I'm trying to do what you hired me for, but you're not making it easy. Do you want your life back or not?"

"Of course. Don't be ridiculous, but based on everything we've seen, the chances of that seem pretty remote."

"Isn't it worth a little personal inconvenience to find out? Surely you can give up working, shopping, drinking, and screwing for two weeks."

"How dare you judge me." Rafe turned away, but not before Jana caught a flash of something hot and primal in her eyes. She'd hit a nerve with the stoic soldier. Was she angry, unaccustomed to being questioned, or jealous? She started to ask, but Bennett rose and wedged herself between them.

"Time to take a break. Kerstin, would you show Jana where she can change for work? Rafe, you and I need to discuss details."

"But I haven't agreed to any of this," Jana objected as Kerstin guided her toward the stairs leading to the second floor.

"So much for being a better client," Rafe said and closed the front door behind her.

"Seriously?" Was she relieved or horrified? Either way, she'd pushed Rafe away. How could she expect a bodyguard to protect her if she didn't cooperate?

Jana eased her timeless Chanel suit out of the carry bag, relieved it wasn't wrinkled beyond use, and spread it across the bed. While dressing, she thought about how to protect those she cared about at work. She made some necessary phone calls and notified the bank to have a hefty cash withdrawal ready for pickup. When she returned downstairs, Rafe was nowhere in sight. "Did she leave?"

Bennett shrugged but didn't speak.

"Are you upset with me, Ben?" Jana asked.

Always the peacekeeper, Kerstin moved to Jana's side. "She's not upset. We're both worried about you. Isn't that right, babe?"

Bennett leaned toward them across the kitchen island. "I don't think you're taking this seriously. Your life is in danger, and Rafe is trying to protect you. I begged her to take this job because Kerstin and I care, but she's not used to working with someone who doesn't want help. Your resistance increases the chances one or both of you could be injured or worse."

"Ben, aren't you being too hard on her?" Kerstin asked.

The two exchanged a loving glance. They looked like toppers on a lesbian wedding cake—Ben a dark-haired, handsome butch, and

Kerstin a petite, blond femme. If Jana played Russian roulette with her life, she would never know a love like theirs.

"No, Ben's right," Jana said. "I've been acting like a spoiled brat, like my life is the only one that matters. This whole thing started because I want to help other people. Now, I've involved Rafe in my mess and made it impossible for her to function. I can't blame her for leaving."

Bennett reached across the island and patted Jana's hand. "She cares about you."

Jana recoiled at Ben's assertion which was completely opposite from her experience with Rafe. "What?"

"Why do you think she's so upset?"

"Because she's a control freak used to giving orders and having them followed without question?"

"Well, that is true," Bennett said. "But I know Rafe, and she never loses her cool. Feelings compromise objectivity and judgment, so Rafe hides hers. I'm just guessing, but I think you're more than a job, and the possibility of letting you down terrifies her."

Jana buried her face in her hands, on the verge of tears. "I'm a horrible person."

"No, honey, your life has been turned upside down, and you're scared," Kerstin said.

She hurried to the front door. "I have to apologize. Get her back." She jerked the door open and stumbled over Rafe sitting on the stoop. Rafe caught her before she hit the ground, and Jana struggled to breathe pressed so tightly against her chest. "Th—thanks."

Rafe gazed at Jana, her pupils dilated, and she licked her lips. Jana recognized that look. Desire. Was she so used to overt signals that the subtle eluded her? Or had Rafe's feelings been there all along or grown so slowly that she hadn't noticed? It was also possible she'd been so distracted by fear and suspicion that she'd missed the obvious.

Rafe brushed Jana's hair away from her face and gently stroked her jawline as she withdrew. "Are you okay?"

"Rafe, I—"

"I can't fail. Not this job." She eased Jana onto the steps and stuffed her hands into the pockets of her leather jacket.

Jana had never seen anyone so conflicted by her emotions, so unwilling or unable to express them. She wanted to help, but she was the problem, if what Bennett said was true. "I'm sorry I've been so difficult. I'll do anything you say."

Rafe struggled not to smile. "Anything?"

Without hesitating, Jana said, "Yes."

"Get the time off if it feels right, quit if it doesn't. I don't think they'll try anything at work but keep Camille close. Ben and Kerstin will drive you to the lake. And, please, leave your electronics at home so you can't be tracked."

"What about your risk assessment?" Jana finger quoted the fake job.

"I emailed a faux report to you last night. Tell Fergus it was a one-time thing, and the security company has made adjustments, which is true. I spoke to their boss."

"Good to know. And thanks."

After a quick good-bye and a few last-minute details with Bennett and Kerstin, Rafe and Jana walked silently to her office building. She dreaded seeing Fergus but decided to get it over with first. She took a deep breath and forced a blank expression on her face before opening his door unannounced. He blanched when she entered.

"Um…Jana, what do you need?"

She wanted to say the truth but stuck with her fabricated story. "I'd like a two-week vacation. I've been promising Camille a decent bonus for years and now seems a good time. I'm taking her, Angie, and baby Skylar away for some fun and relaxation." She wasn't leaving Camille to face Fergus and his questions about her whereabouts.

"You and Camille? Who'll manage your department? We're in the middle of a merger."

"Sonya, of course. She can handle anything that comes up. Dayle is reviewing the Kitamura contract, and if she or Sonya need me, I'll check in periodically." She wasn't sure if that was true, but he didn't need to know.

"Sure. Take the time but let me know where you are…in case I need you."

Not a chance in hell. She relayed Rafe's information about the security company and turned to leave but summoned her courage.

"Mr. Fergus, before I go, are you familiar with a purity test done on the Badin Lake drinking water in the last few years?"

The veins across his forehead bulged, and his scalp flushed red beneath his thin dark hair. "What's going on with you lately? We're a reputable company. Is this about that damned shoebox? I demand you turn any company documents over to Dayle Hargrave immediately. She warned me they might be a problem."

She sucked in a sharp breath. Was she surprised Dayle betrayed their private conversation? They weren't soul mates or even good friends, so her loyalty was rooted in the company. "I can't do that until I'm sure of what's happening or has happened. Will you answer my question?"

"I won't be interrogated by my staff. Your mother wouldn't quit digging into the past either." He glared at her from behind his desk. "On second thought, you're fired. Leave all company property on your desk. If *everything* isn't accounted for, I'll file criminal charges. Get out."

"My pleasure." Not exactly how she thought this meeting would end. Part of her felt lighter than she had in days, but the other part panicked. She struggled to breathe evenly. Her career was over—years of dedication, loyalty, and apparent naivety—and she wasn't ready to consider what that meant. But Fergus invoked her mother to argue his position, and she wouldn't forget that. Ever. If it took the rest of her life, she'd expose his lies.

"What's wrong?" Camille asked when Jana returned to her office.

"Fergus just fired me, and you're going to visit your parents for two weeks. Free."

"You're *what*? I'm what?" Camille was practically jumping in place. "Going to Florida? For two weeks? When? Why? The whole family? *Free*?" She hugged Jana and then stepped away. "Back up. What do you mean fired?"

"We had a serious difference of opinion about what's right and ethical. I have proof the company has knowingly put people's lives in danger and caused deaths for years. I can't continue to work here because I'm compiling a case against them now."

Camille crossed her arms across her chest. "Then I won't either."

"No, Camille, you have a family to consider."

Camille shook her head. "I won't stay."

Jana took her by the shoulders and looked her in the eyes. "Take the two weeks, see your parents, and talk with Angie. I arranged everything this morning, and they're thrilled. You're leaving today. And yes, I'm paying. You deserve it for everything you do for me. There's just one catch."

Camille scanned the office. "I'm on *Candid Camera* and this is all a joke?"

"No. You need to drive and pay for everything in cash, no credit cards so you can't be tracked. I don't want Fergus to know where you are until you've had time to think. Will that be a problem?" Jana wasn't putting Camille and her family at risk if someone tried to get to her through them.

"Oh. My. God." Camille hugged Jana so hard she could barely breathe. "Thank you. You have no idea how much Angie and I need this right now. We'll be able to leave Skylar with my folks and have some time to ourselves. I love you so hard." Her eyes filled with tears. "But can we talk at some point? I'm worried about you and don't like leaving you alone."

"I won't be alone, and we can absolutely talk. Jana stepped away and pretended to straighten her desk. When she looked up again, Camille was staring at her with that "you're not fooling me" look. "What?"

"This is about," she moved closer and whispered, "the threats? It's all connected. And you'll be with Commando Barbie, right?"

"Sometimes you're just too damn smart for your own good. Do you have a problem taking time off?"

"No, ma'am. Just tell me you'll be okay."

"I definitely will. Don't worry. Have a good time with your family. Turn your cell phones off too and get a burner, so you can't be tracked. I'll call your parents' landline when I surface again. If you leave now, you can be halfway there before dark." She handed Camille an envelope stuffed with cash. "If you need more, let me know."

Camille stared at the money and her eyes widened. "You're too generous."

"Go before I change my mind." She hugged Camille and urged her toward the door.

Jana turned to the task of briefing Sonya on current projects. She had just enough time to get home and pack another bag before Bennett and Kerstin picked her up.

After everything that had happened this morning, Jana wasn't sure if her apprehension was about the threats on her life, losing her job, or spending time alone with Rafe. Gut check. All were anxiety-ridden—one with fear, one with desperation, and the other with possibility.

CHAPTER FIFTEEN

Rafe replayed the earlier interaction with Jana on her ride to the nest. Too much touching and closeness, not nearly enough objectivity. The color of Jana's eyes. The softness of her skin. And Rafe's desire to be the kind of woman Jana would consider spending time with. She wheeled into her driveway, and the bike skidded on gravel, nearly dumping her. She righted herself but blasted the perimeter security and set off alarms. Thinking about Jana was dangerous.

She screwed up when she met Jana's gaze. G-ma Carlyle said the eyes were the windows to the soul, and hers were always open if anyone took the time to look. And Jana had looked too closely. Had she seen the way Rafe felt about her—caring, protective, and conflicted? If so, Rafe's job just got harder.

She turned on the coffee pot and unpacked the business suits she'd picked up from her go-bag to refill with work clothes and a backup security system. She poured a cup of coffee and settled by the window to calm her thoughts. Why hadn't she refused this job? A hiatus to reintegrate into society was normal SOP. Time cleared the mind of the debris of war or at least dimmed it, like the breeze rippling across the surface of the lake washing fallen leaves to the edge. If she'd taken time, maybe she'd be ready for someone like Jana Elliott.

But not now. She couldn't talk about her life or her work, and Jana would never accept that. She loved to discuss, analyze, and *feel*.

When was the last time Rafe allowed herself to really feel what was happening around her? Compartmentalizing kept her alive and sane. How could she give up a coping mechanism that was a vital part of her life? Her job and feelings didn't mix, and neither did an outgoing corporate dynamo and a solitary soldier.

Rafe tidied the nest and took in the small space. Other than in full battle gear leading men, she felt most comfortable in this aluminum can. Home. Insulated. Safe. She locked the door behind her and headed toward the water unsure when she'd return.

A small fiberglass dinghy floated under the raised dock, and she tugged the lines free and tossed her bag in. After checking the fuel and connecting the line to the motor, she engaged the choke, and jerked on the cord. After a couple of tries, the engine sputtered to life. She untied from the dock and angled out into wide water toward the Carlyles'.

The engine leveled into a hum as she skirted across the water in the waning light. She scanned the shoreline, alert for anything unusual, but her tiny finger of the lake was unaltered. She tried to shift out of work mode and enjoy the easy ride and cool temperatures, but the image of a young boy she'd lost on foreign soil flashed through her mind. As she guided the boat to the Carlyles' dock and secured the lines, she vowed Jana would not be another casualty, even if it meant she could never acknowledge her feelings.

Rafe climbed to the upper deck and looked back at the Carlyle fishing cottage. She was a teenager the last time she was here and struggling to acclimate to yet another foster family, but the Carlyles were different. Even with four other children, Rafe felt like she belonged, and the small two-bedroom cottage seemed like home. She and Bennett scaled the tin roof to clear leaves in the fall, and during summer, the kids slept on the screened porch. She'd laughed, swam, played, eaten, and talked more than all her years prior, but it ended too soon.

"Hey, a little help unloading, slacker," Bennett called from the house.

Rafe leapt down the steps, grabbed her bag, and sprinted across the lawn. No, she wasn't eager to see Jana, only to help. Right. Jana wrangled an unwieldy suitcase down the steps from the car pad to the house, and Rafe rushed to her. "I've got it." She lifted the bag easily and waved Jana ahead of her. "You okay? Everything all right with the vacation request?"

"That didn't exactly go as planned." Jana kept walking toward the house.

"What do you mean? What happened?"

Jana stopped on the sidewalk and turned toward her but wouldn't meet her gaze. "He fired me because I asked about the water purity test and refused to hand over the contents of my mother's shoebox."

"What? Tell me you're kidding."

"I told you she was fearless," Bennett said as she passed with a cooler.

"Reckless is more like it," Rafe said. "Now he knows you suspect a recent violation and possibly have the evidence to prove it. He won't let that go, Jana."

"But he brought up my mother as if she'd done something wrong, and I...I just had to see his face when I asked about the drinking water. And now I know. Those aren't the actions of an innocent man." She leaned closer to Rafe and whispered, "You've got me, right?"

The flirty gesture registered in the pit of Rafe's stomach, and she stumbled on the last step. Jana was a blitz threatening to overwhelm Rafe if she didn't adapt. One minute, Jana was needy and afraid, and the next, she was daring and rash. Either mode complicated Rafe's job and messed with her head. She rushed past Jana and dropped her suitcase in the guestroom.

Jana stopped in the center of the open kitchen-dining-living space. "How do you know that's my room?"

"Because there are only two bedrooms, and Ben and Kerstin get dibs on the other."

"And you?"

Rafe nodded to the sofas in the living space. "I get a choice."

Jana took in her surroundings for the first time. "This is such a cute, cozy place, and the view of the lake is amazing."

Kerstin chuckled from the kitchen where she was putting away groceries. "Translation, it's small and smaller?"

"I didn't mean it like that. I love the comfy furniture and beachy décor. It's a perfect getaway for a couple or a foursome if they're... close."

Rafe caught Jana's quick glance and elbowed Bennett. "Want to help me set up outside?"

"Thought you'd never ask. If I stay here, Kerstin will give me some domestic chore that I totally suck at. Let's go."

Kerstin gave Bennett a quick kiss. "Would you bring the rest of the water from the car on your way back? And don't take too long. These steaks won't grill themselves."

"Yes, dear."

Rafe led Bennett to the edge of the grass where she'd dropped her gear bag. "Never thought I'd see police captain Bennett Carlyle pussy-whipped."

"And proud of it." Bennett grinned. "You ought to try it. Could do wonders for that sour disposition of yours. Lack of sex leads to horny, unhappy people, and a shorter life."

"Thanks for that."

"Maybe you and Ja—"

"Stop, Ben. What Jana has on Fergus could torpedo his multibillion-dollar merger, not to mention his reputation and career, maybe even totally bankrupt the company. He's going to fight with all his resources. I can't afford to get sidetracked by…by feelings."

"I'm just saying she likes you. And you like her. You may be able to fool Jana, but I see through your bullshit. Soldier or not, you still have feelings. They're just a little dusty."

Bennett resurrected things Rafe buried on her ride across the lake and was in no mood to revisit. "Are we going to talk or set up this security system?"

"I was hoping for both."

Rafe pulled the ground spikes out of her bag and tossed them at Bennett's feet. "I'm thinking we'll put these on the east, south, and west sides of the property. The barrier wall on the north should be sufficient."

"Won't you get a lot of wildlife interference this low to the ground?" Bennett grabbed a handful of spikes and started toward the front lawn.

"This is state-of-the art stuff, Ben. Government castoffs when they move on to the next best thing. I can adjust the array to account for birds and small rodents."

"Of course, you can."

"One of the perks of a government job." Once the perimeter was set, Rafe programmed the system on her watch. "We're good to go. Guess you better get back to your grill master duties." In the kitchen, Jana and Kerstin were huddled together at the counter chopping vegetables and chatting. "What's my job, boss?"

Rafe wasn't sure if she was addressing Kerstin or Jana, but they both turned, and Kerstin said, "Help Ben with the steaks. She gets distracted by the shiny water and overcooks."

"I do not," Bennett protested, but a raised eyebrow from Kerstin had her backpedaling. "Come on, Rafe. I'm smart enough to know where I'm not wanted." She took the platter of steaks and retreated to the patio.

"What was that about?" Rafe asked as she pulled two chairs over beside the grill.

"You really don't know anything about women, do you? They haven't had any quality time alone in a while, so they wanted to catch up. Girl talk, probably about us."

Rafe groaned. "I really can't handle this drama right now. I have to stay focused."

Bennett fired up the grill and placed the steaks on the grate. "I'm telling you, pal, nothing focuses the mind like good sex."

"Yeah, on the wrong thing." She stared at the water for a few seconds. "Look, Ben, even if I was interested in Jana, which I'm not saying I am, I couldn't do this"—she waved her arms to encompass the house and property—"and that." She pointed inside toward Jana. "Both are too important and deserve one hundred percent."

"Is this about the kid in Afghanistan?"

"Jamal." Rafe shrugged.

"Because if it is, that wasn't your fault. You do know that, right? Who puts a single soldier in charge of a dozen children and expects nothing to go wrong? And you spent the rest of your career rescuing people to make up for something you couldn't have prevented. When will it be enough?"

"I just can't be preoccupied, not now."

"I get it. All I'm saying is, don't dismiss the possibility of something more with her after the detail is over. Think about your own life for once. Okay?"

Was it really that simple? Do one thing and then the other? Could she separate the two? Jana's appeal grew daily, and Rafe's resolve weakened. Maybe she could start small, share the unclassified parts of her life, and give Jana a glimpse of the woman underneath the soldier's facade. Would that be enough to interest her, to eventually hold her? The only thing Rafe had ever been good at was soldiering. Even in foster care she'd never quite measured up to the criteria of prospective parents.

"Hey, what are you thinking?" Bennett asked. "Nothing good by that expression."

"Foster care. The memories are like another form of PTSD."

"I'm sure there are similarities. Why don't you start there, with Jana? It's probably one of the few things you can talk about. Just tell your story."

Rafe tsked. She couldn't even visualize how that conversation might go. The guys she worked with were perfect examples of how not to treat women, and the military provided a cover for her inadequacies. No intimacy required. Unpacking and dusting off her social skills would be a challenge. "And who'd want to hear that sad tale?"

"Anyone who wants to know who you really are. Trust me." Bennett flipped the steaks and poked one with the tongs. "I'm calling this done. You and I are rare. Kerstin and Jana medium. Get the door for me."

When they returned to the kitchen, Jana was placing salad and baked sweet potatoes on the bistro table. "What would you like to drink?"

Before Rafe answered with her usual water or Gatorade, Bennett said, "Rafe and I are having margaritas."

"Not for me," Rafe said. "I have to—"

"You have to drink with me. It's been too long, and I'll be here for backup tonight if anything happens. Give yourself a break, just this once?"

Bennett gave her the help-a-sister-out look Rafe couldn't refuse. "Okay, but only one."

"Perfect," Jana said. "Kerstin and I are having as much vodka and tonic as we can hold."

Rafe visualized the fastidious Jana Elliott drunk and herself tipsy enough not to care, but the image deteriorated into them naked, sweaty, and moaning. She took the drink Bennett offered and downed two large gulps to cool her thoughts and her body.

Chapter Sixteen

Jana sat across from Rafe at dinner to watch her while they ate. Rafe wielded her knife and fork like precision weapons. She wadded her napkin to wipe the corners of her mouth in single efficient strokes. Her gaze lighthoused behind Jana constantly searching for danger, occasionally sweeping over but never settling on her. By the time the meal ended, Jana was totally smitten and more than a little tipsy.

"You're very quiet," Kerstin said. She took the final dish from Jana, dried it, and put it away in the cabinet. "Bet I can guess why."

"Is it that obvious?" Jana wiped the counter again, mostly to avoid Kerstin's stare.

"Only to me. Let's join them on the porch before the light is gone." They started toward the back door, and Kerstin caught her arm. "Be patient with Rafe. She's had a challenging life."

The teaser piqued Jana's interest even more. "What do you mean challenging?"

"Not my story to tell." She opened the door before Jana could ask another question.

Bennett had positioned the Adirondack chairs so everyone had a view of the lake. The two butches sandwiched her and Kerstin in the middle like a special filling. How adorably protective.

"I didn't realize it rained while we were eating," Jana said.

Rafe breathed in deeply and exhaled. "I love everything about rain."

"Such as?" Jana asked.

"It's cool, always a plus in my opinion. Water soothes, cleanses the air, and leaves a fresh scent. If you're outside, it's like being kissed by the sky. And nothing beats the smell of rich, dark dirt when it's wet. The scent settles at the back of my throat and slides down easily instead of choking and suffocating like dust and heat in the desert."

The heartfelt words sent a tingle through Jana, and she tilted her head to study Rafe. "That was beautiful and quite poetic."

Rafe blushed and wiped condensation from the side of her glass. "I'm sorry. I didn't mean to embarrass you."

"She's just had too much to drink," Bennett tried to help her out.

"Probably," Rafe mumbled.

"My mother loved rain," Jana said. "We lived in the country, and during showers, we'd strip down to our undies and go outside. Sometimes we'd lie in the garden and look up at the sky. Other times, we'd play tag or catch, slipping and sliding across the wet grass. Those were some of the best memories of my life." When she looked up, Rafe was staring out across the lake, her jaw clenched and lips tight. Jana wanted to ask about her childhood but didn't.

"I've got one," Kerstin said. "What's your favorite childhood memory? Jana has already shared hers. Ben, you're up."

"That's easy. Senior year in high school, backyard basketball game with the family on my birthday. Rafe was there." She nudged Kerstin. "And that thing we did in my bedroom for the first time. Remember?"

"Bennett Carlyle!" Kerstin elbowed her but then leaned over and kissed her. "Of course, I remember. You were fabulous."

"Wait. What? Rafe was there?" Jana had no idea their friendship went back so far. Now, she wanted details.

"Yeah, I lived with the Carlyles for about nine months," Rafe said. "But go ahead with the story, Ben. I like this one."

"You and I were team captains. We started with just the family, and soon, all the kids in the neighborhood joined. When one came through the back gate, Rafe or I would call dibs."

"We played until G-ma made us stop at midnight," Rafe said.

"Marathon game," Jana said. She loved the way Rafe's smile transformed the lines around her mouth and eyes as Bennett told the story.

Bennett laughed. "We stopped for cake and ice cream and ended up in a food fight. Ma washed us down with the garden hose before letting us back on the court."

Beside her, Rafe broke out in a belly laugh, and Jana would've done anything to hear that sound every day for the rest of her life. "What's so funny?"

"I won that fight, as I recall, which means I was slightly less caked and ice-creamed than everybody else."

"You won all the fights," Bennett said. "Okay, Kerst, your turn."

"I don't have any great childhood memories like those. My parents argued a lot and finally divorced before I graduated from high school. But I loved being in my dad's office. He was an architect and patiently answered all my kid questions about his work. Sometimes, I'd sit on his desk while he drafted and create my own plans for a doll or tree house."

Another heavy downpour battered the tin roof, and everyone quieted. The steady rhythm was soothing, and Jana's eyelids flagged until Rafe shifted beside her. If they were taking turns sharing, Rafe was up, but Jana wouldn't be the one to ask.

"Over to you, Silva," Bennett finally said.

"I got nothing."

"You obviously haven't been out socially in a while. That's not how this works, pal."

Rafe held up her glass. "I need a refill. Can I get anybody anything?"

"Bring the drinks tray, please," Kerstin said. "We're all dry."

When the door closed, Jana said, "Don't make her talk if she doesn't want to."

"The problem is she wants to but doesn't know how," Bennett said.

"How is that even possible?" Jana's heart ached for Rafe.

"It's possible," Rafe said from the doorway.

Note to self, never talk about a warrior behind her back, especially one with skills the level of Rafe's. "I'm sorry. I didn't mean—"

"It's fine." Rafe passed the drinks tray, walked to the end of the porch, and stared at the lake with her back to the others. "Imagine a childhood of constant upheaval with little basic parenting, followed by twenty-five years in the army, most during Don't Ask, Don't Tell.

You're conditioned to hide and deny who you are. Deployments are with a team of men who get off talking junk about women, and they're your role models for relationships." Her voice was raspy, her tone laced with pain and loss. "You live and fight in ungodly situations like heat waves, monsoons, ice storms, and sanitary conditions that make people in Third World countries squeamish. You seldom have a private moment to yourself much less a chance to connect intimately with another woman. Is it any wonder I'm an emotional moron?" Rafe chugged her drink.

Their friendly banter and childhood memories suddenly seemed frivolous. Jana struggled for something to ease the pain in Rafe's voice, but everything sounded trite. "I'm sorry isn't enough, but I really am."

Rafe nodded and continued. "And now you know why I don't do well in social situations. Talk about a bummer. But back to the original question. My favorite childhood, and adult memory so far, is Sunday brunch with the Carlyles. I always felt like I belonged."

"You are part of the family," Bennett said softly.

"We still have brunch every Sunday," Kerstin said. "Join us some time. Everybody would love to see you again. You might even interest Ben in a rematch of that basketball game."

"Who won that game, by the way?" Jana asked, hoping to lighten the mood.

"I did." Bennett and Rafe answered together.

"Typical," Kerstin said as she yawned and stretched. "I don't know about you guys, but I'm ready for bed. Rafe, you know where the sheets and blankets are, right?"

Rafe turned to face everyone again. "Yeah. Thanks for dinner and the use of your place. I'll check the perimeter since the rain has stopped. See you all in the morning." She briefly made eye contact with Jana before ducking out.

Jana hugged Bennett and Kerstin good night. "I love you both. Thank you so much for all you've done for me." When they'd gone, she debated going to Rafe, talking to her, comforting her, but she had no frame of reference for what Rafe had been through in her life and no idea how to help. She finished her drink and stood. "I work with people every day. I can do this."

She stepped onto the patio and crept to the corner of the house. Rafe walked the property line and periodically stooped to adjust something sticking out of the ground before tapping the face of her watch. Not since her mother had Jana met a more single-minded or devoted woman. None of her past lovers even came close, and she longed for the dedicated attention to a relationship and building a life. Rafe worked her way to the water's edge and sat on the retaining wall, and Jana cleared her throat to announce herself before joining her.

"Mind if I sit?"

"Wait. It's wet." Rafe peeled off her light jacket and spread it out for Jana.

They sat in silence for several minutes watching the crescent moon over the lake and listening to night creatures scurrying through the underbrush. Finally, Jana said, "I'm sorry if you felt pressured to talk earlier. I can't imagine how difficult it's been for you."

"Thanks for your honesty. Too often, people try to sympathize or pretend to understand and just make things worse because they don't have any idea." Rafe looked at her and her eyes glistened with unshed tears.

"Are you okay?"

"I'm fine. Ben says I need to talk about the stuff I can, but it feels impossible like clearing minute grains of desert sand out of an M4 assault rifle."

Jana took a chance and put her hand on Rafe's arm. Her muscles tensed before slowly relaxing, and warmth shot through her when Rafe didn't pull away. "She knows you. Normalization takes time after what you've experienced. You were honest, heartfelt, and the things you said helped me understand you better. That's all anyone can ask."

"With everything going on in your life, why do you want to listen to me?"

"Because people are naturally curious about those who interest them, and you interest me greatly, Rafaella Silva. We yearn to know secrets and problems, so we can help. And it's how we connect intimately and bear witness to each other's lives." Rafe was studying her like she'd said something profound.

"Guess I never thought of it that way. So, I didn't totally depress you, huh?"

"Not at all. I thought how lonely your service must've been."

Rafe looked at her again and this time didn't turn away. Her bottom lip trembled, and she captured it with her top teeth. "My life has been measured by training, missions, successes, failures, and losses instead of birthdays, proms, first dates, weddings, and births. My default to anything personal is ignore and override."

The pain in Rafe's voice was so compelling Jana leaned forward and kissed her lightly. Rafe grew rigid but didn't object, and Jana deepened the kiss. Her body flooded with heat as she tugged Rafe closer by her T-shirt and claimed her mouth. She'd never felt so swept up in the sensation, or so certain she wanted more. "Oh…God." She gasped and started forward to reconnect, but Rafe withdrew.

"Jana, please. Stop."

She struggled for breath, to make sense of what Rafe said. "But you liked it."

Rafe stood, offered her hand, and pulled Jana to her feet. "Don't get me wrong, I enjoyed the kiss, and you're really attractive, but I'm not one of your playthings. You've got enough of those already. You're paying me to do a job, and this isn't it."

"Did you seriously just say that? I don't pay women to sleep with me." Jana grabbed Rafe's T-shirt and brought them together again. "But you *want* to be with me." She wrapped her arms around Rafe to keep her close. "Tell me you don't."

"That would be a lie." She backed away. "It would be easy to have sex with you, but I'm not like everybody else. Call me old-fashioned, but love isn't like chocolate or an orgasm, one should be enough. I respect your right to feel and live your life differently. So, please just let me do my job."

"What does that mean?"

Rafe studied her boots. "If you make me choose between having sex with you and keeping you safe, I'll choose the job. I have to."

"I really don't understand you."

Rafe took hold of Jana's shoulders and met her gaze. "I would rather know you're alive, safe, and happy in the world with someone else than to have casual sex with you and jeopardize your life in the process. Do you understand *that?*"

The weight of Rafe's words and the truth in her eyes hit Jana like a physical blow. Was Rafe saying she cared about her? Or that she wouldn't be just another tryst? How could she be so crystal clear about everything else and so ambiguous about this? She felt confused by the uncertainty and deflected. "So, you're saying you can't multitask, Silva?"

"Not at all. I just choose not to on some assignments. If your needs are so great, I'll make arrangements for you to meet one of your regulars."

"Jesus, you make them sound like hookers." Rafe was so close Jana felt the warmth of her breath and involuntarily leaned in. She struggled between slapping her for her insulting inference and kissing her again because she aroused such visceral responses.

Rafe retrieved her jacket and then studied Jana's face for several seconds as if memorizing every detail before she said, "We should go in. You need sleep."

"Will you sleep with me?" Rafe raised an eyebrow, and Jana added, "I mean just sleep. A bed will be more comfortable than the sofa, and I promise not to jump you." Talk about ambiguity. She was all over the place as well.

"You don't give up, do you?" Jana chuckled, and they started toward the house. Rafe said, "Will you at least try to behave? I need you to take these threats seriously. You put yourself in Fergus's crosshairs today."

"I'll try, but no promises. You're pretty damn sexy." When they got inside the screened porch, Jana pulled Rafe into the shadows and gave her another breath-stealing kiss and then rushed to her bedroom.

CHAPTER SEVENTEEN

Footsteps. Close. Rafe strained to judge the direction and distance but felt dazed like she'd been in an explosion. She kept her eyes shut a few seconds longer to get her bearings. How much time before the enemy was upon her? She clawed under the pillow for her weapon and tumbled to the floor.

"Stand down, soldier," Bennett said. "Just making more coffee."

"Damn it, Ben. You could get hurt sneaking up on me like that."

"Sneaking? The rest of us have been up since six, but you were totally out. Too many margaritas last night?"

Alcohol explained everything. Except kissing Jana. Did that really happen? She closed her eyes again, and Jana's lilac fragrance invaded her senses, along with the softness of her lips, and the brine on her tongue from the olives in her drink. Yeah, they kissed, and she shut it down quickly by spewing half-truths and judgments. But the surge of adrenaline from their kiss proved more potent than any fight or flight response, and her arousal lingered. "Where is everyone?"

"On the porch having coffee, listening to the birds, and talking. Last night with different beverages and brighter light. Come join us when you're awake."

Rafe folded the covers and returned them to the closet before dressing and brushing her teeth. Neither helped her fuzzy head. She needed all her faculties, especially since her only backup was leaving today. She filled a large mug and joined the others on the porch. "Good morning, everyone."

Jana smiled from the laptop. "Morning. Sleep well?"

"Not usually much of a sleeper, but I guess the tequila helped." Rafe squinted against the sunlight reflecting off the water. The cozy porch atmosphere was transformed from last night. In addition to the glaring light, the melodic chirps and shrill calls of wrens, bluebirds, and geese filled the air. "Damn, those suckers are loud." Bennett tossed her a bottle of aspirin, and Rafe shook some out in her hand and washed them down with another sip of coffee.

"Lightweight," Bennett said.

Rafe looked at Jana for the first time and then focused on the object in her lap. "I asked you to leave your electronics at the condo. Was I unclear?"

"You were very clear about that. The Wi-Fi and locator services are off." She motioned toward Kerstin and Bennett. "What about their phones and yours?"

"This place is pretty much a dead zone for cell service, and if anyone checked, there's nothing unusual about Ben and Kerstin visiting their family home on the lake and no reason to connect them to you. As for me, the government provides excellent geo masking, of which I am still a recipient, in case of recall or reenlistment."

Jana closed the laptop and leaned it against the side of her chair. She gave Rafe a smile that was less than subtle, and one Kerstin didn't miss.

"So, how long did you two stay up last night?"

"Not long. I came in after checking the security system." Rafe hoped Jana wouldn't elaborate or feel she needed to share.

"We sat by the water for a while. There wasn't much moonlight, and the critters kept us company." She wiggled her eyebrows at Kerstin.

"Is there anything I can help with before we leave, Rafe?" Bennett asked.

"I'd appreciate a ride to my place to pick up the bike." She thought through the last couple of days' events for holes. "Could you run down any leads on who gave the burglar access to Jana's building and her condo the night of the break-in? You've seen the video from the fire and the break-in, and it didn't help. Let's just cover all the bases. I'm thinking our accomplice will be an employee trying to make a few extra dollars."

"No problem." Bennett turned to Jana. "Do you want the person charged if I identify him or just try to find out who hired him?"

Jana glanced at Rafe. "What do you think? I don't want someone fired just because he tried to augment his meager salary."

Rafe nodded. "Just put the fear of God in him, Ben. He probably won't know who hired him anyway, and he certainly won't be able to connect Fergus to the threats."

"I agree," Bennett said. "He'll insulate himself from the dirty work. There's a possibility we'll never know who's behind the threats, much less be able to charge anyone. Can you live with that, Jana?"

"Like I said before, I'm not interested in punishing anyone, just finding the truth."

"Okay, Rafe," Bennett said, "if you want a ride, we need to go. I have second shift this afternoon. Babe, would you mind packing our things? I'll pick you up in about twenty minutes."

"No breakfast?" Kerstin asked, poking a fake pout.

Bennett leaned over and kissed her. "I'll get you something on the way home."

"What did I miss?" Jana asked. "Rafe has a place here too?"

"Sort of," Rafe muttered and headed to the kitchen, and everyone followed with their coffee cups.

"She has a small Airstream," Bennett said. "It's about the size of a large eagle's nest, which is why she calls it the nest."

"Could I see it sometime? Could I go with you now?" She followed Rafe until they got to the front door.

"Not this time. I'll be back shortly." She wanted so badly to kiss Jana and see if she'd imagined how delicious she tasted last night, but more importantly, she wanted to keep her safe. She needed to get her bike, familiarize Jana with the area, and stay on task. Reconnaissance and intel. If trouble came, she had to be ready.

"I'll keep digging into those downloaded files and comparing them to the internal memos my mother found."

Rafe nodded and followed Bennett to her vehicle, and as soon as they pulled out of the driveway, she started.

"So…what happened between you two last night? There have been a lot of furtive glances back and forth this morning."

"Furtive glances? Really, Ben? Have you turned into a gossip girl? Nothing happened. Not really." Total lie. That kiss was far from nothing. It sucked her in, opened her up, and rocked her world so hard she had trouble concentrating, then and now. She felt it in places inside she'd forgotten existed.

"You know I love you, Rafe, but your version of nothing and mine differ greatly. Did you kiss her?"

"No." Rafe stared out the side window, more comfortable examining the outdoors than answering Bennett's questions.

"She kissed you. Yeah, I can see that. Jana is a take-charge woman, and Miss Duty Bound would never cross a professional line. Am I right?"

"How the hell do you do that?"

Bennett chuckled. "You won't look at me when you lie."

"Damn it, G-ma. Those windows to the soul. And yes, she kissed me, and I kissed her back, at first. I couldn't help myself, Ben. Does that make me weak and undisciplined or just horny after years of abstinence?"

Bennett reached over and squeezed her shoulder. "It makes you human." Bennett stopped on the street beside Rafe's driveway. "Anything else happen?"

"Nah. She's got enough women to keep her busy the rest of her life. I told her if she needed some recreation, I'd arrange a rendezvous with one of them."

Bennett gaped at her. "You didn't?"

"What? I won't be any number except one. When this is over, she'll move on to the next closest thing. And besides, I can't protect her if I'm in bed with her."

"That would be the perfect position for coverage, just throw yourself on top of her. You really don't know anything about women, but that's a problem for another time. Keep in touch. Let me know if you need anything."

"Thanks, Ben."

"And when this blows over, we'll have you over for Sunday brunch. G-ma will insist on inspecting you personally since you retired, because you're family, and we're your home. Never forget that. Love you, pal."

Rafe nodded, unable to speak after Bennett's kind words. Family. Home. Love. She wanted to believe one day those things would be part of her life, but nothing mattered now except keeping Jana safe. The cold metal dog tags against her chest reminded Rafe of the benefits of focus and planning. But maybe with Jana out of harm's way at the cottage, Rafe could lighten up a little. It wasn't only the mission anymore and not just herself to consider. She'd try to relax and help Jana feel more comfortable with her and the situation. And maybe somewhere along the way, she'd start to feel like a normal person, like a civilian with dreams and a future.

When she returned to the cottage, Bennett and Kerstin were gone and Jana sat on the sofa with her computer in her lap and papers scattered across the cushions and spilling over onto the large ottoman. "Found anything?"

"Look at this." She pointed to her computer screen.

Rafe leaned over the back of the sofa but drew back when the strong fragrance of Jana's perfume reached her. "You showered?"

"Yeah, I tried the outdoor shower. A little chilly but refreshing."

She brought her attention back to the laptop. "What am I looking at?"

"The files I downloaded from the archives. Look at this notation at the bottom of the pages. What do these numbers look like to you?"

Rafe angled the computer toward her so she could put some distance between her and Jana and concentrate. "File numbers?"

"Checked that."

"Cross-reference of some type? A code? Whose initials are those?"

Jana was quiet for several seconds before answering. "My mother's, and the letters *IM* we already know are for internal memorandum, but I'm drawing a blank on the numbers following."

"How long did your mother work for Alumicor?" Rafe shifted some of the papers on the ottoman so she could sit across from Jana without being too close.

"Thirty years. She started as a secretary and moved up to benefits coordinator. Alumicor and her causes du jour were her life. She loved working with employees, helping solve their problems, and spent more time in the plants than her office. She was a blue blood protestor and dragged me along to help with posters, flyers, or any other chore a child could handle. I pretended to hate it, but honestly, we bonded over the injustices in the world and our determination to right wrongs. Oh, the bliss of ignorance."

"You share her devotion to justice. You two were close." Jana wiped her eyes, and Rafe realized her mistake. How many times had she trampled feelings or botched a courtesy proving she lacked the delicacy for intimate conversations? Like last night. "I'm sorry."

"It's okay. She died a year ago, but sometimes it feels like yesterday, especially since I found out why she did what she did. I really miss her." She wrung her hands and then looked at Rafe. "About last night, I'm sorry if I made you uncomfortable. I tend to go after what I want and don't take no for an answer."

"And my comments were insensitive. It's none of my business how you spend your leisure time or with whom. Truce?" The thought of Jana with anyone else made her tense in ways she didn't understand. Maybe Bennett was right, she knew absolutely nothing about women or her own feelings.

"Truce." Jana focused on the French doors and out to the lake. "My mom and I shared some of the best times of my life just talking. She wanted to know about my studies, friends, lovers, and plans for the future. Looking back, it felt like she was packing a lifetime into a short span." She drew her attention back to Rafe. "Enough about me. Why did you live with the Carlyles for nine months?"

Rafe pulled her hand from Jana's knee and straightened. She'd opened this door, but could she go through it? Could she share the most painful part of her life? Her defenses had protected her since childhood, and she had no idea how to be without them. If she wanted to shed the insulated soldier she'd become and someday understand her feelings, she needed to learn. She pointed at herself and tried to laugh, but the stifled sound caught in her throat. "Orphan and foster kid."

"Really? How long?"

"Forever. I was a preemie, abandoned at the hospital the day I was born, and plagued with health issues until young adulthood." A choking sensation threatened to bring tears or screams. She swallowed hard and continued. "So, I was in the hospital for a while and then in so many foster homes I lost count. The Carlyles were the last and best. When I turned eighteen, I joined the army. And here I am."

"I can't imagine life without my mother, much less both parents. That must've been horrible for you."

Jana reached for her, but Rafe pulled back. If Jana touched her right now, she'd break down. Talking brought back the feelings, but a caring touch would render her useless. "I don't have pleasant memories of childhood."

"And no one offered to adopt you in all that time?"

"Preemie with problems. Prospective parents wanted healthy babies. I was passed over year after year as the kids I lived and played with were chosen."

"I'm sorry you went through that, Rafe."

"Yeah, not a path I'd recommend for a well-adjusted child. Now you know why I joined the army. No family, no home, no prospects for furthering my education, and no job skills. The guys I worked with were poor family substitutes, horrible role models, and absolute crap for conversation." She tried to lighten the mood and grinned but imagined it looked as awkward as she felt.

"You said before that you killed, and it took part of your soul. Why did you stay?"

"Turns out I was good at organizing operations, fighting, and ordering people around. I rose through the ranks and became vested in the retirement system. At that point it didn't make sense to leave. What would I do? What *am* I going to do? That's still a mystery. I could always reenlist." Was she trying to scare Jana off with all the horrible things about herself?

"Would you really go back?" Jana stared at her as if the possibility were unthinkable.

Rafe shrugged.

"Have you talked to anyone, professionally? I know cops and soldiers don't like to admit they have issues, but how could they not?"

"I got the name of someone Kerstin recommended, Simone Sullivan, who's supposed to be good with macho types." Rafe tried again to laugh but it sounded like a croak.

"She's excellent and not hard on the eyes either. Bennett and Kerstin saw her after the shooting at Fairview Station, and Kerstin commented on her abilities. If you don't mind my asking, how did the hospital know your name when you were abandoned?"

"They didn't," Rafe said. "One of the nurses chose Rafaella because she loved French and the name means God has healed, which she was certain would happen with all my ailments. And my last name is a combination of the first letters of the last names of the other nurses in the neonatal intensive care unit."

"Very creative. They cared enough to give you a part of themselves."

She'd never thought of it that way, and it felt comforting. "I guess."

"Thank you for telling me about your childhood and your service," Jana said. She nudged Rafe with her elbow. "And that, my friend, is called an intimate conversation."

"O—kay." Awkward. The telling wasn't as hard as Rafe imagined but remembering cut as deeply as her Yarborough combat knife. She rose before Jana could ask any more questions. "I'm going to check the perimeter…again. Try to crack that code."

CHAPTER EIGHTEEN

Jana developed a clearer picture of Rafe Silva every day they were together. Being dumped at a hospital after birth and shuffled from one foster home to the next could totally screw up a child. She couldn't imagine abandoning a newborn. Rafe's mother must've been in serious trouble. And then Rafe committed her mind, body, and soul to the military. Jana wanted to hug her and reassure her until the pain etched on her face disappeared. But how could she alleviate such deep and engrained loss that began at birth and was exploited by years in the army?

She dropped a handful of papers on the ottoman and slammed the lid of her laptop. Not in the mood to revisit her own past. When Rafe returned from the perimeter check, Jana stretched the kinks from her back and said, "I'm over this. Anything to do around here besides hide?"

"As a matter of fact, I'd like to give you a lay of the land in case we're separated."

"Uh-huh. Strategic reconnaissance isn't my idea of fun but lead on."

"I'll get the bike and meet you outside. You'll need your coat."

Jana shivered with the anticipation of riding Rafe's crotch rocket tucked behind her and screaming for dear life. She pulled on a sweatshirt and added her jacket and boots.

Rafe handed her a helmet when she got to the top of the driveway. "Have you ever ridden double on a motorcycle?"

"Nope. Single either."

"Okay, a few rules to remember. Don't mount the bike until the kickstand is up and I tell you to get on. Wrap your arms around my waist. Keep your legs clear of the exhaust pipes because they will burn you. Lean with me when turning, not against me. Try to avoid sudden movements that could affect the bike's handling or throw us off balance. Keep your feet on the footrests at all times and don't put them down at a stop."

"You have rules for everything, Silva." Jana slid the helmet on and watched Rafe check the bike. Her face lit up, and she touched the machine with reverence. "You really enjoy riding, don't you?"

"It's my guilty pleasure. I could've gotten something cheaper, but I wanted speed, dependability, and class. The Kawasaki Ninja H2 has it all."

"If you say so, Ace." Jana nudged Rafe and gave her a big smile. "Let's go."

"One more thing. The helmets have built-in comm devices. Speak normally. Don't yell." She tugged her helmet on and said, "Can you hear me?"

"Nice. Is there SiriusXM as well?"

"Afraid not, but feel free to sing during the non-instructive portions of the program."

"Was that actually a joke, Silva?"

"Maybe. I'll show you the neighborhood first. One thing to remember is this street doubles back on itself, and to the right"—she pointed—"is a dead end. We'll start there." She straddled the bike and offered her hand to help Jana on.

Rafe's thighs astride the powerful machine and her legs holding it upright distracted Jana. When Rafe started the bike, the corded muscles in her hands and arms bulged beneath her leather gloves and jacket.

"Are you coming?"

"Yeah. Sorry." Jana struggled to keep her mind out of the gutter as she wrapped her legs around Rafe's hips and snugged her crotch against Rafe's backside. "Oh. My. Goddess."

"What?"

"Nothing." She already forgot Rafe could hear everything she said. The engine revved, and Jana bit back another moan as Rafe took off. She hadn't mentioned the stimulation factor. How would Jana hold it together after that kiss last night and now this?

Rafe slowed the bike at the end of the street. "This once went all the way through to Badin Lake Road. The Carlyle kids and I used to race to the end. The state stopped maintaining it, so this cornfield stretches to the other side with only glimpses of the previous road."

Jana thought she heard a hint of melancholy in Rafe's voice, but maybe it was just distortion from the sound system and bike noise. After a quick swing through the neighborhood, Rafe turned onto a street Jana recognized as a main road into the subdivision. "Are we leaving?"

"Just showing you the highlights." She slowed again and pointed. "Badin Lake General Store and on the other side, Badin Lake Family Restaurant. Both passable if you need essentials or crave a meal you don't have to cook, but it's true Southern food. The vegetables are usually brown instead of green and devoid of any original nutrients."

"Does the general store sell vegetables and fruits? I'd love something fresh."

"No, but Annette's Produce Barn is right up the road. Hang on." Rafe eased away from the stop sign and gunned the throttle.

Jana tightened her grasp around Rafe's waist and tried to breathe normally barreling down the winding road. She leaned side to side with Rafe in the curves and came back to center in the straightaways. She felt much too comfortable pressed against Rafe's back. Was it simply Rafe's courage and confidence that attracted her, or was it the invisible connection she felt whenever they were close? Rafe wasn't like other women she'd been with, not as easily seduced, understood, or swayed from her principles. Jana had no idea why she was so enamored, but once this scary hide-and-seek game was over, she intended to find out.

Rafe pulled into the parking lot shared by a gas station and Annette's Produce Barn that was more the size of a shed. "While you check out the produce, I need to get some Gatorade. You want anything?"

Jana waved her off and started toward the crates of fruits and vegetables beckoning her. She squeezed and smelled the fruits, chose a selection of apples, pears, and grapes, and paid before diverting to a graffiti-clad pay phone on the side of the building. She wiped the handle and mouthpiece with a tissue from her pocket and dialed Dayle. "What the actual fuck are you playing at, Hargrave?" She tried to tamp down her anger, but the betrayal was too fresh.

"Jana? What happened to you, baby?"

"Don't baby me. You ran straight to Fergus about that damn shoebox."

Dayle was quiet for several seconds. "I tried to call the next day and it went straight to voice mail. I had to tell him, Jana. It's my job to protect the company first."

"And throw me under the bus? Thanks for that."

"Where are you, Jana? We need to talk."

Jana stared at the phone. "Seriously? Not a chance."

"We can fix things with the company and return to our... understanding."

"Dayle, after what you did, I wouldn't—"

"What are you doing?" Rafe grabbed the phone and hung up the receiver. "Meet me behind the dumpster."

"Are you kidding?"

Rafe looped the canvas bag with Gatorade over her shoulder and rolled the bike out of sight to the dumpster.

Jana followed. "Do you mind telling me what the hell is going on? We're not at the house, I wasn't on my cell, so I thought a call from a public phone wouldn't matter."

"So, you called your lover? Who just happens to work for your boss, the man who probably hired the thugs who are after you? Perfect."

"She's not my...never mind. She told Fergus I had the shoebox, and I wanted her to know that I knew she betrayed me. Besides, it's none of your business who I call." She covered her nose from the stench of rotting trash and vegetables. "And why are we hiding? Behind a dumpster?"

Rafe pointed across the road.

A man exited a black SUV and waved his cell around in the air for several seconds. He cursed loudly and then got back in the vehicle.

Fear skittered up Jana's spine. "Was that the—"

"The same guy who broke into your condo. Now you understand why it's important to stay off the grid? These people have money and can locate you quickly from a single contact."

"Rafe, I'm so sorry. But I was on a public phone. How did they even know to look at Badin Lake?" She pulled for breath. This had to be someone else's nightmare.

"They probably tracked your cell until you turned it off yesterday, which gave them a general location." Rafe added the items Jana had bought to her bag and slung it across her body. "And Dayle would be cooperative enough to let them trace her calls."

"And when I did, they zoomed in on my location," she said, almost to herself. "What are we doing now?"

"Waiting to see what they do." Rafe reached into her helmet and pulled out a black elasticized covering with a pull string that resembled a rainhat and slipped it over the license plate. "What did you tell Hargrave?"

"Nothing, and she's not—"

"It doesn't matter what she is, only if you told her where you are."

Jana's stomach roiled because she kept screwing up with Rafe. "I didn't."

"Good. Looks like they're leaving. We'll give them a few minutes' head start. Climb on."

The SUV cruised the area around the gas station and Annette's before pulling back onto Highway 49. Rafe started the engine, and they headed toward the cottage. Jana wanted to say something but had no idea how to apologize yet again. The air whizzing past them and the silence on the comm device made her feel a world away from Rafe.

"Hold on," Rafe suddenly commanded in a tone that offered no alternative. "We're being followed."

Jana clutched Rafe's waist and squeezed her knees tighter around her thighs as they picked up speed. With every bump and dip in the road, Jana felt she was going airborne. "Rafe, I'm scared."

"Hold on just a few seconds longer. When we get to the bottom of the next hill, I'm going to stop really fast. Jump off and run up the path through the cornfield. It's the other end of the street I showed you earlier. It'll take you back to the cottage."

"I can't."

"Yes, you can. Remember rappelling off the balcony. You can do anything after that. Run, but don't follow the path exactly, zigzag so they won't see you. Hide in the boathouse, not the cottage, until I get back. I won't be long. Are you ready?"

"*No*, I'm—" Rafe skidded to a stop so abruptly that Jana would've gone over the handlebars if Rafe's body hadn't stopped her.

"Run, Jana, and don't look back."

She stumbled off the bike and before she got her footing, Rafe was gone. She clambered to her feet but slipped and fell in the ditch. What if they found her lying there like a wounded animal? Would they finish her off for a stupid flash drive and some old documents? The black SUV raced by, and she watched it disappear around a curve before darting into the cornfield. Would they catch Rafe? If so, what would happen?

Her life was unraveling. In no version of her future had this scenario even been a possibility—the vice president of a global corporation scrambling through a cornfield in a motorcycle helmet to escape would-be assassins. She jerked the helmet off and followed Rafe's instructions, weaving back and forth from the barely visible path into the rows of corn. A flock of crows feasting nearby squawked and took flight, and she shrieked but kept running, shielding her face with her arms. "Should've left the helmet on," she muttered.

The path finally ended at the street, but she cowered in the field, afraid to reveal herself. Rafe wouldn't think she was very brave now. What if her pursuers somehow figured out where she was going? What if they caught Rafe and forced her to talk? She almost chuckled at the thought of trying to make Rafe Silva talk when she didn't want to. Jana checked the area, crawled to the edge of the corn row, and then bolted toward the nearest house. She snuck through backyards and hid behind shrubbery to lessen her visibility.

When she spotted the Carlyle cottage with its screened back porch, Jana broke into a full sprint. She jerked the boathouse door open. A large beach towel hug on a nail by the door and an inflatable raft lay folded neatly in a corner. She pulled both on top of her and collapsed on the floor, curling into a fetal position. She shook with fear and adrenaline, her face burned, and she started to cry. Irrationally, she stuck the helmet back on her head. Maybe it would stop bullets.

CHAPTER NINETEEN

The SUV revved behind Rafe and inched closer. Soon, they'd be in ramming distance. She kept her speed steady until she saw Jana run into the field in her side mirror and then gunned the throttle. Corporate execs didn't usually jump off balconies, hide behind dumpsters, dash through cornfields, or run for their lives. Jana would probably be freaking out, but this was just another day in Rafe's high-octane life. She predicted and managed risk for a living, but Jana would need help.

At the next curve, Rafe made a quick turn into a paved driveway, laid the bike down behind heavy vegetation, and moved closer to the road to get the license tag as the vehicle passed. The SUV slowed before accelerating again. She dialed Bennett's cell and asked her to check the owner of the vehicle before heading to the cottage.

Was she the right person to help Jana through this ordeal? She didn't listen or follow orders, even for her own safety. She wasn't a soldier Rafe could cajole or bolster into the next battle. How could she get through to a pampered corporate executive with no concept of danger or death? She probably needed emotional comfort and reassurance Rafe couldn't provide.

The sun was setting by the time she made it back to the cottage. She stowed the bike in the shed and headed to the boathouse. The door creaked when it opened, and she strained to see in the dim light. "Jana, are you here?"

A shuffling sound in the corner drew Rafe's attention to a large, deflated raft. It moved, and Jana stuck her helmeted head from underneath. Rafe almost laughed at the comical sight, but when Jana took off the covering, her eyes were wide, and her face covered with scratches and dried blood. Rafe clenched her fists against the anger that bubbled up inside.

"Rafe, I thought you'd never get here." She started swinging and kicking like she had the night of the fire alarm, but this time Rafe moved quicker. "Where...have you been? I was scared. Do you... have any...idea how much...I hate...feeling helpless? Totally *hate* it."

Rafe's own anger vanished. No point lecturing about Jana's reckless phone call now. She hugged Jana to stop the thrashing and hopefully ease her fear. "Yes. I do. Let's get you inside." She pulled back and looked at Jana. "You're wet. Did you go for a swim?"

Jana shoved past her. "Monstrously heavy rubber float plus beach towel equals hot. And the helmet made my head feel like it was in a sauna. So yeah, I'm a little sweaty."

"Which I'm guessing doesn't happen often in your line of work." This time, Rafe laughed, and Jana glared at her over her shoulder.

"You really need to work on your comedic timing, Silva." She stopped at the back door and dug the key out of her jeans pocket, but her hand trembled so badly she dropped it. "Damn."

Rafe picked it up, opened the door, and waved her inside.

"I'm going to take a long, soaking bath." Her voice was steadier, the wildness in her eyes calmer, but she looked like she was ready to collapse. "If you think it's safe. Where are those guys? Will they find us again?"

"I lost them, and they'll need help to pinpoint our location. As I said, this spot is a tech dead zone. You're safe for now." While Jana filled the tub, Rafe poured a glass of wine and handed it along with her secure phone to Jana before she entered the bathroom. "Why don't you call someone. It might help you unwind. Just please, don't tell them what's going on or where you are."

Jana's eyes filled with tears. "Thank you."

While Jana talked softly in the background, Rafe turned on the gas logs to warm the space. She grabbed a bottle of Gatorade, opened Jana's laptop, and accessed the files containing the mystery notations. It was time to get proactive instead of being on defense. She studied the figures and compared them to other codes and her limited knowledge of codebreaking, but these numbers looked simplistic. She stared into the flames and allowed the sequence to morph as she considered every option. There. Why hadn't she seen it sooner? Simple. "Damn."

"What?" Jana asked from behind her.

The scent of Jana's freshly washed hair and perfumed body wafted over Rafe, and she inhaled deeply to memorize the fragrance. Her light pajamas revealed puckered nipples and every nuance of her curved body. Rafe stared too long before pulling a throw from under the ottoman. "Take a seat in front of the fire." She patted the sofa beside her, gave Jana plenty of room, and decided against revealing what she thought the numbers meant. Jana had been through enough for one day. "Feel better?"

"Much. Thanks." She handed Rafe's phone back. "Talking to Kerstin helped. And I spoke with Camille. They're safe, no contact from the company. Everything is fine."

"Do those cuts hurt? Did you put something on them?" The hair rose on the back of her neck again. She wanted to vanquish the enemy and return Jana to her safe, insulated life. That's what she did, restore peace and normalcy. Jana shouldn't have to endure this kind of upheaval.

"I'm okay." Jana wrapped the blanket around her shoulders and snuggled into the sofa. "You neglected to mention corn leaves are like razor blades. By the way, Bennett said the license plate was reported stolen about ten miles from here this morning."

"That's good."

"Why?"

"Because it probably means they haven't been in the area long, stole the plates as cover, and don't know exactly where we are. So, that's all positive." Which is pretty much what Rafe expected. "Are you hungry?" She needed to keep busy because Jana looked entirely too small and vulnerable draped in the bulky blanket with scratches all over her face.

"Not really, but I wouldn't mind another glass of wine."

The firelight flickered across Jana's face, reflecting tears pooled in her eyes, and Rafe's chest ached. "Stay put. I'll get it." She poured the wine and then assembled a plate of cheese, crackers, and some of the grapes Jana had bought at the fruit stand. "In case you want to nibble."

"My goodness, Silva, is that a nurturing gene I detect?"

At least Jana was joking again. Rafe plopped a cheese topped cracker in her mouth and grinned. "I'm just not as good at starvation as you, and this is the extent of my culinary skills."

"You really are an enigma, Rafaella Silva," Jana said. "Just when I think I have you figured out, you surprise me."

"And that's a bad thing?"

"I'm not sure." Jana pointed to her laptop still open on the ottoman. "What did you find?"

"We can talk about it tomorrow. You've had enough for one day."

"Tell me. Take my mind off what happened." Jana sipped her wine and gave Rafe her full attention. "Please?"

When Jana looked at her with those stormy eyes, Rafe would do anything. She refocused on the files, hoping Jana couldn't read the confusion she was feeling. Giving mixed signals to a woman as intuitive and sexy as Jana Elliott was dangerous. "Was your mother British or Australian or did she spend time in either place?"

"My maternal grandparents were British, and Mom spent her childhood in the Midlands. We used to go back for holidays when I was young. Why?"

Rafe pointed to the numbers at the bottom of the first page. "I think this is a date."

Jana stared at the screen for several seconds. "Of course. Mom always wrote dates with the day first followed by the month and year. I should've noticed immediately. You cracked it, Silva."

"*We* cracked it. You figured out the *IM* part. This means the memos are dated, which will make creating our timeline easier when we sort through the insurance claims, medical files, and media coverage."

Jana fiddled with the hem of the blanket. "But do we have to do it now? I can't think after the motorcycle ride from hell and two glasses of wine. Not that the ride was entirely bad." She shifted uncomfortably. "Probably best not to focus on that." Jana grinned, and Rafe felt her face heat.

"Yeah, probably not." The thrill of 310-horsepower between her legs never escaped Rafe. It was like straddling a plane or wrestling a hurricane. After every outing, she was exhausted from the danger and physical exertion of controlling a machine that was designed for racing. She gazed into the fire and tried to ignore the closeness of Jana's body, but her appeal rivaled the excitement of her bike or any work scenario she conjured. To distract herself, she reached for another cracker but found the plate empty. When she started to kid Jana about not being hungry, her eyes were flagging, and she stifled a yawn. "Maybe you should go to bed. It's almost midnight, and you've had a tough day."

"Not just yet. I like the fire." She stretched her legs onto the ottoman and rested her head on Rafe's shoulder. "Do you mind?"

How to answer *that* question. Did she mind the ache of desire in her body from Jana's touch? Or Jana's heartbeat syncing with hers like a metronome? Did she mind Jana's steady breathing, a lifeline to something she never imagined she could have? "No." She didn't mind any of it but knew it was wrong and yet couldn't stop herself. She put her arm around Jana and pulled her closer. When Jana's breath quickened, and her body heated against Rafe, she asked, "Are you all right?"

Jana looked up into her eyes. "Would you come to bed with me? I need you." She tugged lightly on Rafe's waistband and then smoothed her hand up her stomach to rest between her breasts. "Please."

The firelight danced in Jana's eyes, and her lips quivered. She was vulnerable, and only rogues took advantage. "You're not thinking clearly."

"I know what I want, Rafe."

She should say no, keep her boundaries intact. She wanted to say no. That was a lie. Her body ached and came alive when she was near Jana blinding her to everything except her need. Instead of responding, she scooped Jana's swaddled body in her arms and carried her to bed.

CHAPTER TWENTY

Jana stared up at her from atop the bed, and Rafe stiffened. She never froze in battle, but this was something else entirely. What if she did the wrong thing? Jana deserved a level of finesse Rafe was certain she didn't possess.

"We can take this slow, if you want."

"Just tell me what to do...I mean what you want." Rafe rocked back and forth beside the bed with her hands stuffed in her pants pockets feeling more like a teenager than a retired army major. "It's been a long time for me, and I don't know what women like these days."

Jana grinned. "I'm pretty sure *that* part hasn't changed." She did a twirl with her index finger. "Turn around and undress, and I'll do the same. When I say now, we'll look at the same time. I want to be surprised by you, Rafaella Silva, like usual."

Rafe breathed to release the tension in her body and turned. She'd never done anything like this with a woman. Occasional groping in the dark with a female soldier followed by a quick getaway was the only contact she had time for or interest in during her tours of service, but Jana summoned new desires. Rafe wanted to take her time, touch every inch of Jana's skin, and sate her hunger until Jana begged for mercy. Rafe shucked off her clothes and waited, feeling heat and desire building in her center.

"Now," Jana said softly.

Rafe turned slowly, imagining Jana nude in front of her unashamed of her body or their intentions. She was not prepared.

Jana's pale skin shimmered in lamplight, her blue eyes were wide and expectant, and Rafe swallowed hard. "You're...beautiful doesn't come close." She rounded the foot of the bed and stopped, unsure how to approach someone she wanted to please so much. "May I?"

Jana reached for her, and before Rafe realized she was moving again, she was in her arms. They perfectly fit breast to breast, pelvis to pelvis, and Rafe resisted the urge to slide her thigh between Jana's legs and rock. "So soft. So good," she whispered against Jana's neck.

"Kiss me, Rafe." Jana traced a finger along Rafe's jaw and looked into her eyes.

"Are you sure about this?" One of them should be. Rafe was violating her work code and disregarding the boundaries she'd set between them. She wanted Jana with a fierceness she'd never felt, and one touch convinced her she'd never be able to stop.

Without answering, Jana lifted Rafe's chin and lightly brushed their lips together.

That's all it took. Rafe wrapped her arms around Jana's waist and pulled them as close as breathing allowed. She gently prodded with her tongue requesting entry and exploring the soft wetness of Jana's mouth. She swallowed Jana's moans to quench her soul from years of loss and loneliness. Jana tilted her pelvis for more contact, and Rafe pressed against her to salve the ache knotted in her center. "Jana, I want you so much."

"Then take me, soldier."

Rafe lifted Jana's legs on either side of her waist, walked them backward to the bed, and laid her gently across it. She took a couple of minutes to breathe and soak in Jana's body again. "Now what?"

"Whatever you want, Rafe." Jana brought Rafe's hand to her lips.

She gazed down at Jana streaked by moonlight, certain she'd never seen a woman more beautiful or more vulnerable. The curves of her body were an artist's masterpiece waiting to be explored and cherished. "I want to please you, to be the kind of lover you deserve. If I learned anything in the army, it was how not to treat women. I can't botch this."

"You won't."

Rafe called on the single-mindedness she employed in the field and focused on one thing at a time. She lifted Jana's legs onto her shoulders and massaged from her ankles to her knees and then upward to the join of her thighs and back again. She never took her eyes off Jana's face, drinking in the kaleidoscope of expressions her touches evoked.

"You're so gentle," Jana whispered and bit down on her bottom lip.

"Is it okay?"

"Better. Just not what I expected." Jana captured Rafe's hands and tried to pull her closer.

"I want to look at you."

Jana chuckled nervously. "You sure know how to make a woman feel self-conscious."

"I'm sorry." She'd already done something stupid.

"Oh no, baby." Jana swung her legs off Rafe's shoulders and trapped her between her knees. "I wasn't criticizing. When most women get to this point, they're beyond the looking stage. It's not wrong, just unexpected. Again."

"Their loss." Rafe combed her fingers through Jana's long hair and let it cascade slowly over her shoulders. "Looking at you has been my pleasure and pain since the day we met. I can't imagine not appreciating everything about you while I have this chance. Who knows what—"

"Don't you dare start worst-case scenarizing while we're naked." She scooted to the edge of the bed and buried her face between Rafe's breasts. "Come to bed."

Rafe's knees weakened from Jana's soft command and all it implied. This was really happening. Not just a quick tumble for relief, followed by a hasty exit before a night patrol caught her. She could take her time. "Gladly."

She eased Jana back on the pillows and brought their bodies together slowly. "Oh. My. God. Don't move."

"Why?"

"Give me a minute to imprint the feel of your body against mine. I never want to forget this moment. A first touch only happens once."

She traced her fingers along Jana's cheek, down her neck, over the rise of her breasts, the dip of her waist, and the swell of her hips, enjoying Jana's whimpers. She cupped a breast in her palm, weighed it, pressed its softness, and then tweaked the puckered nipple with her thumb and forefinger.

"Oh, Rafe." Jana's voice was a needy growl.

"You're so warm and soft." Rafe eased her thigh between Jana's legs. "And wet." She stifled the urge to drive against Jana, to rub her sex along her firm thigh, to even think about it yet. "You're killing me."

"Not my intention." Jana kissed Rafe's neck and nibbled a path to her ear. "At all."

Desire swelled inside, and she moaned just before Jana claimed her mouth. The contact electrified a path to her crotch, and she forced her hips still to keep from riding Jana to the world's fastest orgasm.

"You're holding back, Silva." Jana whispered in her ear. "Don't."

"Are…you…sure?" Rafe asked, her breath coming in gasps.

Jana answered with a sharp thrust of her hips. "I need you."

The words were a match to det cord, burning straight to Rafe's sex. "I want to be inside you. Is that okay?"

"God, yes."

Rafe hovered over her on all fours, sucked her middle finger into her mouth, pulled it out, and then eased it inside of Jana. She moaned, and Rafe slid deeper.

"Yes, Rafe, yes."

Rafe would never get enough of this. With each thrust, Jana answered with a moan, whimper, or a scrape of her fingernails down Rafe's back, making it harder to stay on hands and knees and bringing her closer to orgasm. If she lowered herself fully, she'd come immediately, and she desperately wanted to please Jana first.

"On top of me, Rafe. Let me feel you everywhere."

"Not…yet." She slid her thumb to Jana's clit, kept time with her finger, and felt Jana tighten around her. "Come for me. Please."

Jana rocked faster and dug her nails into Rafe's thighs. "So… close. Don't stop."

Rafe lowered her mouth to Jana's breasts and feasted. Maybe she'd violated some code. Maybe this was wrong, but how could it be? Jana panted beneath her, and her face and chest colored bright red. Rafe couldn't last much longer.

"I'm...coming, Rafe. Hold me."

Rafe gave a final thrust, slid her center up Jana's thigh, and collapsed on top of her. Then she was back on the battlefield with explosions all around her, but she must've died because she'd never felt better. Wave after wave of pleasure curled through her. If this was death, she'd die every day. She rocked and came over and over until she couldn't breathe and finally stilled.

"Rafe, are you okay?"

When Rafe registered Jana's question, she kept her eyes closed and assessed her surroundings, just like in the field. She clung to Jana's shoulders with her face buried in her neck and her body still trembling with aftershocks. Her eyes were damp, and her cheeks wet. Was she crying? The orgasm had been intense, and Jana smelled like lavender-scented sex, urging her back for more. And Rafe was ready.

"Rafe?" Jana rubbed circles on her back and teased a blanket from the foot of the bed to cover them.

"Yeah, I'm good." She wiped her eyes and face before raising her head to look at Jana. "Are you? Okay?"

"Never better."

"Thank you for that," Rafe said. "So much."

Jana chuckled. "You don't have to thank me."

"Yes, I do." Rafe cupped Jana's breast and thumbed her erect nipple. "Can we go again?"

"Now?" Jana pulled back and studied her before answering. "Already?"

"Yes, please." Rafe slid her hand down Jana's stomach and paused just below her navel. "I'm playing catch-up."

"So, nothing to do with me, just sex, right?"

"Totally all about you," Rafe said.

"Good answer." Jana traced Rafe's lips with her tongue before kissing her and trying to flip her over.

"Oh no you don't." Rafe rolled them again, topped Jana, and kissed her way down her body. She settled between Jana's thighs and looked up at her. "Is this all right?"

"You're joking? I feel like such a pillow princess."

"Conserve your energy. You're going to need it." Rafe closed her eyes, thanked whatever powers that be for her current position, and lowered her mouth.

Daylight was breaking when Rafe milked Jana's final orgasm from her and moved up her body. She sighed and grinned. She'd been doing a lot of that the last few hours.

"Mercy," Jana said and covered her face with the sheet. "I can't feel anything below my waist."

"I'll be glad to check that everything is still there, if you want," Rafe reached for Jana's thigh, but she grabbed her hand.

"You're insatiable."

"Told you I was making up for lost time."

"And I need sleep." Jana pecked her on the lips before rolling over and taking the covers with her. "Wake me in a couple of hours."

Rafe snuggled up to Jana's back, lightly kissed her shoulder, and inhaled her scent mingled with their sex. How many nights had she lain on desert-heated rocks or wedged between the limbs of a kapok tree in jungle canopy and dreamed of a night like this? So why did she feel as if she'd stolen these precious moments or somehow tricked Jana?

She wanted to sleep beside Jana to wake with her in the morning but feared she'd have a flashback and scare her. Rafe allowed herself one last caress of Jana's naked outline—surprised when her passion reignited the minute they connected. Everything about Jana aroused, teased, and tormented her in a way that made control nearly impossible. Would she ever get enough? Had abstinence caused her ravenous desire or was Jana the reason? If she didn't put some distance between them, she'd be on top of her again. She eased out of bed and tiptoed to the kitchen, turned on the coffee pot, and grabbed a towel from the bathroom on her way to the outside shower.

While the coffee perked, she went to check the perimeter. A mist lay heavy over the lake like a protective blanket waiting to be cast off by the morning sun. Birds caught worms, and squirrels scurried back and forth gathering nuts. Everything looked brighter, more vivid this morning, and Rafe hummed as she walked the lines, trying not to attribute the cheery mood to her night with Jana. She stooped, shoved one of the stakes deeper into the ground, and the enormity of what she'd done hit her.

She'd slept with her employer, violated one of her primary rules. If someone had told her yesterday this would happen, she'd have laughed. But every time she thought of Jana, how she felt, made her feel, the guilt and recrimination vanished. And if she tried to forget what happened between them, it would be impossible.

CHAPTER TWENTY-ONE

Jana woke when the morning sun peeked through a crack in the curtain and splashed heat across her face. She tried to roll over and go back to sleep but couldn't move. She was swaddled in the blanket Rafe had given her last night, her arms pinned at her sides. Rafe. Had she dreamed they made love? She was alone, but her body said she hadn't been. She'd rested her head on Rafe's shoulder, felt safe again, and practically begged Rafe to have sex with her. She hated being needy or at least showing it, but with Rafe it felt like something else.

And then everything came back—Rafe gazing at her like she was golden, touching her like crystal, and making love to her like she was Aphrodite herself. Rafe had been hungry, demanding but also thoughtful and gentle. For hours. Jana finally begged for mercy and felt Rafe snuggle up to her back. It was a perfect night of sex, like no other lover, but how would they interact today? Jana wiggled to get leverage and worked her way out of the covering.

She collected her clothes and dashed into the bathroom for a quick shower eager for some of the fresh-brewed coffee she smelled. When she came out of the bathroom, Rafe was on the sofa in front of the fire where she'd been last night. "Good morning."

"I'm glad you slept."

"Did you?" Jana poured her coffee, added sweetener, and creamer and took the sofa opposite Rafe with a view of the lake. "I imagine it's hard after all you've been through."

Rafe nodded.

"Thanks for taking care of me last night."

Rafe looked up and grinned. "Is that what I did? Took care of you?"

"There might've been some reciprocity involved." Jana sipped her coffee. "Are you okay with…everything? I don't want it to be awkward."

"If I said I wasn't beating myself up a little, I'd be lying. I broke my own rule about getting involved with a client. And for the record, I was serious about not being casual, like the other women you've bedded. But as far as how I feel about it, I'm good. A little sleep-deprived and sore body parts I hadn't used in a while, but otherwise—"

"Okay, stop. Now you're embarrassing me. And FYI, I don't just bed women." Was that true or just her way of denying what her search for Ms. Right had become in recent years. Best not to explore the question too closely. "Thanks for letting me sleep."

"Snoring might've been involved."

"I do not snor—" Jana stopped when Rafe's grin turned into a laugh. "That's not nice." Then she noticed Rafe's wet boots by the door. "You've already been outside?"

"I needed to check the perimeter since I wasn't exactly paying attention last night."

"Do you expect me to apologize?" She playfully raised her eyebrows and then wondered what this protection detail must be like for Rafe. She'd put her own life on hold—retirement, reintegration into society, finding a new career and possibly a relationship—to babysit her. Now, Rafe slept on floors, sofas, or recliners, isolated with someone she didn't know, led henchmen on wild goose chases, and tended the physical and emotional needs of a scared woman who resisted her at every turn. Maybe she deserved twice her exorbitant fee. Would it be worth the trouble then? "I bet you're sorry you took this job."

"Why would you say that?" Rafe placed her coffee cup on the side table and looked at her with those brown eyes that demanded truth.

"I haven't exactly made it easy for you to protect me. I've always been a proud, independent woman, so isolation isn't exactly my idea of a good time, especially when I'm being hunted. And now

I've seduced you and distracted you from your job. What I'm trying to say is, I'm sorry and I really will try to do better for the duration." Rafe brushed her hand through the unruly swatch of curls across her forehead, and Jana wanted to do the same and kiss the tiny scar at her hairline. "Do you want me to keep my distance?" Rafe studied her for a few seconds, and Jana could almost see her deciding how to answer the loaded question.

"Let's put that on hold for the time being. I don't know about you, but I'm tired of playing catch-up. I'd like to do a deep dive into this material and figure out what it means. The only way to get your life back is to find the truth and either confront Fergus or go public."

"Totally agree." Jana stood. "First, we need food. I'll whip up my famous frittata. Care to be my sous chef?"

"I'm pretty good with edged weapons." Rafe followed her into the kitchen.

"Okay, then. Dice some onions, bell peppers, and tomatoes while I set up." Like the night she'd cooked for them in the condo, Rafe followed instructions without question, and Jana acknowledged the pleasure of being in charge. *Control freak.* Rafe hummed quietly under her breath and attacked the vegetables with precision. "Are you humming, Silva?"

Rafe glanced up and blushed. "Maybe."

"Care to share with the class?"

"Not a chance." Jana pretended to pout, and Rafe said, "Okay. I was remembering how proficient you are with your mouth—"

"Again, with the embarrassment. Have you no social etiquette?"

"Thought we'd determined that already."

Jana returned to her prep work so Rafe wouldn't see her blush. She remembered and couldn't wait to do it again. "Do you know where the pots and pans are?"

Rafe pointed to a bottom drawer near the stove with her chopping knife, flipped it in the air, and caught it easily by the handle.

Jana got the same thrill she'd experienced on the back of the motorcycle and in bed last night. Everything Rafe did—mastering her bike, manipulating a handgun, rappelling from the balcony, wielding a knife, having sex—seemed risky and exciting and made Jana want more.

"All done."

Rafe's voice shook her from her arousing thoughts, and Jana pointed for her to put everything in the frying pan. A few minutes later, she plated the cheesy mixture with bacon, toast, and fresh coffee on the side.

"You're an awesome cook," Rafe said. "I could get fat around you."

"I doubt that, and frittata is really easy and mostly protein. Let's eat on the porch."

They settled in the Adirondack chairs facing the lake with a small table between them. Morning mist hung over the water like a droopy canopy, and a low whizzing sound cut through the fog. Jana looked at Rafe, her brow furrowed and mouth full of food.

"Fishermen. The sound of reels releasing the line," Rafe said. "You really are a city girl." She pointed her fork at the cove near the dock. "See?"

Barely visible through the fog, a small boat floated silently on the water, and a man cast his line and pulled it back in before moving farther along the shore. "What a great picture."

"They've been at it since before dawn. What they say about early birds and worms applies to fish too. Maybe I'll find out one day."

"You would actually fish?" When Rafe nodded, Jana gave her a sideways glance. "Really? Seems too tame for you after a career of nonstop action."

"Exactly," Rafe said and rose to collect their plates. "That was really good. Thanks. You cooked. I clean. You plan our next move."

Jana followed and tried to concentrate on the task, but Rafe's retreat distracted her. The tight jeans cupped her ass perfectly, and the muscles across her back and arms were outlined by the stretchy fabric of her thermal shirt. Jana flushed, and her center ached.

"Stop staring at me like I'm something to eat," Rafe said.

Jana's face got hotter, and she considered denying the accusation. "Is that a bad thing?"

"Not as long as you keep it in your pants." Rafe washed a plate and stacked it in the drying rack without looking at her.

"Seriously, Silva, you've been around men too long." Jana was both pleased by the banter and a little annoyed by Rafe's opinion of her. "It's not exactly flattering that you think I'm a promiscuous, indiscriminate womanizer."

"It doesn't matter what I think. You live your life the way you want. No judging." When Rafe finished the dishes, she joined Jana in the living area.

"Does that mean we can't have a repeat of last night?" Jana asked.

"Probably not a good idea because you're entirely too distracting."

"I read you loud and clear. No more sex with the help." The minute the word was out, Jana regretted it. "I'm so sorry, Rafe. That was rude, degrading, and not at all accurate. I meant to say someone in my employ. I'm really attracted to you and totally unaccustomed to not getting what I want. Forgive me?"

Rafe edged toward her but stopped. "I'm not—never mind. It's no big deal. Let's get back to work. Have you figured out what we should do?" Rafe wanted to say she wasn't like Jana's other lovers—that her flippancy was only a cover for deeper feelings and when she made love to a woman, it meant something. But the moment passed, and their easy connection of last night vanished along with the playful banter of this morning.

"I think it's time to take another look at Shelby Mills's list of names," Jana said.

"Do you have it here?"

Jana dug through her carryall and pulled out a folded sheet of Alumicor letterhead. "Shelby said she could get information on the insurance claims and subsequent denials. Maybe I should get in touch with her."

Rafe offered Jana her cell.

"No contact by phone. Shelby insisted. We'll have to arrange to meet her."

"I'll call Ben and ask her to reach out."

When Jana nodded, Rafe dialed the number and stepped out on the back porch. She briefed Bennett on their latest findings and asked her to contact Mrs. Mills. "If she has anything we can use, I'll come get it."

"Glad to help. Anything else going on?" The softening of her voice at the question alerted Rafe that she was asking about personal matters.

"No, nothing else is going on." So not true. She and Jana made love, or had sex, she wasn't sure which, and today things were confusing. She could use Bennett's advice but didn't feel right violating Jana's privacy. Besides, maybe Jana just felt vulnerable last night after her ordeal and needed a supportive shoulder. But that didn't explain Rafe's gnawing feeling that something had shifted inside her.

"Really? Rafe, you beat all. Isolated in a cozy lake cottage with a beautiful woman and nothing is happening? When this is over, we're going to have some serious sister time to discuss the birds and bees. You've been out of circulation too long."

"I don't have time for your ribbing, Ben. Just let me know if you find anything." She started to hang up but heard voices from the living area. "Hold on. Something's wrong." She clutched the phone in her fist, jerked the back door open, and ran into the house.

Her pulse raced, and she felt like someone was squeezing her heart in a vice when she saw Jana heading toward the door. "Jana, no."

CHAPTER TWENTY-TWO

At the frantic knocking on the door, Jana peeked out the window and saw a woman wringing her hands and trying to calm a boy who cried uncontrollably. She reached for the doorknob, but Rafe charged her like a linebacker and shoved her against the refrigerator. "What the—"

"Never open the door. That's my job."

Jana gasped. "But…they look harmless."

"Rafe? Rafe?" Jana heard Bennett's voice from the cell because she and Rafe were so close.

"Yeah?"

"Is everything okay? Do I need to send help?"

"Hold on," Rafe said, "while I check."

"Do you mind?" Jana pushed Rafe away. "I need to breathe."

Rafe raised her hands and peered around the refrigerator through the small window in the door. "Damn," she muttered. "It's my neighbors, Brenda and Teddy. Not sure why they're here, but it's fine, Ben. Guess I blew that."

"You think?" Jana said. "Now can I explain why you acted like a maniac." She opened the door before Rafe could give her instructions. "I'm so sorry. My friend opened the back door, and a gust of wind slammed this one shut. Please, come in."

"What's wrong, Brenda?" Rafe asked. She waved them inside.

Brenda gave Rafe a strange look. "You live here?"

"No, just visiting a friend. What's the problem?"

"Bucky, my dog, is missing." Teddy sniffled and wiped his nose on his sleeve.

"When did you last see him?" Jana asked.

"This morning. A friend called," Brenda said. "He was spotted at the boat launch across the lake from here. We've been searching everywhere close. I'm worried he'll get hit by a car." Teddy cried harder, and Brenda stroked his head. "It's okay, Teddy. We'll find him." She turned to Jana. "We got him two days ago, and we're first-time dog owners. I'm not sure what to do."

"Call your friends and other neighbors and see if they can help with a search," Jana said.

"Can you come?" Brenda asked.

"Of course."

"Not right now," Rafe added. "Remember, we have that thing."

Jana glared at Rafe but spoke to Brenda. "What kind of dog is Bucky?"

"He's a pomsky, a mixture of Siberian husky and Pomeranian, silver coat with gray splotches. He's a rescue and unfamiliar with the area. Teddy is so attached."

As if on cue, the boy wailed like his heart was breaking. "What if a car does hit him?"

Jana wasn't giving up, and Rafe must've realized it because she knelt in front of Teddy and placed her hand on his shoulder. "Remember how we found your dad's watch?" When the boy nodded, Rafe continued, "We'll fix this too." Her expression softened, and she leaned closer and whispered. "He's going to be okay." She looked up at Brenda. "If you have some meat, bring it to lure him out."

"I'm a vegetarian, but I might have a tin of sardines."

"That would probably work better for feral cats," Rafe said.

"We'll find Bucky. Give us a few minutes, and we'll meet you at the dock," Jana said giving Rafe an imploring look. Being so public was a risk, but Jana couldn't bear the child's anguish. A quick search couldn't hurt.

"We might have some hotdogs and leftover chicken in the refrigerator. See you there." Rafe closed the door slowly after Brenda cleared the screen. "This makes me really uncomfortable. Have you forgotten why we're here?"

"How can I after everything we've been through? I'll be careful and promise to stick close to you. My heart is breaking for Teddy and his mom. You save people, and I help them in whatever way I can. Besides, what are the odds Fergus's men will be waiting at the dock on the off chance I'll show up?"

"Any chance is too great, in my opinion."

Rafe's hands opened and closed at her sides as she pleaded, and Jana almost felt sorry for her, but Marian's independent streak ran deep. "I want to help, and I'd feel a lot safer if you'd go with me." Jana peered over her shoulder, and Rafe grabbed her bag, stuffing files and her mother's notes inside as she followed. "Leave it. We'll be back."

"Seriously, Jana. If you insist on going, we do this my way. Take some clothes and whatever else you need in case we don't come back. Humor me while I get the meat." She touched Jana's arm before she reached the porch. "Please. They've found us once already. I can't let anything happen to you, especially not after last…just do this for me. Okay?"

Was that actual caring she heard in Rafe's voice or just concern for her protectee? Either way, it was heartfelt, and Jana couldn't deny her. "Okay. You win. Again." She gathered her clothes, pulled on her coat, and even took time to tidy the bed they'd shared last night. Had it only been a few hours ago since they were tangled together determined to never let go? She wanted to hug Rafe and pretend their lives could be normal, possibly together.

In a few minutes, things had shifted to something heavy and ominous. She took too many things for granted—how she piloted her life with optimism and trust, how much she loved her job, contact with friends, and her unbridled freedom. Rafe had shown her how quickly darkness hijacked good intentions and altered your entire life. Not a welcome education, but a necessary one. She rejoined Rafe in the living area. "I'm ready."

As they walked to the dock, Rafe said, "I'm sorry to put a damper on the day. I really hope we find the dog. We need some good news right now." She untied the boat, held it steady while Jana climbed in, and then demonstrated how to start the motor in case she needed to operate it by herself.

"Why did you change your mind about helping?" Jana asked as they skipped across the water.

"I like children, and you wouldn't give up."

"So, you're just a softie at heart?" Jana nudged Rafe's boot with the toe of her shoe. "I like that about you. Want to tell me why?"

Rafe steered across the water silently for several seconds before answering. "Partly my upbringing, seeing kids mistreated and homed only for the monthly stipend."

"And the other part?"

"On one of my tours, I was watching a group of Afghan children who'd been left in a bombed-out village. One of the boys snuck out of camp and ran across a minefield. He was my responsibility, but I turned my back for a second and…"

"Oh, Rafe, I'm so sorry. Was he all right?" Rafe shook her head and focused on the dock, and Jana felt her pain like a wall between them. "It wasn't your fault."

"I got distracted." Rafe clenched her jaw and stared straight ahead. "We're almost there. Get ready."

Certainly explained the savior complex and why Rafe was so bullheaded about boundaries and distractions on the job. Jana shifted in preparation to disembark. The boat launch doubled as a paved parking lot that sloped from a wooded area near the road down to the water. "I thought it would be bigger."

"Like a marina?" Rafe asked as she backed the boat into a space near the end of the ramp and secured it.

"I guess." Jana waved to Brenda and Teddy standing on the ramp. "Ready for duty."

"Thank you," Brenda said. "Another person saw Bucky here earlier too near the tree line, so we just need to lure him out. I know he's afraid."

Rafe hefted a plastic bag containing chicken, hot dogs, and bacon. "This should do the trick."

"What's the plan?" Jana asked.

Brenda pointed to the wooded area. "There are three paths leading into the woods from the paved lot. Since I'm not sure what Bucky's favorites are, we bait each path with a different treat."

"Great idea," Rafe said.

Jana hadn't sensed Rafe so close but breathed a little easier knowing she was. Being out in the open around strangers after seclusion felt odd and Rafe's heightened vigilance poured off her in waves.

"We need a couple of people to watch the paths and a spotter to relay information." Rafe continued. "How about letting Jana be the spotter?" She pulled a police whistle from one jacket pocket and a pair of binoculars from the other. "We can call the paths one, two, and three from the left looking from the trailhead, and Jana can give a blast on the whistle to indicate which path Bucky is on."

"We have a leader in our midst," Brenda said. "Let's take our places. Bait your trails generously and shout if you see Bucky." She rubbed chicken on her arms, stifling gags as she did so, and took her place near the mouth of path number two after dropping a few pieces along the trail into the woods.

"Would you help me?" Teddy grabbed Rafe's hand and looked up at her with huge watery brown eyes.

Rafe's voice cracked when she spoke. "S…sure. We can take path number one." She touched the boy's shoulder. "Hotdog or bacon?"

"Hotdog!"

Jana nudged Rafe. "Very clever isolating me from the rest of the group to keep me close." Rafe feigned surprise, but Jana wasn't buying it.

"The spotter has a crucial role. Actually, you're the key to the success or failure of the mission." When Jana gave her a skeptical look, Rafe added, "Besides, I like you beside me." She scanned the parking lot.

"Paranoia pure and simple, Silva. Now go. I have to spot a skitzy dog who may or may not take the bait." She raised the binoculars and scanned the paths and surrounding area. No sign of Bucky. Then she looked at Rafe—sexy as hell Rafe Silva, retired army with mad skills, in and out of bed. Just seeing her helping a child warmed Jana's heart.

She turned the binoculars toward the paths again. While she'd been ogling Rafe, the spectators formed a semi-circle near the three paths and closed in on her. "He'll never come out with all those people so close." But Rafe would manage it like everything else. Jana prided herself on independence but leaning on Rafe never felt like weakness. Strange.

CHAPTER TWENTY-THREE

Rafe kept checking behind her to make sure Jana was okay and not too far away. She waved and bounced like a kid on an outing. She wasn't cynical about life and suspicious of everyone like Rafe, and she wanted to keep it that way.

Teddy tugged on her shirt, and she offered him some hotdog pieces and said, "Can you drop these along our trail, about six steps apart?"

"Yep." He walked the trail counting his steps and dropping bits as she'd instructed. "Bucky," he called. "Come, boy." When he returned, he grabbed Rafe's hand and kicked rocks when she did. "Do you have a dog?"

"I travel a lot, and a dog needs a companion."

Teddy puffed out his chest. "I'm Bucky's 'panion, and he's mine. We go to dog school."

"Obedience?" Teddy nodded, and Rafe asked, "Is he learning much?"

"Nope, but I am."

"Smart boy." Rafe ruffled his dark hair. She might've been good with kids before she became jaded by the world. Did Jana like children? A mini-Jana with blond hair and blue eyes enriching their lives and making everything feel new. *What? Wake the hell up, Silva.*

Time crawled like the seconds before a firefight when the team was primed and certain of imminent attack. How long would it take to run the distance from here to Jana? Longer than it took a bullet to reach her. The thought sent a shiver down her spine. She was too far away.

"Rafe," Teddy yelled and pointed. "It's Bucky." At the same time, Jana sounded the whistle once. "He's on our path."

"Let him finish the hotdog and he'll come right to you." But before Bucky got close to them, he stopped and snarled at something on the trail. Rafe stepped forward for a better look. A brown snake lay curled on the path near several pieces of hotdog, and Bucky stalked around him snapping and barking.

"A *snake*," Teddy screamed and barreled toward the dog. "Bucky, stop!"

"Teddy, no!" Rafe caught the boy and scooped him up. "It might be venomous."

"What if it bites Bucky?" Teddy squirmed and kicked. "Put me down."

"Look." Rafe pointed. Bucky charged the snake once, darted away, and circled behind before leaping again. This time, he caught the snake behind the head and slung it side to side in his mouth before releasing. The snake landed in the woods and slithered away.

"Did you see that?" Teddy asked. "Bucky saved us."

Rafe lowered Teddy to the ground but held his hand as Bucky finished the hotdog pieces and trotted toward them. "He's coming to you, buddy."

Teddy knelt and held out his arms. "My Bucky. Good dog." Bucky licked Teddy's face, sniffed his hands, and licked the remnants of hotdog from his fingers.

"Here." Brenda handed Rafe and Teddy some wet wipes. "Thought you could use a few of these." She whispered to Rafe. "Thanks for saving Teddy from that snake. I saw what was happening but couldn't get here fast enough."

"Bucky is the real hero."

Brenda gestured toward the parking lot. "Aren't people wonderful. I even saw a couple of security guards helping with the search."

"Security guards? How do you know?"

"They had guns and that khaki and polo shirt look. Nice men."

"Where?" Security guards didn't usually hang out at boat launching ramps or volunteer to help locate lost dogs. Her unease turned to full blown protection mode when she followed the direction Brenda was pointing. The men were heading for Jana.

Rafe ran toward her and yelled, "Jana, get to the boat. Start the motor."

Jana's expression morphed from joy to panic before she dropped the binoculars around her neck and started running. She reached the boat a few seconds before Rafe and yanked on the starter cord.

The motor sputtered to life as Rafe jumped onboard and loosened the line. "I've got it. Stay low and hold on." She looked back. How much time did they have? The men shoved people aside and ran toward the dock. She took a mental picture of their faces.

As the boat sped away, the dark-haired man raised his arm toward them, and Rafe heard two sharp cracks. "They're firing at us, Jana. Stay down." Rafe zigzagged back and forth in the water so they wouldn't be such an easy target. When she was certain they were out of range, she backed off the throttle slightly, and the small boat evened out.

"How did you know?" Jana's question barely registered above the strained whine of the motor as they lurched across the lake.

Rafe didn't answer. She trained to expect the worst, imagine horrible scenarios, and prevent them from happening, but none of that would comfort Jana. She hunched over her clothes bag and grasped the wooden seat with a white-knuckled grip. She needed security, safety, and a return to her tranquil life. "You're going to be okay. Trust me." But a small part of Rafe doubted her words. She'd gotten too comfortable with Jana and relaxed her guard to help a child. Now Jana was in greater danger because of her.

Who were these guys and how had they found Jana so quickly? If she still had her team, they'd already know every minute detail about them. They would be the hunted, and Rafe the hunter instead of constantly playing defense. But she didn't know anything, and Jana might eventually pay for her arrogant belief that she alone could protect her.

"Where are we going?" Jana had moved from the front seat of the boat to the one Rafe occupied and leaned against her as if needing support. "We passed the cottage."

"We can't go back there now. These guys are good. We're going to my place."

"Can you slow down a little? I feel sick."

Jana's skin was pale and her breathing quick and shallow. "I'm sorry, Jana, we have to keep going. This little skiff won't outrun whatever they've got, so we need to get home and hide ASAP." It wasn't her nature to run and hide. She trained to face an aggressor head-on and eliminate the threat but doing that here could put Jana and other innocent people in jeopardy.

Jana looped her arm through Rafe's. "I'm sorry I doubted you again."

"Danger isn't a normal part of your world, so a level of disbelief is expected." She put her arm around Jana's shoulder and made eye contact. "But I need you to do something for me."

Jana nodded. "Of course."

"When we get to my place, let yourself in and close the shades." She handed Jana the key to the nest. "I have to stow the boat where it won't be seen and then I'll join you. Don't come out, no matter what you hear. Understand?"

Jana's eyes widened. "What do you mean?"

"If these guys find us before we're out of sight, I can't take care of them and protect you at the same time. You need to stay hidden. Promise me."

"I promise, but please, I couldn't take it if you were hurt or…"

"Don't worry about me. Like they say in the movies, 'Live fast, die young, and leave a good-looking corpse.' Warriors are meant to die on the battlefield not rocking on the front porch." Rafe cringed. That was something she'd say to her team not a woman afraid for her life. "I'm sorry. Probably not helpful at all."

She steered the boat to her dock and held it steady while Jana grabbed her bag and climbed out. Once she was safely inside the camper, Rafe slid into the water and secured the skiff under the dock and covered it with the old, mossy tarp. A passerby wouldn't notice the boat at all unless he knew exactly where to look. On the way in, she retrieved her weapons bag from the lockbox in the storage compartment. Time to gear up.

She ducked into the bathroom and changed into dry clothes before joining Jana at the table by the lakeside window. "How are you feeling?"

"Getting back on land helped." She reached across the table for Rafe's hands, but she pulled away. "What do we do now?"

"Wait until it gets dark. I need to retrieve my bike and disassemble the security system at the cabin, if it's not already too late."

"What do you mean too late?"

"If these guys are just looking for you, I still have time. If they realize you have professional help, the equipment I used will point them to someone with a military background. And since we were using the Carlyle cabin, Fergus will make the connection to them because—"

"Because I told him Bennett referred you to me."

"And because he knows I was Delta Force. You're not to blame for any of this. You're trying to help people your company has victimized and abandoned." She took Jana's hands and stroked her palms until she looked at her, wanting to do more but realizing she might never be able to again.

"How could I not help? What Alumicor did was unconscionable, and abandonment is sort of my hot button...after my mother. But I feel like such a coward hiding while some of these people are still suffering and dying. I should be doing more." She withdrew her hands, her body trembling.

"I'm so sorry, Jana. I swear we'll settle this mess once and for all. Are you hungry? I think I have eggs and bacon."

"Not really, but it'll give me something to do. We should probably have something anyway, and breakfast seems like our go-to meal." Jana rose from the table. "FYI, I like your little nest. It's cute, and everything I need is probably within arm's reach."

Rafe pointed to the drawers left of the cooktop. "If it's not in there, I don't have it. We've got about an hour before dark, so I'll check the perimeter if you don't need me."

"I got this. Go patrol, Silva."

Rafe's watch app indicated the security system was working properly, but she needed space from Jana to consider options. She succumbed to her desires, slept with Jana, and lost her objectivity. After Jamal, she'd made promises to herself about anyone placed in her care, and now she'd lost focus again. Maybe she couldn't function efficiently without a team to back her up. She kicked a stone into the lake. Those days were over. Playing catch-up chafed against her years of training and experience but going on offense required that Jana was somewhere safe.

After dinner, Rafe sat across from Jana at the table again. "I need to go back to the cottage, and I can't leave you alone. Are you comfortable coming with me?"

"How will we get there?"

"Either we run or take the skiff," Rafe said.

"Not sure I'd make it that far on foot. I'm not much of a runner."

"Skiff it is. Wait here. I'll signal when I'm ready." Rafe checked the area before sliding the small boat from under the dock again. She whipped the tarp off and signaled for Jana.

Rafe crept close to the shoreline and kept their speed low so the motor didn't make as much noise. The trip seemed to take hours, and she hated being so exposed. The woods or one of the many homes nestled in the trees would be a great vantage point for a sniper if they'd pinpointed their location. When they finally reached the cottage, Rafe helped Jana out, and they collected the security stakes while sticking to the shadows.

"What about your boat?" Jana asked.

"It'll be fine here. No one can identify it as mine. It's not registered." After a quick check of the house, she rolled her bike from the shed, and they gunned it toward the nest. She kept looking behind her on the road, unable to shake the feeling they were being followed.

When they got back, she helped Jana off the bike and followed her inside. "Take your clothes off."

"What?" Jana's eyes grew wide. "Now? Here?"

"Please do as you're told just once without giving me the third degree." Jana handed over her coat first, and Rafe searched the pockets. Nothing. She felt around the sleeves, under the pocket lapels. Maybe she'd been wrong. When she ran her fingers around the collar. "Bingo."

"What?" Jana was unbuttoning her blouse and stopped.

"How could I have been so slack? They bugged your coat. That's how they keep finding us." She dropped the device on the floor and stomped it, then waved toward Jana. "You can stop undressing now."

Jana plopped onto the side of the bed. "Then why didn't they find us at the cottage?"

"Dead zone. The coverage up here is spotty at best, and if there's cloud cover, forget it."

Jana wiped a sheen of sweat from her forehead. "And here?"

"My security system has a state-of-the-art tech damper that I have to disable to even make a phone call. We're good."

Jana shook her head. "I don't understand. When? How did they bug my coat?"

"Probably the first night they entered your condo, during the fire alarm."

"That's right. I left it behind, and you kept me warm. It gives me the creeps that I've been walking around with that thing on me all this time."

Rafe motioned toward the bed. "Why don't you try to get a few hours' sleep?"

"*Sleep*? You can't be serious."

"You'd be surprised how much a frightening experience drains you. Try it. I need to think. I'll be right outside." Rafe closed the door behind her, stripped, and dropped into the water to cool off and figure out how to tell Jana the decision she'd already made.

But soaking didn't help nor bring clarity. She toweled off, pulled another of what Jana called her ninja outfits from a storage cubby along with an old sleeping bag, and eased into the camper to keep watch. She knew what she had to do but had never been so certain she didn't want to do it. She'd strayed from a vital principle of any mission—leave emotions out of it.

Waiting for daylight, explaining her plan, and answering Jana's inevitable questions would be the hardest things she'd ever done. She wanted to stay with Jana, to *be* with her, but her carelessness had made that impossible at least for now, maybe ever.

At daybreak, Jana peered out from the covers. "Are we safe here?"

Rafe couldn't meet her gaze or answer truthfully. Instead, she dialed Bennett's number and waited. "Ben, we've been compromised. We're at the nest. Come get Jana. I can't protect her anymore."

CHAPTER TWENTY-FOUR

*W*hat?" Jana swung her legs over the side of the bed and brought the covers with her. "What do you mean? Have they found us again?" Rafe's bloodshot eyes looked as if she hadn't slept and was in no mood for questions, but Jana needed answers. "Tell me what's going on. I have a right to know."

Rafe untangled herself from the sleeping bag and rolled it up. "Nothing's happened, and they haven't located us. Yet. But I can't provide adequate protection anymore. I shouldn't have tried. You're… the mission is too important for only one operative."

Rafe's words were formal and devoid of the sensitivity Jana had glimpsed recently and cherished when they made love. An invisible barrier loomed between them, and she winced at its cold impenetrability. "I'll hire more people. Just tell me what you need."

"I need you somewhere safe and that's not with me. You should get your things together. Ben will be here shortly."

"You saved me from a burglar at my condo, shook two goons off our trail at the vegetable stand, and yesterday at the boat launch—"

"If I was doing my job properly, they would never have gotten that close. I've been playing catch-up because I'm distracted by—"

"By what? Say it for God's sake and be done with it." Jana evaluated people daily, and Rafe's struggle was obvious the day they met. Attraction ebbed and flowed between them with the persistence of the tides. She'd felt it too but had been more willing to admit it and consider the possibilities. After they made love, she thought they'd reached a new level.

"*You*. You're a distraction I can't afford, especially when you're the target. I can't be manacled by you and fight for you at the same time. Don't you get that? While I've been playing house and make-believe with you, they've been inching closer. I'm a liability."

"No, Rafe, you're scared, and I don't mean of the bad guys." Jana dropped the bed covers, scooped her clothes from the floor, and ducked into the bathroom. The space was as restrictive and unyielding as Rafe, and anger spiraled when she banged her elbows against the walls trying to dress.

She shoved the door open and glared at Rafe. "What happened overnight? Yesterday you acted like you cared about me, but today you want to be rid of me." Rafe stared out the window ignoring her questions, and that was the final straw. "Look at me."

When Rafe met her gaze, conflict, regret, and fear were etched in the lines around her mouth, her furrowed brow, and the dark circles under her eyes. Some of Jana's anger waned. Rafe's decision had not been an easy one. "Will you please explain why you're pawning me off on someone else?" Jana slid onto the seat opposite her.

"From day one, my greatest fear has been that I couldn't protect you on my own. It's come true. Mission failure." She flicked at the army emblem on her metal coffee cup.

"Rafe, I'm not Jamal running through a minefield. I've known the risks since the day I copied those files and lied to my boss. I'm willing to accept the consequences of my actions. This is my fight more than yours. You don't need to do everything alone."

"You hired me for a job, and I haven't been very good at it." She continued as if she hadn't heard anything Jana said. "But I could use your help with something, if you're willing."

Jana wanted to hold on to her anger, force Rafe to face the truth of their connection and work on a solution together, but the resignation in Rafe's voice stopped her. "What?"

"Does Fergus ever use a protection group other than the building security company?"

"Random."

"Answer me." Rafe's soft request was almost a plea.

"Possibly. I've attended events through the years and noticed guys who looked like stone carvings gawking from the corners. I was never sure who hired them or why."

"Can you get the name of the company?"

"If I can use your super-secret spy phone." She dialed Camille's parents and asked for her assistant. "Hey, honey, how are things on your vacation?"

"Excellent. We're about to burn off some calories on a hike. Are you okay?"

"Fine. Listen, I need your brain." She asked the question, and as usual, Camille came through.

"Thor Corporation of Fairfax, Virginia. Not sure why, but a lot of those paramilitary groups, aka government contractors, are based close to the axis of power." Camille's words were laced with sarcasm.

"Thanks, hon. Do you need anything? Has anyone from the office tried to contact you?"

"No to both. We're good but tell Rafe she better take care of you or she'll answer to me."

"I'm sure she's terrified. Speak later." Jana handed the phone back to Rafe. "You heard?"

Rafe nodded. "I'm familiar with Thor. They're not known for their ethics and will supposedly take any job if the money is right."

"So, what are you going—"

"Permission to approach," Bennett called from the driveway.

Rafe tapped her watch and responded. "Clear." She met Ben at the door. "Thanks for coming so quickly."

"Want to fill me in?" Bennett stepped just inside the door with a wide boot box in her hands, and the small camper seemed to shrink around the three of them. "What's the plan?"

"Exactly what I'd like to know," Jana said.

Rafe pointed. "Shoeboxes are becoming one of my favorite things. What you got?"

Bennett squeezed around Rafe and placed the box on the table. "Shelby Mills sent the insurance claims for the people on some list Jana is supposed to have."

Jana elbowed past Rafe and flipped the lid off the box. "This is the last component we need to build a timeline from my mother's notes, the memos, and Shelby's list. We can prove how corrupt and negligent Alumicor has been and for how long. Thank you, Ben."

Rafe opened the door and waved. "Hate to rush, but you guys should get going. I don't want to risk anyone finding Jana here."

"And what are you going to do?" Jana asked.

"Don't worry about me. I'll be fine."

Jana raised and lowered her hands, searching for the right words and failing. "I'm worried you're going to do something stupid, on your own, and then where will we be?"

"*We*?" Rafe stared at her like she'd implied they were committed to each other, and the thought horrified her.

"Just forget it. Forget you've already saved my life, twice. Forget that I depend on you now. Forget we had sex. Forget everything and do whatever you want, like always."

Bennett's head swiveled side to side as she followed their back and forth. At Jana's last comment, she cleared her throat and said, "I'll be outside."

Rafe raised her hands in a why-the-hell-did-you-say-that expression. "I'll help you pack."

"I'm not going anywhere without you."

Rafe grabbed Jana's carryall and stuffed some of her clothes inside.

Jana pulled them out just as quickly. "I. Am. Not. Leaving."

"You're going to make me say this, aren't you?" Rafe released the arm of a sweater she and Jana were both pulling. "This thing, whatever was between us, is over. It's time to move on. And Bennett can take better care of you. She has the resources."

"I can't believe you said that. You don't mean any of it." Rafe stared at her with those sexy eyes as if she hadn't just ripped Jana's heart out, but something told her Rafe was hurting too. Without second-guessing, Jana pressed her body against Rafe and kissed her until Rafe gave in and kissed back. When she finally stepped away, she said, "I care about you, Rafe. Don't make me leave." Her pride screamed at her for being so vulnerable, but if Rafe gave up on her, it wouldn't be because she'd left anything unsaid.

"I can't promise you anything, Jana."

"I don't need promises, only you." They were so close Jana felt Rafe's breath on her face, but she wouldn't make eye contact. She traced the outline of Rafe's jaw. "I've never met anyone as focused as you and I need that right now."

"I'm sorry, Jana, really, but we both knew how this was going to end. You don't have to worry about bedding the help anymore."

"Damn you, Rafaella Silva. You make me trust you, depend on you, even like you, and then you abandon me like everybody else. *Really?* You're just a coward." She grabbed her bag and stormed out the door.

❖

Rafe caught up to Bennett as she trailed Jana to the SUV. "Please keep her safe, whatever it takes. I can't handle this and worry about her too. If I explain what I'm going to do, she'll insist on staying with me and trying to help. I'll be in touch."

"Where are you going to start?"

"I think the guys hunting her are with Thor Corporation, former soldiers, and I have to find them. They've come after the wrong woman and pissed off the wrong grunt."

"Just be careful and let me know if you need backup."

Bennett reversed out of the drive, but Jana didn't look at Rafe again. She saw pain in her eyes when they argued, but she couldn't fix it, then or now. Indulging her feelings got her into this no-win situation in the first place. If she stuck to the rules and just kept Jana safe… The recriminations could go on forever. She rubbed her dog tags between her fingers and thought of her team's motto: improvise, adapt, and overcome. Jana's life came before anything else, even the painful emptiness she felt inside.

She pulled out her sat phone and stared distractedly at the keypad. Jana called her a coward. When it came to chances on love or anything personal, she was one hundred percent, yellow-bellied chicken. She had no training or experience with either. Love should be based on empirical knowledge and certainty like a Trident II missile, not a gut feeling or butterfly-in-the-stomach silliness. Was that what she felt for Jana? Love? She tucked the nagging questions away and dialed the only person who could help, former team member Alpha Six.

"Alpha One, what the hell? Good to hear your voice, dude. How can I help?"

Typical team convo, short on greeting and straight to the point. "I'm good, Six, but I need help IDing a couple of bad guys I believe belong to the Thor Corp."

"Can you narrow it down a little? Thor is a sizeable group."

"One was clean-shaven, blond with strong facial features, possibly Scandinavian. The other scruffier, black beard and moustache, and a seamed forehead. Looks like he lost a knife fight and had a bad doctor. These guys often work in teams, so I'm thinking if I can find at least one of them, the other will be close."

"Way ahead of you." A computer pinged in the background, and Six said, "I'm sending you something now. These two are several years out of active, so probably getting soft, but be careful anyway. They'll be carrying for sure. If this doesn't work, let me know."

"Thanks, pal."

"Rafe, if you need us, we're here. Rules and regs be damned."

She swallowed hard to steady her voice. "Thanks, Six. Give the team my best."

Rafe pulled up the images of the two men she'd seen at the boat launch. Confirmation. She studied their service and disciplinary records, weapons training, and operations, all notable but not outstanding. Tucker and Brand. If she had to guess, Tucker was the brains of the pair with Brand, the dark-haired one, handling the heavy lifting and any wet work. He'd fired at Jana. She bristled at the thought of them getting that close again. Not if she could help it. Time to put the next phase of the operation into action.

CHAPTER TWENTY-FIVE

From the sidewalk in front of the Carlyle family home in Fisher Park, Jana took in the scene of ordered chaos. Two uniformed officers occupied rockers on either side of the front door, marked cars lined the street, and from the cacophony of voices inside, the place was packed.

"What is all this? Has something else happened?"

Bennett shook her head. "I'm just cautious. I put out a call at the department for volunteers to assist an officer in need." She opened the door and waved Jana inside. "Scores showed up, and we had to turn some away."

"But in your family home?"

"None of our other places were big enough to accommodate a small army."

The two living spaces on either side of the entrance now resembled mini communication centers. "G-ma and Ma are okay with this invasion?"

"I strongly encouraged them to visit relatives."

"And they just did?"

Bennett cocked her head and grinned. "You *do* know my family, right? They wouldn't budge until I gave them. all the details and promised we'd leave the place exactly as we found it. Two officers took photos of every piece of furniture and accessory to ensure we replaced it correctly. And you and Rafe have to join us for Sunday brunch after this…if things work out."

Jana started to crack that would be a cold day in hell, but Kerstin bounded down the stairs and grabbed her in a hug.

"I'm so glad to see you." She waved at the officers dashing back and forth, talking on walkie-talkies, and relaying information. "Quite a sight, isn't it?"

"You can say that again. Going from Rafe's one-woman show to this will take some adjustment. Is she here? Rafe? I mean, will she be part of—?"

"I haven't been looped in on that yet. All I know is the subtle approach to your safety didn't work, and Bennett favors the strength in numbers method. Let's get you settled." She guided Jana upstairs and pointed to the second bedroom on the left. "You'll be here next to Bennett and me in the master. The room across from you is empty, right now. Jazz and Finley will be in the rooms at the top of the stairs serving as sentries for the second floor."

"Is this really necessary? It's a bit overwhelming, all the people, preparations, and the constant hum of activity. And what about everyone's normal lives? Will Emory, Dylan, and you be here until this is over?" Jana pressed a hand over her stomach to quell a sick roiling.

"Bennett thinks the manpower is necessary, and I never question my wife about police matters. And yes, the spouses will be together. That's what you sign on for in a law enforcement family."

Jana rolled her suitcase into the bedroom, placed Shelby Mills's boot box on the bed, and collapsed on the settee. "Beautiful room." Part of her wanted to run from the nightmare that had become her life. The other part missed the seclusion of the cottage with Rafe by her side facing whatever came together. She brushed the hair off her forehead and stifled the urge to cry.

Kerstin joined her. "You're going to be fine." She rubbed Jana's back in soothing circles. "You want to talk about what happened… or Rafe?"

"I'm not sure what to say. She gave up and called Ben without even discussing it with me. Shouldn't I get a vote on how my life is managed?"

"Is that really what's bothering you?"

"Of course. Probably." Jana couldn't look at Kerstin, afraid she'd see the feelings that were becoming harder to contain. "I don't know."

"Something happened between you two at the lake."

It wasn't a question. "Bennett told you about our argument. What she heard."

Kerstin nodded. "We don't keep secrets. And we're concerned about both of you."

Jana stared out the window toward Fisher Park and gathered her thoughts. Nothing she said would adequately convey what happened between them or the impact it had. "We talked about our pasts. I thought it meant something." Jana brushed her lips with her finger remembering their kisses and the intense emotions that had claimed her.

"And?" Kerstin leaned forward so Jana would have to look at her.

"We had sex, nothing more."

"Nothing more? From the look on your face, I'd guess it was pretty awesome sex."

"Transformative." Jana blushed, and the heat of it flooded her body. "Sounds corny, I know, but I've never felt anything so amazing. One romp and everything changed for me, but I have no idea how she felt. We didn't talk about it, and then, she…"

"Left." Jana nodded, and Kerstin continued. "And you're usually the one who leaves relationships. Right?"

"If you can even call what I have relationships."

"I'm sorry, Jana, but don't give up on Rafe. She'll be back. Trust me."

"Why would you think that? She said what we had was just a fling and it's over. But after the way I've acted, why would she think I wanted anything else?" Why wasn't she more open about her feelings when they were together? She could've pressed for more conversation, more intimacy. She thought they had more time. Now, nothing was certain.

"I'm so sorry, hon." Kerstin hugged her again.

"How could I expect anything different?" Jana mumbled under her breath.

"Why don't I give you a few minutes to settle in and catch your breath?" Kerstin said. "Feel free to use your laptop or whatever. Ben has a secure network that's monitored constantly. Come down when you're ready." Kerstin gave her another hug. "It'll be fine. We've got you."

Jana sorted her casual clothes into neat stacks in the closet, plugged in her devices by the bed, and considered looking in the boot box. Distractions. She didn't want to think about what could happen next with her life or Rafe. Her employer fired her over something that should've been resolved years ago. A solitary and maddeningly attractive soldier swooped in and altered her life in tangible and subtle ways and then vanished. Criminals chased her out of her home and across the state. And now police officers were assembled to fight for her, probably with no idea why they were called into service. The rally spoke to their respect for Bennett but only reminded Jana what a total train wreck her life had become.

Where the hell was Rafe and what was she doing? The short time they spent together altered Jana. Her pulse quickened. She'd fallen for the reserved major, granted her trust, shared her life story, grieved with her, made love with her, and longed for her in ways she'd never wanted another. Rafaella Silva was not the kind of woman to quit. Righting wrongs was in her blood. No one had ever fought for her like Rafe, so why had she given up? Because Jana seduced her? Forced her to feel things she didn't want to feel and couldn't understand or manage? Whatever the reason, it didn't change the fact that Rafe *left* her.

She grabbed the doorknob and twisted. "Damn it, Silva, you better come back to me unharmed because…" The truth settled in her chest with the awe of a breathtaking sunrise and the warmth of an aged whiskey. She placed a hand over her heart to settle her stampeding pulse. "Because I love you."

❖

Rafe slumped in the seat of a generic rental car outside the Alumicor building and adjusted the settings on the long-range camera lens. A black SUV with tinted windows pulled up a few minutes later, and Tucker and Brand exited. If she got a picture of these two with Fergus, it would establish a connection.

While she waited, her mind wandered to the days with Jana at the lake cottage—confusing and challenging days. She plunged into civilian life where social and emotional skills mattered more than operations and action and was tested on all fronts. Personal protection details demanded focus, but Jana proved a formidable rival for Rafe's attention. Their first kiss took Rafe to new physical and emotional heights, and their sex altered her. It broke her heart to push Jana away and pretend she didn't care.

The distant hum of an engine starting drew her attention back to the SUV, and a few seconds later, Fergus came out of the Alumicor building. She snapped photos as both men flanked him from the entrance to the vehicle, and then she ducked as the vehicle passed heading north on Elm Street. She made a U-turn and followed behind other cars to maintain her cover.

The SUV turned into Old Irving Park, one of the richest neighborhoods in the city and home to US ambassadors, senators, philanthropists, and captains of Fortune 500 companies. The vehicle stopped in front of a massive Colonial style home across the street from the Greensboro Golf Course and Country Club. Rafe clenched her hands around the steering wheel. Fergus lived in exclusivity while the people his company exploited were predominately residents in low-income areas unable to afford insurance or decent health care. This injustice had gone on too long and was the kind of inequality she, and now Jana, fought against. She took more pictures, waited for the SUV to leave, and again followed.

Tucker dropped off his partner in a less affluent area of town before pulling up outside a ranch style home near downtown. Rafe parked half a block away between other cars and waited until the lights went out. She decided to approach Tucker because the thinker of the team was more likely to consider other options and less likely to be as hotheaded as the muscle man.

She crept around the house, found a bathroom window ajar, pulled on her gloves, and hoisted herself up on the ledge enough to leverage it open farther. The bathtub was underneath the window, so she snagged a towel from the rack and threw it into the tub to mask her footprints before lowering herself down. She eased to the doorway, scanned the layout of the home, and then checked each room before finding her target in the master bedroom alone.

A Ruger 9mm semi-automatic handgun rested on the nightstand. Rafe grabbed the weapon, flicked on her flashlight, and aimed it at his face to blind him. "Don't move."

Tucker lunged sideways and reached for his gun.

"Looking for this?" She waved the weapon in the light. "I asked you politely not to move. Try it again, and I won't be so nice." She didn't want to use the gun or fight him. Her combat days were supposed to be behind her. "We need to talk."

"Who the hell are you?" Tucker asked as he sat up.

"What's important is I know you, your partner, where you both live, and who you work for. I also know Thor doesn't pay you guys enough for the crap jobs you do, and I'm wondering if you're smarter than your neanderthal partner."

"Depends." He reached for the bedside lamp.

"Don't," Rafe said.

He waved his mitt-sized hands to block the light. "The flashlight is blinding me."

"That's the idea. Are you interested in providing a few answers?"

"What do you want to know?"

"What is Alumicor paying you to do and how is Jana Elliott involved?"

Tucker chuckled. "Now I know who you are. Ex-Delta Force badass hired to keep the inquisitive Ms. Elliott safe."

Rafe clutched the flashlight tighter. His knowledge of her identity didn't irritate her nearly as much as the implied threat to Jana. She lowered the light but held the weapon trained on him. "Now that the introductions are out of the way, do you want to talk options?"

Tucker yawned and stretched his arms. "I'm bored with this already." He swiped his left hand behind the lamp and sent it flying toward Rafe.

She ducked but not quickly enough, and it struck her on the right cheek. Warm blood trickled down her face. Tucker flung back the covers, but Rafe lunged on top of him and pounded with her fists and the butt of the weapon. He grabbed her around the waist and rolled them off the bed with Rafe still punching.

"Don't…make me…hurt you," Rafe said between blows. *Please let those days be over.*

They tumbled on the bedroom floor before rolling into the narrow hallway and exchanging positions. Tucker ended up on top and landed several jabs to her ribs and belly. Rafe grunted but kept working at his face and head as she flipped him over.

"Damn, woman, ease up," His blows slowed. "Maybe…we should…talk."

"Truce?" Rafe asked and waited for him to nod before she stood and backed away, ready to pivot if he came at her again.

Tucker raised his arms and sat up against the wall. "Truce." He wiped his bloody face on the tail of his T-shirt and shook his head. "You're a hell of a fighter, Delta Force."

She lifted her chin but didn't answer.

"It's simple, man. Fergus knows the Elliott woman has evidence of recent water contamination in the Badin Lake drinking supply. He wants the flash drive she copied, the contents of some damn shoebox, and her silenced."

"And how far is he willing to go to get all that?"

Tucker stared at her hard before answering. "Orders were whatever it takes."

His words sent a chill through Rafe. "Does that include hurting her?"

"You served. You know what it means. He wants her silenced permanently. This was supposed to be a simple document retrieval job, but when you screwed that for us, he upped the ante."

Rafe moved forward with her arm cocked but stopped just before striking him. "It's in your best interest not to follow those orders."

"He'll just send someone else, and I need the work."

He had a point. The best option was to remove the threat entirely by exposing the truth before Fergus got to Jana. She backstepped toward the kitchen. "Do you know where she is?"

"Not since you found our bug and left the lake, but it won't be long."

Good news, bad news. Jana's suspicions about why Fergus was after her were accurate, and he was willing to do anything to shut her down. The good news was he didn't yet know where Jana was hiding, so for the time being, she was safe. Rafe should feel better about that, but the bad news outweighed the good, and she wasn't sure Tucker would take her next offer.

"Are you really going to kill someone for a corporate sleaze like Fergus?" Tucker swallowed hard, and Rafe continued. "You're already on the hook for breaking and entering the condo, arson, and attempted murder at the boat launch."

Tucker shook his head. "No. I snuck in the condo during the fire alarm to place the tracker. Brand set the fire, broke in later to finish the job, and shot at you at the lake. None of that was me. I swear."

"How far are you willing to go? You're already an accessory to Brand's crimes, and Fergus will hang you out to dry when you're caught."

"Look, I'm a soldier. There's a big difference between killing on the battlefield to protect yourself and cold-blooded murder. That's where I draw the line. Can you help me?"

Rafe took her time answering to let the severity of his situation sink in. "I might have a way out for you." She stepped closer and offered her hand to pull Tucker to his feet. "But you're not going to like it."

CHAPTER TWENTY-SIX

Jana woke in an unfamiliar bedroom with raised voices in the distance and bolted upright. The Carlyle home. Safety. Then the events of the past few days flooded back. Sex with Rafe. Elation followed by a stab of pain. Being chased, again. Rafe abandoning her. Leaving the lake. Police everywhere. The voices on the first floor grew louder. If they were discussing her, she needed to be part of the conversation. She threw a robe over her pajamas, took the stairs two at a time, and almost toppled over the policewoman standing at the bottom.

"I'm so sorry. What's going on, Ben?"

"I just talked to Rafe." Bennett hesitated. "The rest of us can discuss this outside. We don't need to bother you with the details."

Jana shook her head. "You'll do no such thing. I have a right to be included. Actually, I insist on it."

"Rafe knew you'd say that." Bennett waved toward the dining room. "Let's have a seat, a cup of coffee, and talk about next moves."

Jana clutched the bathrobe to her throat and tried to contain the comingled anger, frustration, love, and desire rushing through her like a powerful narcotic. How dare Rafe Silva *send word* about her situation and not have the courage to face her. She followed to the long dining table and dropped with a thud. "Tell me."

"Rafe may have found a way to set a trap for Fergus without further endangering you."

Bennett summarized, leaving out the details Jana was most interested in hearing. "And how the hell did Rafe come up with the plan?"

"I'm not sure."

"Damn it, Ben, I need to know all the facts so I can make an informed decision about what to do. This isn't your life and livelihood or Rafe's. Neither of you can control it."

"We're both painfully aware, Jana. We're just trying to insulate you from danger or anything that might jeopardize your future."

"It's a little late for that."

Kerstin moved to Bennett's side. "Tell her everything, Ben. That's what we'd want if the roles were reversed."

Jana nodded her appreciation to Kerstin and returned her attention to Bennett.

"Rafe talked to one of the men who followed you to the lake."

"She talked to him. Alone, I assume? One of the same men who shot at us?"

Bennett didn't look at her. "The good news is they don't know where you are. Yet."

All the horrible things that could've happened to Rafe flashed through Jana's mind and her pulse quickened. "After I begged her to be careful, not to risk her life for me."

"Cut her some slack, Jana," Bennett said.

"Slack?" The word hit Jana with a jolt. "You heard the things she said at the nest. How easily she abandoned her job…and me. You're all right with that? Because I'm certainly not."

"I thought you were good at reading people." Bennett gripped the back of a chair.

"Bennett Carlyle." Kerstin's voice was sharp.

"Don't, Kerstin, let her talk," Jana said. "I definitely want to hear this."

Bennett brushed a hand through her wavy dark hair and inched closer to Jana. "Rafe said those things so you'd leave with me, be safe, and so she could keep you that way. It's what she does. And if she can't help the woman she…" Bennett wrapped an arm around Kerstin's waist. "I imagine she'd feel pretty damn useless. I know I would."

The resignation in Bennett's voice along with the word she didn't say tightened around Jana's heart. She wanted to apologize to her and

Rafe for involving them in her mess and for being so unrelenting but sensed doing so in a roomful of cops wouldn't be welcome.

Bennett kissed Kerstin and headed for the front door. "I'm going to set up the perimeter security system Rafe sent."

Jana stood, still processing Rafe's recklessness. "You can cordon off the entire block if you want, but I'm going to decide what happens next. And once I make that decision, I *will* follow through whether I'm being chased by assailants or a pack of wolves. Are we clear?" She made eye contact with every officer in the room and waited for any objection before heading back upstairs.

After a quick shower and change of clothes, Jana pulled Shelby's boot box from beneath the bed and placed it on a table under a window overlooking Fisher Park. She'd hidden for the last time. If the information in this box confirmed her mother's suspicions about Alumicor's disregard of hazardous materials and their effect on people's lives, she'd know the truth today.

She placed the paper with Shelby's list of names on one side of the table and the insurance claims on the other. Referring to the list, she separated the claims into a *denied for pre-existing conditions* stack and another *died before resolution*. On the floor around her, Jana created a Post-it note circle with the dates Alumicor had been notified of filed claims according to her mother's notes and internal memos. One by one, she read each insurance packet and placed it under the appropriate date.

The problem multiplied with each confirmation, and Jana finally felt the weight her mother had carried for years. She understood why her mother kept her in the dark but wished she'd been able to help. "I'll make up for that now, Mom. I promise." Next, she added private internal memos between Alumicor executives that showed a continuous, calculated attempt to deny claims and cover up the core issue of hazardous contamination. She topped each stack with any reference to EPA restrictions and/or remediation orders, and what the company had done or not done in response. Finally, she added the water purity tests from the Badin drinking supply, the most recent violation.

When the last piece of paper fluttered atop the stack, Jana stared at the results and a sick feeling churned inside her. All these people, and probably countless others who hadn't filed claims, were victims of Alumicor's criminal negligence. Her mother and Travis Mills questioned the company and were either threatened, intimidated, or ignored. She could only imagine the pain and anguish they experienced carrying this deadly secret. Jana covered her face and screamed until some of the rage subsided and her throat felt raw.

A few seconds later, Kerstin burst through her bedroom door and rushed to her side as officers gathered in the hallway. "What happened? Are you okay?" She held Jana at arm's length and examined her from head to toe. "Talk to me, please."

"I'm okay, just angry as hell at the death and destruction Alumicor has caused. The injustice is almost unfathomable. Oh my God."

"Here, sit down, hon." Kerstin guided her to the bed, waved the other officers away, and closed the door. "Do you want some water?"

"No, thanks." Jana brushed away tears before looking at Kerstin. "We can't let this stand. They've hurt too many people."

"We won't. I promise. Tell me what you need us to do."

"I'm going public," Jana said. "I want to meet with the executive editor of the newspaper, a North Carolina Environmental Protection Agency representative, the Alumicor claims manager, the district attorney, and Shelby Mills. And if anybody knows one, a reputable environmental attorney in case we decide to pursue a class action suit."

"I can make that happen. Where do you want this meeting to take place?"

"Here, if Bennett has no objections. Could you have a couple of officers transfer these documents to the dining table and ask them to keep the piles in the proper order."

"Absolutely," Kerstin said. "Now you sound like an executive vice president."

❖

Rafe sat astride her bike down the street from the Carlyle home wondering how Jana had taken the news about her plan. Rafe should've had the courage to tell her. Maybe she was a coward. Maybe she was afraid Jana would see through her lie about leaving. She fought and won battles on many fronts, so why did a simple look from Jana make her feel like surrendering? Who was she kidding? She already had. The only thing left was waving the white flag and saying the words.

She was in love with Jana. She searched for any glimmer of doubt at the idea but found none. What was she going to do? No one taught her how to love a woman like Jana who deserved the best of everything. The fight-or-flight reflex kicked in, and she struggled to breathe.

"You okay, Rafe?" Bennett leaned against a parked police car and stared at her.

"I'm in trouble with Jana, and I've screwed everything up. I can't tell her how I feel. I'm an emotional moron. You know that."

"Don't worry. Love makes morons of us all." Rafe glared at her, and Bennett added, "I'm messing with you. It's the most awesome feeling, and all you have to do is tell her the truth. You're notoriously honest, so that part should go smoothly."

"You're not helping, because I already sent her away with a lie."

"That's why I leave the emotional advice to Kerstin. Don't overthink it, just let it happen, whatever *it* is." She gave Rafe's shoulder a squeeze and nodded back toward the house. "She decided to go public. Kerstin and I are making phone calls to arrange a meeting for this afternoon."

"Is she okay?"

Bennett pursed her lips and stared at her. "What you don't know about women really is a lot. She's furious you dumped her, FYI her worst nightmare, and then used me as a messenger. Guess she expected more from a Delta Force major."

"Yeah, I get that. Sorry I put you in the middle." She got off her bike. "I need to get some air before I face her."

"Body armor wouldn't hurt either." Bennett headed back toward the house.

Rafe walked across the street to a bench in Fisher Park dedicated to the Carlyle patriarch and matriarch, Garrett and Norma. She sat here occasionally during her time with the family thinking and often giving thanks for their presence in her life. Now she needed the kind of strength another person couldn't provide. Jana had opened something inside her, and Rafe had no idea how to handle it.

She hated this part of operations—waiting for something to happen—but in combat that thing was another advance, reconnaissance, or firefight. Here she had no idea what to expect, with Jana or this detail. If she acted, shared her feelings with Jana, where would it lead? Did she feel the same?

Rafe picked up a stick and doodled in the earth as she'd done in the sands of the Middle East, but this time the exercise failed to calm her mind or her nerves. Was the protection detail over? Once Jana's information was out in the open, the threat would likely disappear. Would they ever see each other again when that happened?

A shrill whistle pierced the air, and she turned toward the sound. Bennett was talking with two officers in the front yard and waving for her to come back to the house. Not a casual wave. She sprinted across the street and took her post at Bennett's side. "What's up?"

"These officers have a warrant for Jana's arrest." Bennett gave her a look that said let me handle this. "Who is the complainant?"

One of the officers handed the warrant over, and Bennett unfolded it to the affidavit. "William Fergus." She held the paper so Rafe could see as well. "It's for misdemeanor theft of company property, taken out the same day he fired Jana. She can post bail and walk today."

Rafe hadn't seen that one coming. Fergus didn't seem the type to involve the legal system in his corporate affairs, especially when he had so much to hide, but that meant he was scared and out of ideas. She pulled Bennett away from the officers' hearing. "You can't let this happen."

"I can't stop it, Rafe. Anyone can take out a warrant for just about anything, and then an officer has to serve it. The rest is hashed out in court."

"Apparently, all it takes is placing your hand on the Bible and lying to a magistrate."

"Not exactly. Fergus listed the shoebox and a company flash drive." She turned the warrant over. "And he has a witness. Dayle Hargrave."

"Seriously?"

"You know him?"

"Her. She's one of Alumicor's corporate attorneys...and a *friend* of Jana's. What a dick move," Rafe said.

"Apparently she was sincere enough to convince a magistrate the claim was legit."

"I can't let Jana go to jail alone, not even to post bail. Can you at least work that out?"

"These officers don't work for me, but I'll give it a shot." Bennett gave the officers a brief rundown of the problems Jana encountered on Fergus's orders, waved to the extreme measures she initiated at her own home to protect her, and then explained the protective nature of Rafe and Jana's relationship. "If I arrange a closed appearance with the magistrate for Ms. Elliott's bond hearing, will you allow us to meet you at his office?"

The officers looked at each other, and both nodded. "Sure, Captain."

"Better let me tell Jana," Rafe said and started toward the house. This was a hazardous assignment she preferred to pass off, but Jana deserved to hear the bad news from her, especially after she'd sent Bennett to do her dirty work earlier.

CHAPTER TWENTY-SEVEN

Jana rose slowly from the dining table when she heard Rafe's voice outside the door. Her pulse galloped, but she refused to react physically or verbally. Rafe dismissed her for whatever reason, so she didn't deserve to know how Jana felt. When she looked up and saw the red cut across Rafe's cheek, her resolve vanished. "What happened? Are you okay?" She started toward her but stopped.

Rafe fingered the injury and nodded. "Just a scratch."

"From your talk with Fergus's man, I assume?"

Rafe nodded again and toed the hardwood floor like a nervous kid. She fought for Jana and the information she needed to make critical decisions about her life, but that didn't change the painful words she'd said. "Why are you here, Rafe? You were clear about how you felt."

"I was wr—I mean…Can we talk about that later?" She looked over Jana's head toward the kitchen without making eye contact and waved back toward the front door. "There are some police officers outside with a warrant for your arrest. You have to go to jail and post bond."

Surely, Rafe hadn't said what she thought she heard. "I have to go *where*?"

"Jail, well, actually a magistrate's office at the sheriff's department."

Jana shook her head. "And what am I being arrested for exactly?"

"Theft of company property. Fergus issued the warrant the day you were fired with Dayle as his witness, but we've been—"

"Yeah, I know where we've been. You really are something, Silva. You use Ben as your mouthpiece for bad news and then show up to deliver worse news in person." She glared at Rafe, mentally vowing not to kill the messenger. "No. I won't be arrested for that."

"You don't really have a choice."

Rafe inched closer, but Jana put her hand up. "I always have a choice."

"True, but this might not be the best time to choose the greater of two evils. All you have to do is appear before a magistrate so he can set a court date and then sign the recognizance form saying you'll appear."

"In the meantime, one of Fergus's flunkies photographs the whole thing, blasts it over social media and the news outlets, and my reputation and credibility are ruined. After that, no matter what information I release, Alumicor's victims will never receive justice."

"Bennett arranged for a closed initial appearance, and we'll both be there to make sure that happens. And anyone who hears what you've been through will realize this is just another of Fergus's attempts to keep the truth from coming out. I promise I won't let everything you and your mother did and the lives of innocent people be in vain."

Rafe reached for her, but Jana stepped back. "I can't. Not like this." She wouldn't accept Rafe's charity consolation. She had friends to comfort and console her who hadn't crushed her heart. Now was the time for strength and action. Just when she thought she was near the end of this nightmare, Fergus lobbed another grenade. She nodded to the officers waiting near the door. "Let's get this over with."

Jana was quiet while they followed the police car to the magistrate's office. If not for Bennett, she'd probably be in the caged back seat of that car and soon sharing a cell with real criminals. She shivered, stifled a whimper, and then straightened. Damned if she'd let William Fergus get the best of her. He declared war when he sent his thugs after her, and with or without anyone's help, she'd show the world what kind of man he was and what kind of corporation he ran. Her mother, her friends, neighbors, and coworkers would be vindicated.

Rafe offered her hand as they exited the vehicle and approached the brick and glass-fronted building, but Jana didn't take it. If anyone was watching, they'd see a composed woman entering a government building to conduct business unsupported and unfazed. Her roiling insides told a different story.

Bennett preceded them to the service window, and in a few seconds, a door to the side opened and a sheriff's deputy ushered them through to a conference room barely large enough for them. One of the officers read the warrant while Jana concentrated on the gouges from chair backs and scuff marks that marred the walls. She tried not to imagine who'd last occupied the space and what his crime was.

"I need your license, ma'am," the deputy said.

An older man she assumed was the magistrate sat at a small table typing. "You're charged with…" The words oozed into the institutional gray walls, and his voice was drowned by the static buzzing of a fluorescent light overhead. She was being arrested. Never even a speeding ticket until today.

The man pushed a piece of paper across the desk toward her. "Sign here."

"What?"

"I'm releasing you on your own recognizance to appear in court on the date listed."

She signed the document and asked, "What happens now?"

"You're free to go, Ms. Elliott. And good luck." The magistrate nodded for Bennett to join him outside, and Jana moved quickly toward the front door with Rafe close behind.

"Are you okay?" Jana gave her a scathing glare, and Rafe tried again. "Stupid question. I'm sorry you had to go through that, but we'll get it cleared up. Trust me."

"Trust you? Really? You walked out on me yesterday. Tell me why I should trust you again."

"Jana…I—"

"And will this ever truly be over, or will this fiasco follow me the rest of my life? Every time someone googles my name will this show up?"

"No. I promise." She opened the car door for Jana and then scooted in beside her. "We have to concentrate on the meeting now.

You've worked too hard to let him win. The folks need to see the evidence you uncovered. When you've turned over your findings, then we'll concentrate on shutting Fergus down once and for all."

"Do me a favor. Stop saying we." Jana turned away from her and stared out the window.

On the way back to the house, Bennett said, "The magistrate was actually the one who issued the warrant for Fergus. You can't repeat this, but he had doubts about the credibility of his information and Hargrave's testimony. Unfortunately, he doesn't try the case. I'm betting it's thrown out before it ever gets to court."

"Thank you, Ben, for keeping this private. Now, I want to change clothes before the others arrive. If you'll excuse me."

She reached for the door handle, but Rafe stopped her. "You want me to come with—"

"I'd like to be alone." Truth and lie. Rafe's strength, confidence, and support were exactly what she wanted, but she and her mother had started their journeys separately, and it seemed fitting she should finish the final piece of her mother's legacy alone. Maybe when her life was finally her own again, she and Rafe could talk. Maybe, if she was willing to risk more rejection.

An hour later, Jana checked the fit of her Dolce & Gabbana suit in the hallway mirror. Gray suit with white pinstripes and white pussy bow blouse. Perfect business attire. She raked her fingers through her hair to fluff the curls and started downstairs.

"Everybody's here," Bennett said as she reached the bottom. "Do you want anyone else in there with you?"

Could Bennett's relationship with the reporter and district attorney be beneficial? Would Rafe's presence do anything except distract her? "No, I'm good."

Bennett closed the pocket doors of the dining room that led into the kitchen and hallway, and the room became an intimate conference space. Jana waved for the attendees to be seated. "First, thank you for agreeing to meet with someone you don't know to discuss something you might or might not be interested in. But I promise by the time I've finished you'll be glad you came. Why don't we start with introductions?" Jana gave a brief rundown of her credentials and history with Alumicor and waited while the others did the same.

Shelby Mills started to speak, but Jana waved a hand to stop her. "And this is Shelby Mills, wife of former Alumicor executive Travis Mills who recently died from toxic poisoning. If there's a hero in this tragic scenario, it's Shelby. She brought this information to me originally and asked for an investigation. I can never thank her enough on behalf of all those who have suffered and died because of Alumicor's blatant disregard for human life."

Shelby nodded and dabbed her eyes.

The district attorney, a formidable woman with graying hair, spoke next. "Bennett said you uncovered a hazardous waste situation that rose to the level of criminal neglect and malfeasance."

"Yes." She handed a copy of the chronological summary she'd prepared to each of them. "This will give you the bullet points, and I can answer any detailed questions."

"Who else knows about this?" The *Greensboro News and Record* executive editor asked.

"My mother and her coworker Travis Mills knew, but they're deceased. Mrs. Mills, of course, and my bodyguard is aware. No one else knows the extent of the problem."

"You have evidence Alumicor knowingly disregarded EPA recommendations and sanctions?" The state environmental representative pointed to her summary. "I see no evidence of that here."

Jana placed her hand on the stack of her mother's notes and corresponding internal company memos. "These documents will clearly show not only a disregard for EPA abatement orders and recommendations but an ongoing conspiracy to cover the company's knowledge of hazardous pollution. You'll find a recent water purity test conducted on the Badin water supply that shows contamination as well." She shifted her hand to the other stack. "And these will establish a pattern of denying workers' insurance claims for illnesses directly related to the very chemicals the aluminum smelting process produces."

"If all this is true, Ms. Elliott, you have a compelling criminal case as well as grounds for civil litigation against the company on behalf of the victimized employees." The district attorney pointed toward the two stacks of documents. "May I take these to formulate the state's case?"

"Not right now. I've prepared each of you a copy of the information. When you've read and researched it and are ready to proceed, I'll provide the original documents for evidence. In the meantime, I'll keep them with me."

"Understandable after what you've been through," the DA said. "Bennett informed me that you were followed, harassed, shot at, and had your home burglarized. If we can identify any of the culprits, we *will* prosecute."

"Thank you. Do either of you need anything else from me?" When no one spoke, Jana continued. "I plan to hold a press conference soon to release this information, and I'd like all of you present."

"Could you give us a couple of days to review what you've got?" the EPA rep asked.

"Of course, but don't wait too long. I'm anxious to get on with my life."

"And we can't risk anyone else scooping the story," the newspaper exec said.

The group rose and headed toward the door, but the DA remained. "You do realize we may not be able to charge William Fergus personally?"

"I'm prepared to accept that only if we've exhausted every effort to do so," Jana said. "As CEO he's responsible for so much death and sickness, not to mention my mother's suicide. And I'm sure he's behind the men who've been tormenting me. We have to do our best to hold him accountable. Promise me?"

"You have my word."

She ushered the group out, leaned against the doorframe, and pulled a long breath.

"Better?"

Jana felt Rafe's breath on the back of her neck, and it both excited and calmed her. "Much." She turned and put distance between them, unable to trust that her presence wasn't a precursor to another vanishing act. "I still don't understand why you're here."

"Jana, I had to send you away to protect you. But if you're so anxious to get rid of me, my former team is urging me to reenlist."

"You called me a manacle."

Rafe closed the distance between them. "Manacles can be fun in the right scenario."

"Stop it, Silva." Rafe kept advancing until Jana's heels hit the doorframe. "What am I supposed to do while I wait for everyone to review the evidence?"

Rafe winked. "I have a plan."

Rafe's stare turned Jana into a quivering mass of needy emotions and aching flesh. She fake coughed, poked her index finger in Rafe's chest, and pushed her back. "Of course, you do."

CHAPTER TWENTY-EIGHT

Rafe snuck downstairs the next morning to finalize her plan for the day. When Bennett came into the kitchen, she raised her coffee cup and finished her call. "Make sure you do exactly what we agreed." Rafe hung up and turned to Bennett. "Excellent."

"Care to fill me in?" Bennett poured coffee and joined her at the banquette.

"Can you stick close to Jana today? I'll let you know when the plan is set in motion and where you need to stage. I'd like you both at a safe distance from the action but close enough to see and hear what's going on. She'll need to be ready to move when I call." She finished her coffee and rushed out.

Alpha Six was seated in the back at Krispy Kreme Doughnuts on Battleground Avenue with a box of fresh glazed in front of him. "I'd forgotten what a sweet tooth you have."

"This is breakfast, dude." He slid a ring-sized box toward her and an object that resembled a large smart phone. "This should do the trick, but I'll need them back."

"Roger that." She tucked them both in her jacket, ordered coffee, and snagged one of his donuts. "I owe you."

Six licked donut glaze off his moustache. "You could repay me and the rest of the team by reupping. We need you."

"Don't think it hasn't crossed my mind."

"What's stopping you?"

Rafe watched as Six lined up the remaining donuts like a wedge of soldiers. "Stuff."

Six laughed. "Okay, that's the vaguest, bullshit answer you've ever given to anything. You must be in love."

"What?" She snapped her eyes to his and immediately looked away. Lying to each other had never been part of their team dynamic. "Damn, man, I'm not sure what I am."

"You've got the look." He took a sip of coffee. "I'm happy for you. Everybody deserves someone to care about them, even hard-assed soldiers. And you definitely need a honey-do list or you'll go crazy in civilian life."

What could she say? Denial equaled lying. "Thanks, Six. Gotta run."

He waved a half-eaten donut as she headed for the door.

She texted Bennett to meet her down the street from her house and handed her the larger device.

"What's this?"

"An audio-video receiver. I assume you've used one before?" When Bennett nodded, Rafe added, "I want Jana to see and hear everything from a safe distance. The meet is set for the first picnic table beside the lake in Country Park. We'll need a couple of unmarked cars to cover the exits in case he runs, but have them stay out of sight. Get there an hour early and find a place to hide."

"I know how to conduct a UC operation, Rafe. Are you sure you don't want to be with Jana during this?"

"She doesn't want me around right now...and I can't blame her. Besides, she'll just distract me. I need to make sure this thing goes off without a hitch."

Bennett nodded and headed back to the house.

Rafe spent the rest of the morning and early afternoon conducting reconnaissance of the meet location in Country Park and staying away from Jana. Until Fergus and his men were dealt with, she wasn't safe, and the best place for her was with Bennett and her officers. Her phone pinged, and she texted Tucker her location and how he should approach.

"You sure we can do this?" Tucker asked as he broke through the bushes beside the path that encircled the park.

"If you do exactly as I told you. Did Fergus question meeting in a public place?"

Tucker shook his head. "He seemed relieved. Not sure if he's more worried about me or the possibility of being bugged. He'll meet me at the picnic table we chose at four o'clock."

She pulled the box Six had given her out of her pocket and stepped closer. "This will give me eyes and ears. If it goes to hell, I'll move in." She attached the tiny buttonhole camera to his shirt. "You know what I need to hear, right?"

"We've been over it a dozen times. I'm good. And you'll get me a deal with the DA?"

"I'll try my best. Give me a test count." She moved away and waited.

"Testing one, two, three. Tucker to Delta Force."

"Read you five by five. I'll be just behind that rock in the bushes. Take your mark and stay cool." Rafe called Bennett to get into position and resisted the urge to talk with Jana.

The minutes waiting for Fergus to arrive stretched like hours and gave Rafe too much time to think about the hurtful things she's said to Jana. Would she ever be forgiven? Her attempts to protect and care for Jana led back to where she'd started—alone and miserable.

The sound of a car door closing brought her back to the present. William Fergus walked toward Tucker. "You and that brainless partner of yours have caused more trouble than you can possibly imagine. I should've handled this myself. The girl?"

"She's close. I want to renegotiate terms before I hand her over."

"Hand her over? I want her taken care of like we agreed." Fergus shook his finger in Tucker's face.

"Well, you see, that's the problem right there. I agreed to recover company papers, nothing else. I'm a soldier not a killer for hire."

So far, so good. Tucker's voice was strong, his demeanor commanding, and Fergus was rattled.

"Brand didn't seem so discerning when I told him to silence Jana Elliott permanently. Remember *that* conversation? But he blew it at the lake because he's such a horrible shot." Fergus's face reddened. "I won't allow *anyone* to bring down my company. If you want more money, name your price."

"I won't get an innocent's blood on my hands for any amount of money, Fergus. Find yourself another patsy. I'm not it."

When Turner walked away, Fergus stared after him, his eyes wide and mouth moving wordlessly. Rafe started to call in the troops, but movement from a clump of azaleas caught her eye. Jana. Running toward Fergus.

CHAPTER TWENTY-NINE

Jana jumped out of Bennett's car, crashed through a stand of bushes, and ran full throttle toward Fergus. "Pathetic coward. How could you?" She just wanted a few minutes with him to have her say before Bennett carted him off to jail. Her mother deserved nothing less.

Fergus moved toward his vehicle, but Rafe dove from behind the rock and shoved him against the side of the car. Bennett joined her and jerked his hands behind his back, handcuffed him, and turned him to face Jana.

"What do you think you're doing?" Fergus bellowed. "Do you know who I am?"

"All too well," Rafe said. "You're a disgrace to the army."

Jana stepped closer to Fergus. "Is your precious company and reputation worth having me killed?"

"If you'd just given the documents back and kept your mouth shut, extreme measures wouldn't have been necessary, but you're just like your mother. Neither one of you knows when to leave well enough alone."

"Well enough?" Jana started toward him, her face red with anger, but Rafe held her back. "*Well enough*? You killed people. There's no justifying that."

"Every worker in our plants knew the risks associated with spent potliner. They chose the jobs. I forced no one."

"Did they choose to become sick because Alumicor refused to provide protective gear or to properly clean their dump sites?"

Rafe wanted to step in, but Jana needed this confrontation for herself, her mother, and the others who'd paid dearly for trusting Alumicor.

"And did those same workers *choose* to have their insurance claims denied, healthcare withheld, and families shattered?"

"You can't prove any of that, Jana," Fergus said.

"Really? I have my mother's notes, along with internal company memos confirming you conspired to cover up the effects of hazardous materials on your property. And I have the purity test on the Badin water supply."

Fergus stumbled back as if he'd been slapped. "You have...a... the..."

"I think the word you're grappling for is evidence." Jana crossed her arms over her chest and nodded. "Now who's got proof?"

"Too bad no one will ever see it."

"I'm afraid they already have," Rafe said, pointing to Tucker who'd hung back during the confrontation.

Two unmarked police cars raced onto the lot with lights flashing, and officers surrounded the group. Bennett guided Fergus toward one of the officers. "You're under arrest for conspiracy to murder and a lot of other stuff the district attorney will explain later."

"You can't arrest me," Fergus tried to wrench free. "I run a multibillion-dollar enterprise."

"And you broke the law."

Jana turned to Rafe. "You planned this whole thing? When?"

Rafe nodded toward where she'd parked her rental car. "Fancy a ride back to your place? I can explain on the way." Jana agreed, and Rafe called to Bennett. "Catch you later. Thanks for the backup."

Jana started to loop her arm through Rafe's as they walked but wasn't sure if she should or if she wanted to. There were so many things still unresolved between them. "You set this up so I could hear Fergus's confession, confront him, and watch his arrest, didn't you?"

"There's a certain satisfaction in facing your enemy after winning the battle."

"Thank you for that." Jana leaned closer to Rafe as they approached her car. "Does this mean I'm no longer in jeopardy from Fergus and his cronies?"

"Probably, but just to be safe, I'd prefer to wait until after your press release to claim victory. Once your news goes public, the threat will be neutralized."

"So, I can't fire you yet." Jana stopped at the car door. "Are you coming home with me?" Even if she wanted to, she couldn't stay angry with Rafe. She'd fought for her since the day they met, put her own life on hold and in jeopardy, and given her the best sex she'd ever had. Maybe it was the relief of knowing Fergus would pay for his crimes, but all she wanted now was to be alone with Rafe to find out where they stood.

"You're not getting rid of me until I'm certain you're safe. And we have some things to talk about. Don't we?"

"I can't believe you just said that Rafaella Silva. Talking? Really?" Jana reached across the console and took Rafe's hand. "Please drive faster."

When the condo door closed behind them, Jana was suddenly nervous and uncertain. "Do you want something to drink? Are you hungry? I can fix something, besides breakfast. I'd really like to change into something less business." Rafe was grinning at her, and she asked. "What?"

"I haven't heard your machine gun rattling in a while. It's cute."

Jana's skin heated. "Cute, huh? I'm a little edgy, aren't you?"

"Terrified."

"Why, Rafe?"

"We're venturing into uncharted territory for me."

Jana couldn't resist the vulnerability in Rafe's voice or the sincerity of her words. She shucked off her suit jacket, took Rafe's hands, and guided her to the sofa. "Okay, so let's just get it all out in the open. No filtering, just honesty." Rafe nodded, so Jana continued, "And, I'd like you to go first since you did sort of dump me once already. Please."

Rafe's Adam's apple worked up and down, and her dark eyes widened. "Okay. Bear with me." She brushed at the shock of hair on her forehead, released a deep breath, and said, "I'm so sorry I hurt you at the nest. I was trying to protect you the only way I knew how."

"I know."

"And—you do?"

"Ben told me." Jana waited, willing herself not to touch Rafe, unwilling to rush or save her from the honesty they both deserved.

"Since you already know that, the other thing I have to say is I love you." This time when she spoke, Rafe met Jana's gaze and tears welled in her eyes. "I love you so much it's like a living thing inside me. When we're apart, I ache for you. And the thought of you hurt or unhappy is worse than any injury in battle. I know I'm not an ideal potential partner but—"

"Stop," Jana said. "You're perfect for me because I love you too." Unable to wait any longer, she straddled Rafe's lap and kissed her softly at first and then deeply. "I love you."

"I can't believe it. A woman like you with someone like me." Rafe cupped Jana's chin and brought their lips together for another kiss. When they parted again, Rafe held Jana at arm's length. "You know this won't be easy. You're a city girl. I'm more the woodsy type. You're all about people, and I'm more of a recluse."

"Opposites attract," Jana said and tongued her ear.

"I'm serious, Jana. We have things to figure out. I don't even have a job."

"As long as you don't reenlist, I don't care what you do. And I'm currently unemployed as well. Isn't it wonderful? We'll have time to get better acquainted."

"And I want a wife, a real home, and kids."

Jana almost toppled off Rafe's lap but righted herself. "Kids? We haven't had our first date yet."

Rafe drew her closer again and whispered, "No, but we had sex, so I'm thinking a date is a sure thing."

"I'm going to reserve dating until we have sex at least a dozen more times. I need to know you can keep up, Silva." She slid her center along Rafe's thigh and moaned.

"Hold it. I just need to hear two more words before we go any further."

"Take me?"

"You're fired," Rafe said. "I can't handle the guilt of sleeping with the boss again."

Jana twerked her pelvis against Rafe and said, "You're definitely fired."

"Thanks. Never thought those words could make me so happy."

"In that case, make love to me, Rafe."

"Here?"

"Absolutely. Right here. And in the kitchen. Then the guest bedroom. The master bedroom. And the shower if you'd like." Jana slid off Rafe's lap, unbuttoned her blouse, and wiggled out of her slacks.

"You still sound like a boss," Rafe worked her hand up the inside of Jana's thigh.

"I like telling you what to do."

"I have a feeling you'll always be my boss, Jana Elliott."

CHAPTER THIRTY

Two weeks later

Rafe woke from another night of restful sleep, propped up on her elbow, and stared at Jana asleep beside her. The morning sun drenched the condo in light and cast a warm glow over her skin. It took everything inside Rafe not to kiss her, run her hand up her thigh, and take her before work. Instead, she snuggled close and placed her head between Jana's breasts, listening to the heartbeat now tethered to her own. She'd never imagined feeling this connected to another person, this eager for her affection, or this certain they were meant to be together.

"Good morning, my love," Jana said and hugged Rafe closer. "Did you sleep well?"

"Uh-huh. I always do with you beside me. Maybe it's because you wear me out first."

"Glad to be of service." She brushed the curls from Rafe's forehead and kissed her scar.

"In that case." She snaked her hand under the cover.

"Don't you dare, Rafaella Silva."

"What? Only two weeks and the passion is gone?"

"Never." Jana kissed her deeply before rolling out of bed. "Have you forgotten it's the first official day of my new job?"

Rafe grabbed for her, but Jana sidestepped. "No...but it's right next door. You just go down a few floors and walk across the skyway. Sure you don't have time?"

"Not this morning, love. Camille starts today too, and I want to be there when she arrives."

"I'm afraid for the Lincoln Financial Group with the two of you onboard. You'll be running the place soon."

"I can't believe how eager they were to hire me after the Alumicor article broke. They said my courage and integrity were exactly the qualities they needed to spearhead their corporate brand and advertising division."

"They're lucky to have you." Rafe jumped out of bed, caught Jana around the waist, and pulled her close. "Is that a fancy way of saying you sell the company image?"

"Exactly and you know how good I am at selling things." She wiggled her hand into Rafe's boxers and flicked her clit before rushing into the bathroom.

"Damn, woman." Rafe followed, stripping as she went. "Can I shower with you?"

"Only if you promise not to touch me." Jana waggled her eyebrows suggestively.

Rafe crossed her heart and waited until Jana adjusted the water temperature and motioned for her to enter the enclosure. She'd follow Jana anywhere, do anything she said for the rest of their lives. She was her heart and her home.

Jana placed her forefinger between Rafe's breasts and edged her back against the tiled wall. "Spread 'em."

Rafe did as instructed, and Jana knelt in front of her. The minute Jana's tongue touched her, Rafe's body started spasming. "Oh, babe. I'm not going to last."

Jana looked up and grinned. "Four more tiny little tastes. Don't come yet."

"*Jana*." Rafe tried to count but only made it to one. Her knees trembled, and she grabbed Jana's shoulders. "Please."

"And…four." Jana rose, slid their bodies together and rocked. "Almost, baby."

"I need…you…" Rafe's voice sounded weak. She needed so much from Jana and felt everything so deeply. "I love you."

"Come for me, Rafe." Jana panted, and her thrusts quickened. "Now."

Rafe's orgasm exploded and tumbled through every nerve head to toes. She clutched Jana close and held on as they finished together and collapsed to the floor. "Damn."

"I know, right?" Jana kissed her face and then stared into her eyes. "I'm the luckiest woman in the world."

Rafe shook her head. "That would be me. And I am the boss."

"Of Silva Security Solutions. And don't forget who your first client was. Guess you could say I started the business for you."

"Oh crap." Rafe tried to get up, but Jana didn't budge. "I have to meet a new client this morning. Might be some travel involved."

"Just don't be gone too long. You know how I feel about you leaving me." She arched her back, stuck her head under the shower, and finger combed her hair off her face.

"You have no idea how hot you look when you do that." She pulled Jana back onto her lap and buried her face between her breasts. "Time for one more?"

"Who's the boss?"

"You are, babe, always."

About the Author

A thirty-year veteran of a midsized police department, VK Powell was a police officer by necessity and a writer by desire. Her career spanned numerous positions including beat officer, homicide detective, vice/narcotics lieutenant, captain, and assistant chief of police. Now retired, she devotes her time to writing, traveling, and volunteering.

VK can be reached on Facebook at @vk.powell.12 and Twitter @VKPowell.

Books Available from Bold Strokes Books

Boy at the Window by Lauren Melissa Ellzey. Daniel Kim struggles to hold onto reality while haunted by both his very-present past and his never-present parents. Jiwon Yoon may be the only one who can break Daniel free. (978-1-63679-092-3)

Deadly Secrets by VK Powell. Corporate criminals want whistleblower Jana Elliott permanently silenced, but Rafe Silva will risk everything to keep the woman she loves safe. (978-1-63679-087-9)

Enchanted Autumn by Ursula Klein. When Elizabeth comes to Salem, Massachusetts, to study the witch trials, she never expects to find love—or an actual witch...and Hazel might just turn out to be both. (978-1-63679-104-3)

Escorted by Renee Roman. When fantasy meets reality, will escort Ryan Lewis be able to walk away from a chance at forever with her new client Dani? (978-1-63679-039-8)

Her Heart's Desire by Anne Shade. Two women. One choice. Will Eve and Lynette be able to overcome their doubts and fears to embrace their deepest desire? (978-1-63679-102-9)

My Secret Valentine by Julie Cannon, Erin Dutton, & Anne Shade. Winning the heart of your secret Valentine? These award-winning authors agree, there is no better way to fall in love. (978-1-63679-071-8)

Perilous Obsession by Carsen Taite. When reporter Macy Moran becomes consumed with solving a cold case, will her quest for the truth bring her closer to Detective Beck Ramsey or will her obsession with finding a murderer rob her of a chance at true love? (978-1-63679-009-1)

Reading Her by Amanda Radley. Lauren and Allegra learn love and happiness are right where they least expect it. There's just one problem: Lauren has a secret she cannot tell anyone, and Allegra knows she's hiding something. (978-1-63679-075-6)

The Willing by Lyn Hemphill. Kitty Wilson doesn't know how, but she can bring people back from the dead as long as someone Is willing to take their place and keep the universe in balance. (978-1-63679-083-1)

Three Left Turns to Nowhere by Nathan Burgoine, J. Marshall Freeman, & Jeffrey Ricker. Three strangers heading to a convention in Toronto are stranded in rural Ontario, where a small town with a subtle kind of magic leads each to discover what he's been searching for. (978-1-63679-050-3)

Watching Over Her by Ronica Black. As they face the snowstorm of the century, and the looming threat of a stalker, Riley and Zoey just might find love in the most unexpected of places. (978-1-63679-100-5)

#shedeservedit by Greg Herren. When his gay best friend, and high school football star, is murdered, Alex Wheeler is a suspect and must find the truth to clear himself. (978-1-63555-996-5)

Always by Kris Bryant. When a pushy American private investigator shows up demanding to meet the woman in Camila's artwork, instead of introducing her to her great-grandmother, Camila decides to lead her on a wild goose chase all over Italy. (978-1-63679-027-5)

Exes and O's by Joy Argento. Ali and Madison really only have one thing in common. The girl who broke their heart may be the only one who can put it back together. (978-1-63679-017-6)

One Verse Multi by Sander Santiago. Life was good: promotion, friends, falling in love, discovering that the multi-verse is on a fast track to collision—wait, what? Good thing Martin King works for a company that can fix the problem, right...um...right? (978-1-63679-069-5)

Paris Rules by Jaime Maddox. Carly Becker has been searching for the perfect woman all her life, but no one ever seems to be just right until Paige Waterford checks all her boxes, except the most important one—she's married. (978-1-63679-077-0)

Shadow Dancers by Suzie Clarke. In this third and final book in the Moon Shadow series, Rachel must find a way to become the hunter and not the hunted, and this time she will meet Ehsee Yumiko head-on. (978-1-63555-829-6)

The Kiss by C.A. Popovich. When her wife refuses their divorce and begins to stalk her, threatening her life, Kate realizes to protect her new love, Leslie, she has to let her go, even if it breaks her heart. (978-1-63679-079-4)

The Wedding Setup by Charlotte Greene. When Ryann, a big-time New York executive, goes to Colorado to help out with her best friend's wedding, she never expects to fall for the maid of honor. (978-1-63679-033-6)

Velocity by Gun Brooke. Holly and Claire work toward an uncertain future preparing for an alien space mission, and only one thing is for certain, they will have to risk their lives, and their hearts, to discover the truth. (978-1-63555-983-5)

Wildflower Words by Sam Ledel. Lida Jones treks West with her father in search of a better life on the rapidly developing American frontier, but finds home when she meets Hazel Thompson. (978-1-63679-055-8)

A Fairer Tomorrow by Kathleen Knowles. For Maddie Weeks and Gerry Stern, the Second World War brought them together, but the end of the war might rip them apart. (978-1-63555-874-6)

Holiday Hearts by Diana Day-Admire and Lyn Cole. Opposites attract during Christmastime chaos in Kansas City. (978-1-63679-128-9)

Changing Majors by Ana Hartnett Reichardt. Beyond a love, beyond a coming-out, Bailey Sullivan discovers what lies beyond the shame and self-doubt imposed on her by traditional Southern ideals. (978-1-63679-081-7)

Fresh Grave in Grand Canyon by Lee Patton. The age-old Grand Canyon becomes more and more ominous as a group of volunteers fight to survive alone in nature and uncover a murderer among them. (978-1-63679-047-3)

Highland Whirl by Anna Larner. Opposites attract in the Scottish Highlands, when feisty Alice Campbell falls for city-girl-about-town Roxanne Barns. (978-1-63555-892-0)

Humbug by Amanda Radley. With the corporate Christmas party in jeopardy, CEO Rosalind Caldwell hires Christmas Girl Ellie Pearce as her personal assistant. The only problem is, Ellie isn't a PA, has never planned a party, and develops a ridiculous crush on her totally intimidating new boss. (978-1-63555-965-1)

On the Rocks by Georgia Beers. Schoolteacher Vanessa Martini makes no apologies for her dating checklist, and newly single mom Grace Chapman ticks all Vanessa's Do Not Date boxes. Of course, they're never going to fall in love. (978-1-63555-989-7)

Song of Serenity by Brey Willows. Arguing with the Muse of music and justice is complicated, falling in love with her even more so. (978-1-63679-015-2)

The Christmas Proposal by Lisa Moreau. Stranded together in a Christmas village on a snowy mountain, Grace and Bridget face their past and question their dreams for the future. (978-1-63555-648-3)

The Infinite Summer by Morgan Lee Miller. While spending the summer with her dad in a small beach town, Remi Brenner falls for Harper Hebert and accidentally finds herself tangled up in an intense restaurant rivalry between her famous stepmom and her first love. (978-1-63555-969-9)

Wisdom by Jesse J. Thoma. When Sophia and Reggie are chosen for the governor's new community design team and tasked with tackling substance abuse and mental health issues, battle lines are drawn even as sparks fly. (978-1-63555-886-9)

A Convenient Arrangement by Aurora Rey and Jaime Clevenger. Cuffing season has come for lesbians, and for Jess Archer and Cody Dawson, their convenient arrangement becomes anything but. (978-1-63555-818-0)

An Alaskan Wedding by Nance Sparks. The last thing either Andrea or Riley expects is to bump into the one who broke her heart fifteen years ago, but when they meet at the welcome party, their feelings come rushing back. (978-1-63679-053-4)

Beulah Lodge by Cathy Dunnell. It's 1874, and newly engaged Ruth Mallowes is set on marriage and life as a missionary…until she falls in love with the housemaid at Beulah Lodge. (978-1-63679-007-7)

Gia's Gems by Toni Logan. When Lindsey Speyer discovers that popular travel columnist Gia Williams is a complete fake and threatens to expose her, blackmail has never been so sexy. (978-1-63555-917-0)

Holiday Wishes & Mistletoe Kisses by M. Ullrich. Four holidays, four couples, four chances to make their wishes come true. (978-1-63555-760-2)

Love By Proxy by Dena Blake. Tess has a secret crush on her best friend, Sophie, so the last thing she wants is to help Sophie fall in love with someone else, but how can she stand in the way of her happiness? (978-1-63555-973-6)

Loyalty, Love, & Vermouth by Eric Peterson. A comic valentine to a gay man's family of choice, including the ones with cold noses and four paws. (978-1-63555-997-2)

Marry Me by Melissa Brayden. Allison Hale attempts to plan the wedding of the century to a man who could save her family's business, if only she wasn't falling for her wedding planner, Megan Kinkaid. (978-1-63555-932-3)

Pathway to Love by Radclyffe. Courtney Valentine is looking for a woman exactly like Ben—smart, sexy, and not in the market for anything serious. All she has to do is convince Ben that sex-without-strings is the perfect pathway to pleasure. (978-1-63679-110-4)

Sweet Surprise by Jenny Frame. Flora and Mac never thought they'd ever see each other again, but when Mac opens up her barber shop right next to Flora's sweet shop, their connection comes roaring back. (978-1-63679-001-5)

The Edge of Yesterday by CJ Birch. Easton Gray is sent from the future to save humanity from technological disaster. When she's forced to target the woman she's falling in love with, can Easton do what's needed to save humanity? (978-1-63679-025-1)

The Scout and the Scoundrel by Barbara Ann Wright. With unexpected danger surrounding them, Zara and Roni are stuck between duty and survival, with little room for exploring their feelings, especially love. (978-1-63555-978-1)

Bury Me in Shadows by Greg Herren. College student Jake Chapman is forced to spend the summer at his dying grandmother's home and soon finds danger from long-buried family secrets. (978-1-63555-993-4)

Can't Leave Love by Kimberly Cooper Griffin. Sophia and Pru have no intention of falling in love, but sometimes love happens when and where you least expect it. (978-1-636790041-1)

Free Fall at Angel Creek by Julie Tizard. Detective Dee Rawlings and aircraft accident investigator Dr. River Dawson use conflicting methods to find answers when a plane goes missing, while overcoming surprising threats, and discovering an unlikely chance at love. (978-1-63555-884-5)

Love's Compromise by Cass Sellars. For Piper Holthaus and Brook Myers, will professional dreams and past baggage stop two hearts from realizing they are meant for each other? (978-1-63555-942-2)

Not All a Dream by Sophia Kell Hagin. Hester has lost the woman she loved and the world has descended into relentless dark and cold. But giving up will have to wait when she stumbles upon people who help her survive. (978-1-63679-067-1)

Protecting the Lady by Amanda Radley. If Eve Webb had known she'd be protecting royalty, she'd never have taken the job as bodyguard, but as the threat to Lady Katherine's life draws closer, she'll do whatever it takes to save her, and may just lose her heart in the process. (978-1-63679-003-9)

The Secrets of Willowra by Kadyan. A family saga of three women, their homestead called Willowra in the Australian outback, and the secrets that link them all. (978-1-63679-064-0)

Trial by Fire by Carsen Taite. When prosecutor Lennox Roy and public defender Wren Bishop become fierce adversaries in a headline-grabbing arson case, their attraction ignites a passion that leads them both to question their assumptions about the law, the truth, and each other. (978-1-63555-860-9)

Turbulent Waves by Ali Vali. Kai Merlin and Vivien Palmer plan their future together as hostile forces make their own plans to destroy what they have, as well as all those they love. (978-1-63679-011-4)

Unbreakable by Cari Hunter. When Dr. Grace Kendal is forced at gunpoint to help an injured woman, she is dragged into a nightmare where nothing is quite as it seems, and their lives aren't the only ones on the line. (978-1-63555-961-3)

Veterinary Surgeon by Nancy Wheelton. When dangerous drugs are stolen from the veterinary clinic, Mitch investigates and Kay becomes a suspect. As pride and professions clash, love seems impossible. (978-1-63679-043-5)